Carla

Michael Gryboski

Carla
Michael Gryboski

Republished September 2018
Little Creek Books
Imprint of Jan-Carol Publishing, Inc.
All rights reserved
Copyright © 2017 Michael Gryboski
Original work published 2017
InknBeans Press

This is a work of fiction. Any resemblance to actual persons, either living or dead, is entirely coincidental. All names, characters, and events are the product of the author's imagination.

This book may not be reproduced in whole or part, in any matter whatsoever without written permission, with the exception of brief quotations within book reviews or articles.

ISBN: 978-1-945619-74-8
Library of Congress Control Number: 2018958658

You may contact the publisher:
Jan-Carol Publishing, Inc.
PO Box 701
Johnson City, TN 37605
publisher@jancarolpublishing.com
jancarolpublishing.com

For God, Family, Country

Table of Contents

Chapter I   1
Chapter II   18
Chapter III   32
Chapter IV   53
Chapter V   72
Chapter VI   85
Chapter VII   104
Chapter VIII   120
Chapter IX   140
Chapter X   162
Chapter XI   179
Chapter XII   201

I

Uptown was a peaceful neighborhood. There was the occasional blue collar crime, the periodic robbery or battery. However, where two or more members of the human race are gathered, there is also the potential for wrongdoing. In the exercise of comparability, it scored low next to the suburbs but high next to downtown, old town, and other cities in general. People could go about its light brown sidewalks and dark gray streets under the presupposition of security. Nightlife was decent, with more people going to the drunk tank than to the prison. A mild concrete wilderness.

It was a relatively prosperous neighborhood. Its skyline was defined by several tall buildings comprised of middle class and high end apartments. Office buildings stood vigil with the living quarters, their walls of glass shimmering during the morning and afternoon. Most of the parking was done underground. Garages housed rows and rows of compact cars separated by thickly painted white lines. Some of these garages were quite compact themselves, causing much angst for the driver attempting to turn into a space or back out without nudging the vehicle on the other end of the confined space. Others were immense, with several levels and room for a couple hundred vehicles.

Most of the people living in the uptown were middle class, rising businessmen and young professionals. Nearly all were single, with a tiny minority being newlyweds. Few children and even fewer big families. Those family units were either in the downtown area or comfortably ensconced in their suburban palaces. These people worked mostly regular hours though not paid by the hour. Most were saving for that dream domicile outside of the city while also paying off the new car or the student loans. Few were past the age of 35, very few past 40. Business casual was their frequent outdoor attire and privately owned cars were their preferred means of transportation. Some used public transportation, especially those who ventured towards lower income areas of the city. Those who worked for the government were known to use it to get to the halls of power.

They were an industrious lot. While officially the office hours for the majority of them were nine to five, many were known to have the occasional late night. Professional occupations and a general commitment to personal advancement forbade lethargy, with so many seeking and in due time achieving promotions and raises. These people were known to watch and sometimes buy tickets to sports events, have expensive dinners to celebrate special occasions or first dates, or go to the bar on the weekends with friends to drink, dance, and flirt the night away. A small percentage were involved in church, social clubs, community events, and the political process, though for most such civic participation was not to come until after they had settled down or when the first child entered the world. No surprise that the largest congregations were located on the outskirts of the city.

The relative security of this urban neighborhood was generated through a mixture of machine and man. Police occasionally patrolled the streets and guards more or less watched the garages in case something or someone suspicious arrived. Cameras were affixed to numerous buildings and traffic lights. Most of the time, the footage helped nab a person running a red light or being drunk in public. Sometimes the more wicked part of society was viewed through those mute black-and-white lenses.

She was looking at the lone camera. Like most of them, it had a white body and dark transparent lens. It was bolted to the side of the skyscraper across the street from the parking garage, though it had a second part that allowed it to slowly move from side to side. A single bright red light was on the lower left hand side of its front, indicating that it was in operation. Its eye caught a few cars going by, typically at a pace four or five miles above the speed limit. The dense population of vehicles on the road prevented greater excess. There were some pedestrians also, though most were still asleep or inside preparing for the work day. The spring weather made sunlight pierce the windows early.

For the past couple of weeks, she had studied the observing technology, tracking its movements, timing its gradual systematic swaying. A watch upon her wrist, she looked down at the morning time, quickly exchanging glances between the digital timepiece and the monitor attached to the building. She was in the blind spot, peering around the side of the brick-and-mortar corner of the structure. A small purse filled with various objects hung from her left shoulder. She wore a black collared t-shirt whose sleeves were a couple inches away from the elbows and ordinary blue jeans that were too loose to be considered tight and too tight to be considered loose. Normal shirt, normal pants, and a normal pair of slightly worn black sneakers comprised her outfit. There was no jewelry, no piercings, or tattoos. Most of this she shunned for either personal or economic reasons.

As to her physical beauty, this was beyond the ordinary. Even with the lack of makeup or cosmetic modification, she was an attractive creature. She lacked blemish or scar, with no birth mark or deformity. Her skin was fair but not too pale, her eyes dark brown, and her hair a silky black which ran down behind her back, the hair halting at the bottom of the shoulder blades. She had lips that were full enough to be noticed but not large enough to be distracting. The demands of her life did allot some early lines on her face, yet these simply added depth to her countenance, offering an aura of attractive maturity. They showed a woman who was a thorough adult, properly seasoned before her fading. Expressions of joy or sadness were amplified when expressed, filling the immediate social environment with whatever emotional state her attention-getting face harbored.

The camera panned away, rearing its monitor to the other end of the short street. On the proper schedule, she moved the moment the electronic eye was away. Walking fast but not awkwardly so, she crossed the street after another car whizzed by to try and turn onto a major road. She almost jumped as she got onto the sidewalk, which was parted by the entrance to the parking garage. Someone was leaving as she neared the opening. This was an unexpected bonus that made her entry into the facility go without notice. As the lone guard was distracted by pleasantries with the departing inhabitant, the woman walked in, searching for a specific vehicle. She knew the description, having studied photos and videos of the automobile in action, as well as having a written report with basic details.

It was only a few minutes after entering the cavernous garage that she found the sports car with the right make, model, color, and above all license plate. All the marks of identification verified, she approached the vehicle. Another woman walked by, oblivious to the casually dressed female to her right. With the other person gone, Carla al-Hassan walked to the side of the car, a red compact parked between two similarly aged vehicles. Kneeling, she placed her purse near the side of the car and then carefully rolled onto her back. She then used her left arm and left leg to push herself underneath the automobile. Back on the asphalt, above her was the intricate body of the vehicle.

With both hands, she pushed up her black shirt, revealing an ominous device taped to her abdomen and covering her stomach. She ripped at the tape, removing the mostly silver-hued item from her hairless belly and flipped it over so that the side which was resting on her stomach was now facing the bottom of the car.

She pressed the tape upon the frame of the vehicle, allowing for it to adhere to the automobile frame. After getting the first couple pieces of tape to stick, she used one hand to secure the remainder of the tape to the frame while the other hand instinctively dragged her shirt back over her belly. It was an automatic reflex for Carla, even when she knew no one was watching.

To make the attachment less precarious, Carla went for her purse and took out more tape. This further secured the device to the frame. After completing this, she opened a small compartment on the item. It revealed a calculator keypad, with ten digits and no letters. Pressing the right code on the first try, a small screen that initially showed the numbers in bright red instead showed the all-capitals message of ACTIVATED. Compartment closed, Carla put the unused tape into her purse, zipped it up and then, after a few people walked by without incident, used her right leg and right arm to push herself out from below the car.

She neared the exit without notice, another car blocking the attention of the guard. The camera outside was looking at her general direction, stopping her from leaving the lot. She remained hidden in the shadowy corner of the garage until the artificial eye again turned away. At once she speedily walked out of the parking garage without being noticed. Guard and commuter alike had their minds on other matters. Upon exiting the covered facility, she crossed the street at the intersection that was about a hundred feet away and from there walked to the public park a few blocks away.

Several minutes later an elevator dinged and its semi-reflective light gray doors parted to allow eight people to exit into the parking garage. He was among them, wearing a bland brownish tie and pants with a white long-sleeved shirt. With dark-rimmed glasses and a clean shave, he looked like hundreds of thousands of other civil servants and office building dwellers across the city. Carrying a suitcase with important contents, he took out his keys from his pocket as he neared the red sports car. With a couple presses of his key, the car lights lit up and made a corresponding beeping noise to verify that all was unlocked. Opening the passenger side front door, he nonchalantly dropped his case onto the chair. Slamming the door, he made his way to the driver's side and opened the door.

The park was beautiful in the spring. Flowers coalesced in large clusters, the grassy expanse glimmered when beams of light struck the morning dew. Daycare centers and stay-at-home moms often brought children there. Dogs played catch with their masters while the elderly played chess with one another. Several acres in size, it was the location for many of the citywide observances, like Founder's Day and Fourth of July fireworks. Ceremonies connected to Memorial Day, Veterans

Day, Easter, and Christmas also took place there. It was a common hangout for families, churches, and youths. For its extensive presence in city life, the grounds were well maintained, with the grass cut, playground equipment up to date, and solid dark green benches alongside gravel walkways.

    Carla was sitting on one of these benches. Her spot oversaw the two streets that intersected at the corner of the public park. She was relaxed in her appearance, seated with her right leg crossed over her left. The purse was perched on her lap, with her left hand holding her mobile phone. The purse and the phone obscured the right hand, which was holding the trigger for the bomb. She looked about the road, looking for the sports car. There was a close call when a ruby colored vehicle stopped at the traffic light in front of her, but she soon noted that it was the wrong model.

    After exchanging the usual quick greetings with the guard, he flipped the turning signal and went left onto the small street. The route was barely a few blocks long and in the opinions of some was little better than an alleyway. Turning right to merge into traffic, the man turned the radio to a classical music station, the volume low. There was much on his mind about what he needed to do that day. When not focusing on the road he kept looking at his briefcase, its unassuming leather exterior hiding documents of great significance. His thoughts kept proliferating about the fallout.

    A few blocks after turning onto the major road, he could see the more vibrant portion of the uptown area. There was a group of school kids waiting for the bus, scores of adults heading to work via car, bus, or walking. Crossing guards aided some of the pedestrians, helping when interests conflicted. He saw the taller buildings, their cells holding a growing number of on-the-clock people. Attention turned to the park, a beautiful place. As a child, he played there with his friends. As an adult, he attended many public events there, sometimes even being on the temporary stage they constructed for said ceremonies. On a bench near him, he saw an intriguing figure, a black-haired woman who looked to be around his age.

    BOOM! A great explosion ripped through the monotony of the morning commute, met with hundreds of screams and gasps. The red compact shot its metal and gears in every direction, striking other cars and pedestrians alike. After the flame of the blast went outwards, a thick gray plume of smoke encircled the immediate vicinity, blotting out even the bright red of the nearest traffic lights. People ducked, people ran, panic filled the intersection and the park. As vehicles stopped, wounded groaned, and crossing guards attempted to maintain order amidst the chaos, Carla got up from the bench and walked away.

Her stride was brisker, partly to flee the scene of the crime and partly to blend with the panicked folk around her. Putting her phone into her purse, she walked fast along the sidewalk while fidgeting with the trigger device. After a little bit of effort, she got the upper third piece of the device removed from the other two. This one included the button she pressed to bring anarchy to the uptown that morning. Seeing a public trashcan coming up on her right, she tossed the piece into the bin without stopping.

The smoke cloud went farther, covering the intersection as several people were unconscious due to their proximity to the explosion. Others lay on park ground or in the street, bleeding profusely from shrapnel wounds. Mobile phones were used in abundance, flooding emergency services with their calls, some under a forced calm while others were exasperated and to the point of screaming. More nearby crossing guards and police officers who were patrolling on foot arrived.

Meanwhile, Carla increased her distance from the destructive sight. A growing number of people were fleeing the scene, making her a mere face in the surging, horrified populace. She removed the second piece of the trigger, giving one piece per hand. One of them went into the next trashcan she found on her way. After that, the crowd of people started to use the road to get away from the destroyed car. Vehicles on the street were facing that intersection and were therefore stopped. Some rolled down their windows, shouting for information. Walking along the side of the road with several others, Carla threw the final piece of the trigger into a sewer vent, the metal object clanging as it went down before a deep-noted splash indicated that it was lost to investigators forever.

Emergency services were on the scene, navigating their alarm-laden vehicles through a maze of stopped cars. Firemen quickly subdued the blaze, fiery embers landing on a few automobiles that had been beside the red sports car. EMTs treated the dozens of injured, whose wounds ranged from cuts and bruises to temporary deafness and severe bleeding. Eight were severe enough that they were evacuated from the intersection with the park and sent to the main uptown hospital. With the police securing the area, crossing guards went to work attempting to get the throng of cars away from the crime scene and towards assorted detours. It was a frustrating task.

Meanwhile, Carla was about a half mile away from the epicenter of the explosion. Returning to the sidewalk, her traveling was still fast, though not as much, lest she engender curiosity from the increasingly calmer crowds. When the occasional police car zoomed by on the street she always looked towards the buildings on the other side. Her route was a planned one as she neared a certain alleyway between two closed stores. While others minded their business, carrying on with their lives, Carla trained herself for the alley and then in a precise moment suddenly turned into the narrow space.

The park became a crowded space as detectives talked with the large number of witnesses. Some were still wounded, getting treatment from emergency personnel. Others were simply shaken, unnerved, or crying. Officers jotted notes while bystanders explained what they were doing and who they saw. Banal happenings until the loud noise drew their attention to the horror with its smoke, fire, and mangled metal. While the compact was, to say the least, totaled, a detective did find one of the license plates. It was thrown over fifty feet, landing all the way across the intersection.

She exited the alleyway a new woman. The purse and the informal clothing were stored in a large blue duffle bag, whose long white strap was slung along her left shoulder. She now wore a pair of mostly white sneakers, a white pair of work pants, and a white collared shirt with a white undershirt. Her once free-flowing black hair was controlled with a pink scrunchie that fashioned it into a ponytail. Carla looked at her watch and widened her eyes upon seeing the time. Her walk became an awkward jog as she rushed along the sidewalk while trying to balance the duffle bag slung upon her shoulder.

Turning a corner, she saw it. The large blue and yellow bus, with its wide shaded windows and four tires to each side. The door near the front was open, but the kneeling transport was lifting upwards. In a mild panic she increased her jog, nearly colliding with another pedestrian on her way. The bus remained there, as though taunting her all the more to go quicker. She caught up with the stagnant behemoth, running along its right side she desperately pounded the frame with her left hand. The slapping of the bus's side, while not loud compared to other regular city noises, nonetheless prompted the driver to wait a little bit longer. Carla finally reached the two gray steps and then ascended into the body of the large vehicle. Meeting her was a familiar driver, a middle-aged, heavy-set African-American man who smiled at her while she smiled back.

"Thanks, Max," said Carla between breaths, hastily taking out her fare card from her bag and swiping it on the machine.

"No problem. Anything for my Carla," he replied in a good natured tone while she quickly found a seat. There were only about a dozen people seated in the bus, with Carla taking a window-side armless chair for her that had an empty seat beside it. She placed her duffle bag upon the vacant seat, slowly moving her left shoulder around to deal with some soreness. Another passenger, a forty-something man in a suit and tie, mildly protested.

"Hey Max, when are you going to hold up the bus this long for me?" he protested from the opposite side of the bus, seated next to a couple of his work buddies.

"When you're as pretty as her."

"Whatever," smiled the dissenting passenger as his friends laughed. The bus doors revolved to close and the large machine pushed forward, moving ever faster towards the next stop along the way. The line began on the fringes of uptown and got as far as the downtown area, the last stop being a few blocks from a train station and about ten blocks from the waterfront. Carla did not look back. Her gaze went only forward through the window, seeing a faint mellowed reflection of herself within the glass. As the bus went its typical route, about a mile behind it a dissipating cloud of smoke hung over the uptown part of the city; the part that was known to be so peaceful.

***

It was originally a factory. The large edifice was constructed during the Second World War as part of that grand democracy arsenal. Specifically, it churned out the frames for the Sherman tanks. Black-and-white newsreels were recorded showing the mostly female employees working long shifts to mass produce the mechanized weaponry. Everyone did their part: welding, pounding, pushing along. Thousands made it off the assembly line and were used to fatal effect over there in Western Europe.

Initially the end of the global conflict was a time of prosperity. Factory owners did a double switch, from producing tanks with a predominantly female workforce to producing civilian cars with an almost exclusively male workforce. The transition went with little incident and, to the dismay of feminists everywhere, with little protest for the former employees. Most of those ex-employees ended up marrying the men who took their place. Thanks to a postwar boom and a GI bill to boot, these people formed the first suburban neighborhoods, expanding the reach of the city, and becoming good citizen consumers.

By the 1960s however, things went sour. Union pressures, combined with a freer market down South, led factory owners to pack up their jobs and leave town. This was one of the many empty shells left as the jobs went to the New South and sometimes beyond the borders of the country. While the jobs and the employers left, the buildings remained. This particular site became the headquarters for a cleaning service, which hired a mostly immigrant workforce to clean the middle and upper-class homes.

News of the bombing did not equal a surprise holiday from their workloads. Of the many homes scheduled for cleaning, only one family phoned in that morning to cancel. Everyone else wanted to get on with life. Most of their clientele did not live near the uptown region, being able to afford their own spot of land in the suburbs. And most of their workplaces were either downtown or even in other cities. Besides, in that time and place these violent acts were not as uncommon as they should have been.

Carla rushed once more down the block. Having thanked Max again for the ride, she scurried towards the warehouse. Turning a corner, she entered the large open space. This largest of the rooms at the former factory resembled a loading dock, with a small fleet of vans that were emblazoned with the name, logo, and contact information for the cleaning service. Already present were her coworkers, whose backs were turned towards her. Only a couple of managers saw her enter through the open space, the same area where completed tanks used to be driven off the line and into a parking lot.

"Ah, Carla, you are just in time," shouted one of her superiors, prompting about half of the cleaners to temporarily turn their heads. "We were just about to go over the agenda for today."

Carla smiled in relief. Standing behind most of the employees gathered, she was next to Concepción, an older woman from Central America that she had known since her first day. "Wow, Carla," she commented in a whispery tone and an amused look. "You do Salvadoran Time better than the Salvadorans."

"Gracias, mi amiga," replied Carla, with enough English accent to reveal her lack of Hispanic background yet not so much as so botch the pronunciation.

"Okay, so we're going to need six people for the Carl Boulevard route. Do we have any volunteers?" asked the manager, who saw several hands go up. Maids had their preferences, as some had come to befriend those whose houses they cleaned. Carla and Concepción raised their hands and both were selected for the route. "Okay, good. Mario, take van number five with you for this one." Mario, who was one of the few in the group to have a driver's license, nodded and soon they were off.

Even with the occasional terrorist attack within the city or elsewhere in the state, the suburbs prided themselves on being a safe environment. So much so, that the people off Carl Boulevard who had the maid service left their doors unlocked. Robberies were scarce for that neighborhood. Either way, most families had someone there until the arrival of the service. It was typical for there to be communication between cleaner and family. Carla was the best English speaker of her group. As a result, generally she was the one who interacted with the person on their way out the door, planning in advance to run some errands so that the maids could clean without interference.

The first house they entered was vacant. Front door unlocked, the six maids entered the house and began to do their invisible job. They placed coverings over their shoes to prevent tracking from the outside world. Two worked on mopping the hardwood, another vacuumed, and another dusted. Mario surfed the Internet and watched videos on his smart phone while waiting in the van. Being a driver gave him these privileges. It was a curious profession, as one became immersed in the lives of strangers.

Carla was meticulous in her labors, carefully removing a row of ceramic horses from a mantle in the living room. A thin layer of dust was upon the fixture, the only oases of cleanliness being the rounded spots left by the removed equestrian figures. She set about cleaning the mantle top and then the shelves that bore books located in that room. However, before that, she turned on the television located in the corner of living room and tuned it to a news station. Graphic images showed the wounded and the terrified. A reporter reading from a teleprompter off-screen was in the background as Carla continued working: "Reports are still coming as police and investigators comb the intersection at Gavins Park for more evidence. Currently, officials say that at least thirty people have been injured and it appears that one individual, the lone passenger of the vehicle, is the only fatality ..."

After an hour, the cleaning was complete and the maids gathered their equipment, removed the shoe coverings, and then packed up the van. Going only a few blocks farther they went back to work, cleaning up another large middle-class family home. Carla and Concepción were tidying up the rec room for the space. It was the fun chamber, located at the basement level. It included a ping-pong table, pool table, and a bunch of board games on a few shelves. It also had a large screen TV, which Concepción turned on.

"Prefiero mirar las noticias, por favor."

"Estas practicando, Carla. Muy bien."

"Gracias," smiled Carla as her friend used the remote to change it to another news station, different from the former but still covering the same developing story. This time it was an older man interviewing a city spokesperson.

"And what of the explosion? Do you believe it is terrorist-related?"

"Most likely," replied the spokesperson. "It fits the MO of past incidents; though earlier victims have never been this prominent before."

"So, you're saying it is the Cicero Organization?"

"Once again, Bob, at this point I cannot say with full certainty. But we are definitely working under the assumption that it is."

"Thank you for your time."

"No problem."

"And to confirm, 34-year-old District Attorney Myles Talbert has died. He was murdered when a bomb went off in his car, killing him instantly and wounding at least forty other people. They, at least, are expected to survive."

"Muy horrible, no?" asked Concepción.

"Sí, mi amiga, sí," stoically responded Carla as she finished dusting off the ping-pong table. Constant gameplay meant that it had several little spots lacking grayish white particles. As they finalized their efforts in the rec room, Carla hid her relief as the correspondent continued.

"At this point, police have been unable to identify the perpetrator. While it is believed that the person was working for the Cicero Organization, witnesses have failed to give authorities an agreed-upon specific description of the bomber. As with similar attacks, it is feared that the culprit will again be lost in the smoke."

The next house was adjacent to that one, so the van stayed where it was, with the six cleaners carrying or dragging their equipment. A housewife greeted them, a kind woman in her fifties who had aged well. A nice soul, she and Carla talked some about specifics, like leaving a couple of the bedrooms alone. Carla informed Concepción of this. While her friend was largely fluent in English, she occasionally struggled with auditory comprehension and did better when certain things were explained by Carla at a slower pace. Once understood, she explained it to the other maids in Español.

This house was cleaned right around the lunch hour, so once done with it the cleaners took a break. Mario ordered some pizza and bottled water for the maids. There were also some sodas in the refrigerator which the housewife said they could have. While everyone else ate in the van, Carla remained inside. She ate her pizza on a paper plate and had a can of soda, while draping one of the towels over her lap while she ate, just in case. The television in the living room was on and the talking head gave the update: "While police continue to struggle to find any evidence of who the bomber was, it is increasingly agreed by authorities that the ultimate guilty party is the Cicero Organization. According to a statement released by the district attorney's office, Talbert was the lead investigator in an operation meant to expose the Cicero Organization and its titular leader ..."

***

Closer to home and after her shift was over, Carla was at a seamier locale. It was a clearing between two reddish brick apartment complexes. Neither building was more than five stories tall and each unit within it was small. Spaces for singles barely went above the 400 square foot mark and family units were only slightly larger than that. It was squalid, with piles of filled trash bags scattered on the ground, broken up asphalt for a surface, and a few rusty dumpsters. Connected to the large cubic brick buildings were a collection of dark steel ladders and porous platforms.

The sun was setting. As usual the cleaning crew had completed its rounds about six in the afternoon. Although one family had canceled, their time was increased when one home owner accidentally locked them out. So time was wasted while Mario called the head office who then had to make a few calls before getting the owner to return and finally unlock the door, apologizing at every step onto the front lawn. Still, the work had to be done and was done. By that time, the news programming was offering nothing original regarding the evidences from the crime scene or the suspects they had in mind.

Carla stood there in the silent alley between the two brick complexes. All seemed nonorganic, yet this was not so and she knew it. Her blue duffle bag was lugged about with her, the white strap resting upon her left shoulder. She was still in her maid outfit, having eaten dinner out with a couple of coworkers at a nearby fast food restaurant before catching a bus back to her neighborhood. Max drove during the day so she did not recognize the man behind the wheel. Still, she was her usual pleasant self, saying hello with a smile upon entering the bus and thanking him when she got off.

Putting the bag down to give her sore shoulder a rest, she walked over to where one of the ladders descended to just above the ground level. Using the twilight visibility, she was able to locate a rough-looking wrench several inches below the bottom rung. It was left there on purpose. Had someone stolen it, Carla had a small hammer in her bag as backup. Taking it with her right hand, she struck the side of the ladder five times in a quick manner, then paused, and then five more times in a slower manner. Placing the wrench back upon the ground, she straightened as someone from the darker parts of the alley emerged. He was wearing what looked like a flowing raincoat or maybe a cape. The hood was over his head, shadowing his face. The flowing garment obscured most of his body, which was itself fully clothed with a long sleeved shirt and pants.

She stood her ground with a straight-faced expression as he got closer, making little noise as he navigated the bagged refuse on the ground and walked beside one of the rusted dumpsters. His face betrayed an older man, early to middle fifties she guessed. Like Carla, he carried a bag slung on one shoulder. His cargo was smaller, more medium sized and was either black or Prussian blue. They were three feet apart from each other when he began to speak, a sinister smile appearing on his wrinkled face.

"Ah, Carla," he said in a pleasant tone. "Once again you have done an excellent job. The news has told me much about your accomplishment. It has the perfect balance of confirming your success while not telling me who did it. You excel at that. Indeed, I often ponder which is your greatest attribute: your talent in carrying out Cicero's will, or your nonpareil beauty." Carla remained silent. "Of course, you did not come here merely to have me endlessly compliment you on your obvious strengths." The man turned to his bag, unzipped it, and then took out a few bundles of money. Carla was handed her payment for works rendered, but unlike her initial transactions, she went through the bills. She counted them in silence, her lips moving as she spoke the numbers to herself.

"There is only seven thousand here."

"Yes, dear Carla. And it is money well earned."

"The rules say I am supposed to get nine thousand."

"I beg your pardon?" asked the man, a bit awkward at the comment.

"I remember the rules for compensation. Four thousand for nonhuman targets. Six thousand for low level human targets. Nine thousand for medium targets. And at least fifteen thousand for high level targets."

"Your memory is as good as your appearance," he conceded. "Yes, you technically deserve nine thousand, but for circumstances abounding we can only give seven at this time."

"Seems like every time," she protested softly.

"Pardon?"

"I said, it seems like for the last several times you have short-changed me. Come on, Cato," she pleaded using the only name she knew the man to have. "You can get me an extra two thousand dollars. There is more than that in your bag right now."

"As I explained the last time we had this little discussion, the treasury is a little harder to get at these days. When we have more control of the purse-strings, I promise that you will get what you need from me."

"Cato," she persisted. "You need to pay me what you owe me."

"Carla," Cato sternly responded, "you, my dear, need to remember the order of the Cicero Organization. I am your superior. You have no right to complain. If you do not want the money, then you can find work elsewhere. And needless to say, Cicero's money will not be the only thing you lose if you quit us."

Carla knew what Cato was getting at. She looked down at the money, sifting through it again as the twilight fled before the evening. With a breath, she looked up towards the old man in the hood and flowing robe. "Seven thousand," she said emotionless. "That is seven thousand more than zero."

Cato smiled. "Exactly. Seven thousand more than zero. Now that is the Carla I know and love. Good evening." Cato turned and walked into the alley. Carla looked at the money some more before turning to her blue duffle bag. Unzipping it, she threw the bundles of cash into the bag before zipping it once more. Slung upon the right shoulder to give the left one a rest, she walked eight blocks to get back to her apartment.

***

The elevator was broken at her complex. Earlier that afternoon, it was stuck between the second and third floors, trapping one of the tenants. Fortunately, the person was an able-bodied soul and successfully crawled out of the lift onto the third floor. A repair man came in but lacked the proper tools to fix it. He diagnosed the problem and promised to fix it the following morning. For the needier tenants, of which there were many, the landlord agreed to let them temporarily use the service elevator, provided that one of the maintenance team members was present at all times to oversee its proper usage.

Keeping her complaints to herself, Carla simply took the stairs, carrying her duffle bag up four floors before getting to the carpeted hallway. As apartment complexes went, hers was not too shabby. The piping worked and the water was clean. They had the occasional malfunction with the power or the climate control, but as with the elevator these issues were fixed in a range of several hours to a couple of days. While it lacked a regular security guard, the complex was only a few blocks from a police station, giving it several patrol rounds by default. Yawning as she walked down the hallway, Carla spotted her door amongst the identical portals distinguished only by number. Unzipping her bag and then going into her purse, she found the right key for the lock. Earlier someone else was entering the complex itself as she did, so this was the first time that night she needed to access her chain. Key inserted, turned, and the door was opened.

"Hello?" asked an accented voice from the dining room.

"It's me, Giddo," replied Carla as she walked in and closed the door behind her, the duffle bag immediately falling to the hardwood floor.

"Oh, Carla! Glad you are back," said her grandfather as he wheeled himself from the dining room to the living room, where Carla was removing her shoes. After doing so she approached her seated grandfather and kissed him on the cheek before they hugged. "How was your day?"

"Busy as always," she said as the two made their way to the television and the furniture that surrounded it. Her grandfather grabbed the remote from a small table that had a lamp upon it and turned it on. Carla collapsed onto the couch, still in her work clothes. They happened upon a network channel, which had the news of the day. This of course included the car bomb that killed the district attorney.

"Horrible, just horrible," commented her grandfather. "When I left Syria years ago, I had hoped this would stay there. Were you near any of this?"

"No, not at all," she said while looking up at the ceiling. One arm lay over her stomach while the other had the elbow pointing at the ceiling, hand near the head. Her legs were bent at the knees, her feet dug into the couch. "That happened uptown. I was in the suburbs all day. The usual cleaning up nice houses."

"Thank God," he said as the segment ended and the commercials began. "Otherwise noted, a normal day?"

"A normal day," she said and then yawned. "How was yours?"

"Ah, the usual," smiled George al-Hassan. "Watched the television, dreamed big, and then had lunch with the landlady."

Carla giggled some. "How did that go?"

"I had a good time," said George. "She makes an excellent lasagna. And she thinks I have a beautiful smile."

Carla laughed. "My giddo. He never stops being a ladies' man. You know, I can only imagine the trouble you caused for the women of Damascus back in the day."

"One of them said yes," pointed out George. "And you should be thankful."

"I am, if for no other reason than that it means I would eventually meet you," smiled Carla as she shifted in the couch and eventually got to a seated position, yawning once again. "I think I need some coffee."

"You stay put, I'll get it."

"But Giddo—"

"No, no," stressed George as he wheeled himself around to face the kitchen, which had no barrier between it and the living room, "just because I am paralyzed does not mean I am a vegetable. You relax on the couch, I'll get the coffee."

As her grandfather exited, Carla pondered whether she should indulge. It was late and momentarily she was going to be readying for bed. Then again, her energy was low and there were quite a few tasks that needed completion before she could go to sleep. She leaned back into the couch as she yawned once more, her blinks getting longer. As the commercials ran once again, she concluded that struggling to go to sleep later that evening was an acceptable risk to be able to have the strength to do final preparations for bed. A few more minutes went by before her grandfather returned. During pauses like these she wondered if he was all right. A bad habit, although the occasional past incident fractured her assurance of his abilities to act independently.

"Here you go," he said, handing her a warmed cup. She drank it readily. A few swigs into it and she remembered that she was still wearing her all-white work clothes. Setting the coffee on a coaster on a table beside the couch, she went into her bedroom. A small space, she stored her clothes in two large suitcases under the bed to forgo the spatial demands of a large dresser. She took out her pajamas and a worn t-shirt she usually slept in and changed into the informal outfit. A couple of minutes later she was back in the living room and she finished off her cup in a matter of minutes. "You should see a doctor about that."

"Oh please, Giddo," smiled Carla. "There is nothing wrong with drinking coffee. Decades of research have found nothing."

"Alright," he agreed, dropping the intentionally manufactured controversy.

"Did you take your medicines today?"

"Yes, mother."

"Seriously, Giddo."

"Yes, seriously," he said with feigned apprehension. "I do not like them, but I respect their purpose."

"Good."

Carla asked because there was a time when her grandfather refused to take the medicines. He also at one point refused help when he struggled to get in and out of his wheelchair. This disabled life was a new one for George. As a youth, he was known as a fast runner. He served in the Syrian army, being part of the force that violently suppressed a revolt against then President Hafiz Assad in the city of Hamah. From there, disillusioned with his actions, he started to help resistance forces and dissident groups. He was involved in the early Arab Spring revolts, which led to him and his family fleeing the nation. The stresses of the protests combined with a nasty wound he got from a government soldier during one of the suppressions gradually devastated his health. It came rapidly several years earlier, but had only taken away his ability to walk about two years before that evening. Dependence was something he despised, but had to deal with in a measure usually doled out later in one's life.

They chatted for a few more minutes while they watched the news. Seeing the hour getting later, Carla got up from the couch and went about getting things ready. She placed the cups and plates into the washer, pouring just the right amount of cleaning liquid into the machine before closing the door and turning it on. She closed the drapes and curtains, turned off the climate control to save on the bills, and did her own dental care in the bathroom as the sports updates were rolling in on the TV.

"Ready for bed?" she asked.

"Yeah sure," replied George dully. "I will never understand why they report on sports so much in this country. I bet you half the news is about basketball and baseball and American football."

"Probably," said Carla as the two went into his bedroom. Stopped right before his bed.

"Now like I said before, Carla, I just need you here in case something bad happens. I am pretty sure I have it down."

"Go ahead," grudgingly replied Carla with arms folded.

"Remember, I dressed myself this evening. You would not realize it, you would think I wore this house coat and stuff all day, but I did not."

"Okay, okay. Go ahead."

"Just wanted to say that," he added as he shifted out of his maroon housecoat and left it on the chair. She observed him seemingly in deep thought, as though trying to remember some password to a secret chamber. Then he got to work, wheeling himself a little bit closer to the foot of the bed. There, he used his right hand to grip the short post and his left to balance himself. Heaving himself upwards with what little strength he retained in his limbs, George raised himself up, for a moment being taller than his granddaughter. Then he fell forwards, giving Carla a moment of concern that ebbed as he kept moving and moments later was properly placed with his head on the pillow.

"Can I at least help with the sheets?"

"Sure," said George, who added with a smile, "but I did the hard part all by myself."

"Yes, you did," she replied as she tucked him in. "Yes, you did."

"Good night, sweet Carla."

"Good night, Giddo."

II

They were gathered at the steps of the capitol building. It was a sunny day, as pleasant in temperature and humidity as the day that Myles Talbert was killed. A blue sky with some clouds canopied above the small crowd outside of the pillared building. On the top of the steps was a group of government personnel, representing various tiers of the state. In the center was Governor Claire Voxner, who read a prepared statement regarding the murder of Talbert and the tireless service he rendered for his state. She wore a string of pearls around her neck and matching earrings as well as a green skirt with a matching jacket and white blouse. She spoke with stoicism as she read the statement, occasionally looking up and seeing the collection of press filming or taking notes.

To her right was Attorney General Kyle Brown, the man who, a couple of years before, lost the gubernatorial election to Voxner. It was a close and vicious race, with both resorting to attack ads, the spreading of false rumors, and, according to some sources, violence against assorted campaign volunteers. Nothing was ever officially linked to either campaign, though a good circumstantial case probably could have been assembled. As an apparent act of reconciliation, Voxner appointed Brown as state attorney general. Since being sworn in, the two had often found themselves at odds on various public policy initiatives, especially whenever they were challenged in court. Regardless, Voxner felt better personally for having granted the political olive branch.

Among the group in front of the microphones were members of the state government, including an assistant district attorney named Josiah Sharp. The son of a minister at a rural community church several miles from the city, Sharp had recently turned thirty and was a last minute addition to the group assembled on the steps. His primary purpose was to stand around and help show an imposing presence for the media to describe, photograph, or film for the paper, the Internet, or the evening news. He took it in, knowing that this level of importance was, like all worldly matters, a fleeting one.

Another reason Sharp was tapped to be in the presentation was that a community leader and former mayor was invited, but refused to attend. Rafael Sanchez-Vargas was a constant presence in state politics for the past several years. He was twice elected mayor, both times vowing to clean up crime amongst the cities and succeeding. However, his results tended to be temporary and he struggled with economic reform. Short but known for his commanding presence, Sanchez-Vargas was an inflammatory fellow who was known on the campaign trail to ignite violent and uncivil protests. He was also known for his cruel and at times slanderous allegations against ideological opponents. Whenever he lost an election or ballot initiative, it was often because his foes stooped to his level. There was a melancholic sense in many intellectual circles that even when he failed to win office, he still successfully stole the soul of whomever vanquished him.

The statement completed, the reporters shouted questions with their hands raised and recorders running. However, Mayor Mary Bhatia said there was not going to be a question-and-answer session. The statement was enough. Undaunted, correspondents still shouted things out as the mass of officials and subordinates walked away towards their respective offices. For Sharp, that meant following his immediate superior, District Attorney James Colbert, and the attorney general back to the Justice Department's building.

Back at his office, Sharp had an excellent view of the city. Located on the fourth floor, he had a window to his back that overlooked both the downtown and old town portions of the city. There was some dispute among residents as to where downtown ended and old town began. Old town had the more historic structures and a few cobblestone streets, so perchance when the buildings became newer was where downtown ended. Others countered that this was simpleminded, as downtown had a few historic sites in its own right and old town was the sight of a few recently constructed homes.

Sharp's desk was simple, including a computer with flat-screen monitor, a notepad with a couple of pens and some jotted down comments, and a landline telephone used exclusively for business calls, one of which he was going to make shortly. While many of his coworkers had photos of family framed on their desks, Sharp had two seven-by-five inch framed images placed on his desk, one to the right of his keyboard and another to the left. Each image was a simple white background with a biblical quotation in black text. The one to his left was Leviticus 24:22, "You are to have the same law for the foreigner and the native-born. I am the LORD your

God." The one to his right came from James 2:10: "For whoever keeps the whole law and yet stumbles at just one point is guilty of breaking all of it."

Working on his computer, Sharp searched his files briefly to find the correct case he was working on. Several tenants from a downtown condominium were filing a class action lawsuit against their landlord, who reportedly was syphoning money from the funds meant to maintain the facility. Allegedly these funds were going into a personal bank account used by himself and for the benefit of his board members. Windows opened on his screen showing the information he needed. Picking up the receiver, Sharp dialed the number written on a post-it note pasted on the bottom right hand corner of his computer monitor.

"Hello, this is Jim."

"Good morning, Jim. This is Josiah Sharp of the Justice Department. You agreed that we could talk now regarding the condo lawsuit."

"Yes, I remember."

"Good. Have you gotten a chance to look over the settlement terms I sent you and your lawyer via email last week?"

"Yes, we did."

"Can you accept them?"

"Well," began the landlord, offering an awkward change of tone. "My legal friends think that the suit is frivolous and feel that, if fought out, will result in my vindication."

"Really?" sarcastically replied Sharp.

"Yes, Sharp. Really."

"You are aware of the fact that the tenants want to remain at the condo, right? They simply want the money allocated for repairs to be used for repairs."

"Yes."

"You are also aware of the evidence that I have compiled for my case, correct?"

"Yes."

"Including the information I pulled a couple hours ago from the bank?"

"I'm sorry?" inquired Jim, his arrogance leaving quickly.

"Your bank account, Jim. The one that I was able to get transcripts of courtesy a formal request from the manager. Sound more familiar?"

"What did you find?"

"You mean you do not know?"

"I say you're bluffing," angrily countered the landlord.

"You can believe that. It is your right," Sharp replied calmly. "And I can believe that it is strange that at the same time you told the tenants that you were unable to afford necessary repairs for their condo, you were busy buying a dozen travel tickets for an excursion out to Paris and from there, to Prague. And these started at the not-so-cheap price of $3,200 a ticket. I can also believe that it is strange that when the first complaints about insulation issues were sent your way you spent approximately $15,000 renovating a ten-room villa with swimming pool, which you and your family proceeded to host a beach party at for friends."

There was silence on the other line.

"Jim?"

"What?"

"Good, you're still there," smartly commented Sharp. "Anyway, how about you and your legal team agree to the terms of the settlement? That includes repairing everything wrong with that condo, as well as awarding each tenant the amount of money for personal and emotional damages rendered. What do you say?"

There was a long pause, then what sounded like a moan on the other end of the line. "Fine, whatever you want. I will bring my lawyers and me, you can come and bring the lead condo tenant reps."

"How does next Monday at 12:00 noon at the Old Town Courthouse sound?"

"Agreed."

"Thank you very much for your cooperation and as the old hymn goes, 'God be with you 'til we meet again.'"

Jim hung up without a response. Receiver hung up on his end, Sharp wrote in his agenda book the date, time, and location for the settlement meeting. He clicked some of the windows closed and the computer screen showed only his work email, which was constantly up during the day until he clocked out. He was feeling proud of his accomplishment and its eventual fulfillment. Spurts of jovial sentiment welled within him until one of his coworkers approached his desk for reasons he foreknew. The coworker was a fellow attorney and similar in age, size, and appearance.

"Did you get an update from the Homicide Division, Tom?"

"Nothing promising," said Tom, motioning with his hand for Josiah to follow him, which he did.

"That bad, huh?"

"You'll see what I mean when I show you the footage."

The two men walked towards a room cut off from the open air desks and cubicles abounding on the fourth floor. Josiah entered the room, which had many television screens, recording equipment, and video files in both hardware and software formats. A third man, less formal in his attire than the two wearing ties and slacks, looked at the main screen, which featured the surveillance footage. The screen showed a black-and-white rendering of the parking garage's lone entrance.

"Anyway, Josiah, this is how it is," began the disappointed coworker. "We did not have a good amount of video to use, because the street outside the garage has only one camera. And that camera revolves at a 180-degree motion."

"In other words, it won't even show us the entrance 24-7," responded Josiah.

"Correct," nodded Tom. "So as a result, you will be seeing some brief disruptions. That is the footage only showing the rest of the street edited out." Tom tapped the seated man facing the screen on the shoulder. The video got darker, indicating a later hour as it was being fast-forwarded through. After a few moments, Tom told the controller of the footage to pause it, which he obliged. The image shown on the screen was a sports car that if colorized would be a shade of red.

"Myles' car."

"That's right," noted Tom. "As you can see, he is just arriving at the garage at this hour. As you know, since the murder of Withers last year, office security always checks employee cars for explosives or tracking devices. His car got the all-clear and according to other surveillance video from other streets he apparently went straight home that night."

"Which means that whoever planted the bomb did so in the garage. You think it was during the night or the following morning?"

"Well, since our forensics team was able to deduce that it was a remote-controlled explosive, my guess is that it was morning."

"I think that's a good guess," commented Josiah as the controller fast-forwarded through the footage for a couple of minutes.

"Here we have the parking garage at morning. You have a fair amount of people going in and out. Some walking, some driving."

"And that camera probably missed about half the people who did so," said Josiah with annoyance drenching his voice. "Have the police interviewed the guard?"

"Yes. He said that he saw nothing out of the ordinary."

"Nothing?"

"Nope."

"Not even people who may have been unfamiliar?"

"He explained that enough people visit or move out within a year or two that it's hard to keep track of everyone. So he only knows a few people by name or face."

"And he was the only guard, correct?"

"Unfortunately so."

"Wait a minute," thought Josiah aloud. "This is a fairly upscale neighborhood with a want for security. Doesn't the garage itself have a camera?"

"We looked into that already. Apparently, the building's system was malfunctioning and was scheduled to be repaired later that morning."

"That sounds too convenient."

"The detectives looked into it and said it was legit. It was just very bad timing for old Myles," solemnly commented Tom while Josiah shook his head.

"A guard who does not know when a suspicious person shows up. A street camera that likely missed our perp. And now a security system that was broken. This is amazingly absurd."

"If you like, we can tell Homicide's techies to zoom in on the faces and run them through the system. It's possible we'll hit something."

"Go ahead, but I doubt it," sighed Josiah. "If this person planned this hit as well as we think they did, then they probably were adept enough to avoid camera time."

***

They were in another city that evening. Not far from the one where she lived, within the same county in fact. It was not as large, nor as populous. They had complexes and skyscrapers, though theirs tended to be shorter. Being a different city did not make them immune to the reach of the Cicero Organization. Their tentacles seemed to reach into most major cities in the state and, according to some, even a few cities outside those porous borders. Rumors strengthened the Organization, as conspiracies were alleged, making them seem ever larger. Secrecy abounded, even among the members as though they were some esoteric occult brotherhood in which full knowledge came only to a select few.

Carla al-Hassan and her fellow Cicero Organization member took turns looking at the building across the street. Both women were wearing tight-fitting black clothing and ski masks. Carla's hair made it appear like she had a hunchback. She noticed this the first time she and Tiffany were assigned to break into a bank. Tiffany pointed it out and, while troubled at first, Carla decided it did not matter. After all, she reasoned, the hunchback appearance will aid in her disguise. Tiffany conceded this to be true. For her part, Carla's friend kept her hair short and usually put it in cornrows.

"Time?"

"11:00," replied Carla as she looked at her wrist watch.

"The guard should be leaving soon."

"You sure the scouter got it right?"

"Of course, she did," countered Tiffany. "After all, I was the one scouting it."

"Oh, sorry Tiff."

"That's okay."

"I thought you might be busy with another gallery."

"Nope," said Tiffany as she looked at the bank building through the binoculars. "I have not had one for two months now."

"That's rough."

"Yup. It means I have to take more assignments for Cicero."

"Hey if I had more money, I would buy a painting or two from you."

"I've been to your place, Carla," said Tiffany, looking away from the building briefly. "I do not recall you having the room for it."

"I am sure I can make room for it."

A door opened in the tranquil night. Both women drew their attention to the front of the building. There across the street a lone shadowy man exited and locked the doors behind him. Tiffany examined more closely with the night vision capable lenses. Sure enough, it was the stern-faced uniformed man who was checking on the security. An engine ignited and the car parked to the side had its lights turned on. Soon after, the gear was put in drive and the man was gone from the scene.

"Just as scheduled," said Tiffany as she put away the binoculars. The two gathered their things and descended to the lonely streets. A couple more cars whizzed by on the street, failing to see the duo as they made their way towards the bank. Originally, they wanted to be situated on the same side of the road as the bank itself, but Tiffany learned through advanced scouting that both facilities were well occupied and well-locked during the evening hours. By the time the next automobile drove by on that lonely stretch Carla and Tiffany were already at the back of the bank, making their way into the place.

Using specialized equipment provided by the upper echelon of the Cicero Organization, Tiffany was able to identify the numbers used to open the service entrance at the rear of the financial structure. After a couple of tries, she got the exact order correct and the door made a clicking noise, confirming it unlocked. The amount of money they could steal was limited, as the main vault was on a timed lock. However, large sums were in a couple of safes in the manager's and assistant manager's offices.

"Opened," boastfully stated Tiffany as she pushed away the door to the safe and with Carla holding an open duffle bag threw several bundles of bills into it. Bag zipped up, the two closed the two safes, spinning the dial some to add to the deception of it having not been opened over the evening. Out the door, the two went along the rear side of the bank, within an alley space between it and another adjacent business building. From there, Carla unzipped her blue duffle bag with white straps and handed Tiffany her change of clothes. Quickly the two changed into some business casual clothes, with Tiffany's including a short skirt while Carla's included one half of a pantsuit. Alteration completed, the two each took a duffle bag and then walked at a normal pace onto the sidewalk.

"So, you're saying they fixed it?"

"Yes, they did."

"That's good," smiled Tiffany.

"Especially for my grandfather. He hates being shut in all the time."

"I was just about to ask how he was doing."

"Well," began Carla as the two turned left to be on the sidewalk of a well-lit major road, "he always believes he's doing just fine."

"Now, now, that can be something," replied Tiffany. "I have heard of plenty of people who were really sick, but then because of having a positive outlook they got better."

"If only that would happen."

The two kept walking, getting the occasional look or catcall from a man. They were used to it. Soon they were at the predetermined meeting place. The alleyway was between two warehouses. Carla had never been there before, but Tiffany had and knew where to find a broken lead pipe on the ground. There was a pipe on the side of one of the warehouses and it was this item that was struck five times quickly, and then five times slowly. While the setting was different, the character in the hooded cape was the same. He approached slowly, beckoning the two women to come closer. This time, Cato paid the two women what he and the rules promised from the onset. As planned, Cato took both duffle bags after the women took their purses from them. Cato then disappeared from their sight into the space between the two warehouses, presumably on his way back to home base. Tiffany and Carla casually walked out of the alleyway and into the nightlife.

"You okay?"

"Yeah," replied Carla. "I just feel a little weird without that bag of mine."

"I'm sure Cato will take good care of your little baby," remarked Tiffany, eliciting a smile from Carla.

"Sounds good."

"You don't work Fridays, right?"

"Right."

"Then how about we have a night out?"

"I thought we just did."

"You know what I mean," said Tiffany with a laugh. "Come on, I have a couple friends who live near here."

"I don't know. I mean, my grandfather might get worried."

"Oh, Carla, you know he never gets worried about you. You worry more than he does."

"I guess you have a point."

"Besides, my friends will love you."

"You think so?"

"Yeah. Especially when they learn you'll be the designated driver."

"We will see if I can remember how to drive."

"Even if you don't, you'll still be better than the rest of us drunk."

***

Sunday morning in the city. For a small yet sizable minority of the population, the time meant attending worship at one of the metro area's roughly 4,000 churches. Most met in the traditional sanctuary setting, though several congregations were small enough that they worshipped at school buildings or hotel meeting rooms. There were a couple of megachurches whose facilities looked like concert halls as well as a handful of satellite campuses for large nondenominational communities.

Josiah Sharp's congregation was closer to the traditional mainline avenue of design and ceremony. Sharp worshipped at St. Ives Methodist Church, a congregation with approximately 700 members that averaged 250 regular weekly attendees. As usual, the worship attendance numbers peaked during the Christmas season and Easter then ebbed during the summertime and Spring Break. Raised Methodist and confirmed when he was a teenager, Sharp transferred his membership to St. Ives from his home church, which was shepherded by his father, who took the reins from his father before him.

Sharp was active in the church. Besides his regular presence for Sunday worship, he also went to a Wednesday evening Bible study and the occasional social event usually scheduled for Saturdays. He tithed each paycheck and refused to engage in all but the most urgent of work on that first day of the week. Ushering was another contribution. The way St. Ives' head of ushers organized it, there were three teams that did four months each in a rotating fashion. Sharp's team did January, April, July, and October. Being a friend of the head usher, he occasionally stepped in whenever someone could not make it to the service. Such was the case on that particular morning.

"Welcome to St. Ives," he said once again, reinforcing the greeting given at the nearby open door. The elderly couple smiled as he handed them bulletins that gave the agenda for the worship service. The trickle of people who had entered in the past several minutes was increasing as 11:00 AM was drawing near. "Good morning, welcome to St. Ives," he repeated as another few people showed up. A middle-aged couple that Sharp was friends with showed up and they chatted briefly. They brought with them their daughter, who smiled and simply said thanks when handed a program. She was fairly attractive, prompting the head usher to walk over to Josiah after the family entered the sanctuary.

"You know she seems like a nice girl," commented the head usher, an expert matchmaker, with a smile. Josiah simply laughed it off; that was what she said of every young woman he gave a program to.

Unlike the other ushers, Josiah remained in the narthex during worship. He was not obligated to do so, but felt that it was good to help any latecomer with a bulletin and, if necessary, hold open the door to the sanctuary. On one occasion his vigilance within the narthex fulfilled a different aid. One Sunday a traveler who had lost their way en route to see family came in and asked for instructions. Fortunately, Josiah knew the exact location of the restaurant they were supposed to meet kinfolk at, and gave them the simplest way to find the family gathering.

This service was not as eventful. There was the sexton and a couple of youth who showed up as was typical to set up the refreshments the congregation would enjoy following the service. There were a few people who exited the sanctuary to go to the restroom down the hall and returned within a couple of minutes. Otherwise all was still. Not being amongst the pews, Josiah felt no guilt in checking his phone for messages and for the time. While generally a predictable examination, around 11:30 AM Josiah noticed that his phone, on silent, had a new text message. He recognized the number and swiped the phone screen to investigate. A meeting was to happen at 3:00 PM on Monday. Listed as "VERY important", the text said that he was to go to room 1018. It was a curious request, as he knew what type of chamber room 1018 was. He texted back his affirmation.

The following afternoon Josiah was riding pretty high. The meeting with the landlord and the tenant representatives went without problem. The defendant agreed to their terms, and even sent verification that repair crews were working on the condominium that very day. He sat between the two framed Bible verses with a sense of confidence, though not at the expense of attending to other matters and similar cases put before him. The clock was nearing 3:00 PM and so he gathered a notepad and a couple of pens and went to room 1018. There were a couple of security folks present, stoically standing on either side of the entrance. One asked for identification, which Josiah provided. Tacitly nodding, the security allowed Josiah in and he closed the door behind him.

"Assistant District Attorney Josiah Sharp," said Attorney General Kyle Brown. He was one of four people seated at a table in the center of the room. A rectangular shaped furniture piece, all four people sat facing the recent entrant. Brown was to the left of the others. On his right was Mayor Mary Bhatia and to her right was Governor Claire Voxner. At the far right was District Attorney James Colbert. "Do you recognize everyone seated before you?"

"Yes," replied Josiah, who also noticed the empty chair facing the four prominent public figures. It was pushed into the table.

"And do you know what makes this room significant?" asked the attorney general.

"I know we occasionally conduct confidential meetings and depositions here. Hence why there are no windows and the walls are sound proofed."

"That's correct, Mr. Sharp," chimed in Mayor Bhatia. "This meeting is in the strictest of confidence and cannot be discussed by anyone outside of this room."

"Take a seat, Josiah," said Brown in a welcoming yet formal voice. Josiah walked forward and pulled back the chair, sitting in it before pushing himself forward and placing his notepad and pens on the table. He took a pen and removed one of the caps, readying to jot down notes for the information he was about to consume.

"Those will not be necessary," said Brown. "This will not be a detailed meeting, but it is of great importance nonetheless."

"Yes, sir."

"The purpose of this meeting is to offer you the deadliest position I can possibly offer any staff member under my watch," solemnly spoke Brown. "I am offering you the lead position on the Cicero investigation."

"Okay," said Josiah, his word choice not clarifying if he meant understanding or was indeed taking the presented offer.

"I specifically chose you for consideration because I feel that you are a competent and passionate professional. Your sense of justice and studious researching are seldom matched amongst the other assistant DAs."

"Thank you, sir," replied Josiah as Governor Voxner spoke next.

"We wanted this offer to be made in confidence. As you are obviously aware, the Cicero investigation has been the costliest investigation our Justice Department has ever undertaken. We have lost more witnesses, persons of interest, and staff members than any other case I am aware of. So, we are taking the added provision of keeping the identity of our lead investigator anonymous."

"I respect that decision," said Josiah, "and I am honored that you have selected me for this position. I promise to do my best."

"Josiah," interjected Brown. "Just to clarify, you do not need to accept or reject the offer now. Let me know your decision tomorrow at some point."

"Tomorrow?"

"Yes, Mr. Sharp," said Voxner. "You surely understand that by agreeing to this you are effectively signing your death warrant. Your life will be that much more dangerous should you agree to this."

"My apologies for any disrespect," began Josiah, "but I have already made up my mind on this and that position is not going to change within the next twenty-four hours. I understand the danger, the possibility that I may end up like Myles. But I also understand that for all their power the Cicero Organization cannot kill the soul. As the Good Book puts it, they can only kill the body. Instead of fearing them, we should be far more afraid of Him Who can kill both body and soul. Cicero cannot kill my soul, and therefore I am not afraid."

"Very well," said Brown. "You will report your updates to either me or Colbert and we in turn will report them to the governor and mayor respectively. When possible, you will report everything to us as a quartet."

"Sounds good to me," replied Josiah. "Anything else?" Then four prominent individuals either said no or shook their heads. "Then if it is okay with you, I would like to get started on my research."

"Very well," said Brown. "Godspeed, Josiah."

***

Droning noises emanated from the dark mysterious pit below the sink. The cubic impression upon the counter was gradually losing its fragile structures of unconnected dishes and scattered utensils. Water plunged downward in a constant thick cylindrical column, feeding into the growling blades below. Its other victims were the remnants of a couple meals that day, as remains of various food items were pushed down by the clear liquid deluge and from there obliterated by the rapidly moving parts.

Her grandfather, having just finished taking his medicine, was seated in his wheelchair a few feet in front of the television. Carla was nearing the completion of the evening chore. She was using a spoon to scrape the undesired leftovers off of the plates and bowls before carefully putting them in the washer. The remaining utensils were placed into the cleaning machine, the shelf pushed into the mouth of the device. There were only a couple of plates left when the pain began.

She had to stop as the surge rushed through her head and chest at the same time. Her eyes closed tightly at the internal jabs. Moments after that, there was an aching within her joints, especially the wrists and knees. There was no cry of agony, no alert sent to her elder kin in the adjacent living room. Instead, she kept at her chores. Acknowledgment of the uncomfortable sensations were quick and then back to work. She was almost done, almost ready. Just a little longer.

"Come on, come on," urged George al-Hassan, his two fisted hands gently striking the arms of his wheelchair. "You are getting there. Keep at it."

"I thought that you gave up shouting at the television for Lent," smartly remarked Carla, hoping to distract herself from growing internal agony.

"Shouting, that is what I gave up," responded her grandfather, raising a wrinkled index finger in the air as part of his rebuttal. "Talking forcefully is different."

"Of course, Giddo. Whatever you say," said Carla, putting the last plate in the upper shelf and pushing it into the dishwasher. Down went the cleaning solution, poured into the hole designed for its presence, and then up went the door, sealing the contents shut. Carla flipped a switch near the sink that caused the groaning within the counter to halt and then turned the knob to discontinue the stream. It was getting worse, and coursing through her body as though it were its own thick stream going through her veins.

"Mmmmmm," muttered George, making the noise not because he thought something tasted well but rather to subdue his own profound annoyance at another missed goal attempt. "Sunday's game will be easier to handle."

Carla did not respond to the comment. She did not hear it. Rushing into her bedroom as the dolorous affair was abounding even more so, she looked for the way to end it. The pain was ratcheting up in its intensity, causing her to grimace more. It was a matter of mistiming, a poor estimation for how long things were going to take. Last night she was early and now the expanse of specific hours was longer. This lapse was undiscovered until she started to feel the minor pounding within her cerebrum and chest. It descends quickly and then gets worse and worse. She knew from experience.

Upon entering the room, she dived to the left side of her bed. She threw the sheets that shielded the clearing under the frame of the bed to get at the wooden box. She dragged out the box while down on both knees, her proximity to the solution helping her mind to stem off the rising anguish. The top was removed, revealing several dozen little packets. They were clear, tightly securing an odd bright green gelatinous substance. Desperately grabbing at one, she pulled it out of the box and put it in her mouth, swallowing the packet in its entirety. It was going to be another half hour or so until full relief came.

 In the meantime, she shifted herself so that she was sitting on the floor, her back to the bed with its tossed sheets. Leaning back offered some relief, but not much. With her right hand, she put the top back on the box and shoved it underneath the bed. Moments like this made her remember those days many years ago. It was something to think about, anything as the pain continued to rush through her body. Her eyes closed as her right hand grabbed her head. Moments like these traced their origins to the events of years ago, when her life was realigned in its priorities and savageries.

III

A different world, a different world. The same person, the same place. The same city, with a community college all its own. She was taking night classes there, having done so for the past two years. There was still some pending discernment on what she was going to specialize in. There was a passion for English literature, its prose and poetry alike. Tennyson, Dickens, Shakespeare, and Poe. However, there was also an undercurrent of financial realism, prompting a fair number of math and economics courses.

At this point she was two semesters away from having enough credits to transfer to an official university. She was looking forward to the transition. Her retail employer at the time was made aware of her coursework and was given advanced warning that her night classes may become daytime ones instead. Small issue, as the store was often open until late evening, especially during sales. The young woman struggled to pay bills, but living with her grandfather helped square away some costs. For the longest time, she needed him more than he needed her. This changed on that day years ago.

A relative who later moved halfway across the country alerted her. A call that happened a couple of hours before class. Later on, she realized that the class period before that one was going to be her last college level course. Her boss allowed her to leave early. She sped in her used car to the hospital. After struggling to find a space among the large parking deck, she hastily walked the equivalent of a half mile from the outside spot to the waiting room. She huddled in her seat, her insides spurting with nervous acid. Whenever a uniformed medical professional walked by her, she looked up, only to see them keep walking and at most give her a glancing smile. Minutes felt like hours, hours felt like days.

"Carla al-Hassan?" asked an inquiring voice. The woman, still dressed in her bright retail uniform, looked up at the voice. It was a woman maybe a few years older than herself, wearing a white coat, glasses, and having her dirty blonde hair in a bun. Carla stood with dreaded anticipation.

"Yes, that's me. Is he alright?"

The doctor took a breath. "He is doing fine now. We have him stabilized. It was touch and go at first, but he stayed conscious the whole time."

"Can I see him now?"

"I recommend that you wait a little while," answered the doctor. "He is resting now and I think it would be best if he stayed that way."

"Okay. Fair enough," said Carla, brushing her fingers through her hair as the anxiety levels lowered. "How long will he be here?"

"I would say no more than a couple days. I highly advise that he be put on some medication for his heart, at least for the next several months."

"Okay."

"All right, then. If you could provide the front desk with some insurance information, then we can get started."

"Insurance?"

"Yes, of course," reiterated the doctor with a puzzled expression. "Your grandfather does have insurance, doesn't he?"

"No, um, I don't think he does," said an equally confused Carla.

"That's strange. You mean he does not even have government insurance?"

"My grandfather is not a United States citizen."

"Oh," said the doctor with surprise. "Well, you can still purchase the medication. It's just that you will have to purchase it at full price."

"How much?"

College was the first thing to go. Carla barely made enough to afford tuition and with George al-Hassan's declining health and advanced age, he was no longer capable of working. As his ailments increased, the amount of funds required to keep him alive went up as well. She had a minor scare when the accounts office accidentally billed her for the semester she would never take. However, through a series of frantic phone calls, the accounts office offered their deepest apologies and removed the charge.

Next was her car. For the past three years, she scraped enough from extra shifts at work and borrowing textbooks from friends and the library to pay the dealer for the used car. It was a sufficient vehicle, with windows being manual and the climate control being mediocre. However, the automobile fulfilled perfectly its basic purpose of getting her from one location to another in faster time than running or cycling. With her grandfather in need of a series of treatments at the hospital, the vehicle was sold off for a mere $3,000. This was about a fourth of its actual worth, but time and haggling and the need for immediate cash made for a steal of a deal for one individual.

"Carla?" the doctor asked, prompting the former student to rise from her chair in the waiting room. It was the same woman as before, whom she had come to know over the past couple of months.

"Yes, Stephanie?"

"Your grandfather is going to need another surgery."

Carla took a breath. Hand upon her forehead she paced about before returning to face the doctor. Stephanie could only look at the granddaughter with pity as Carla gathered herself together to deal with the cruel turns of reality. "How much is it going to be?"

"Somewhere around $8,000, assuming there are no complications," responded Stephanie. Carla looked down, trying to form the words to communicate. Her lips moved some as she looked down at the cold sterile floor. Taking another breath, she faced the doctor.

"I don't know if I can pay it," she said, attempting to hold back a great wave of emotion. "I-I don't know if I can pay for it. What happens, what happens if he doesn't get it?"

"If he does not get the operation, he will not have long to live. Maybe a few months."

Her eyes closed, the tips of her fingers touched her cheek and forehead. She again struggled to grasp the situation. Objectively she knew everything, she understood all that was spoken to her. Subjectively, it was a challenge, an overwhelming challenge that rocked her within and throughout. An idea slowly incubated and birthed in her mind, a contemplation she had briefly entertained but mysteriously dismissed time and again during the past couple of months of financial struggle.

"Is there a way my insurance can pay for it?"

"It is possible," replied Stephanie. "I am no expert in the field, but unless I am mistaken you should be able to add him as a dependent."

"Really?" she asked, lightening up even as the weight of the current situation was pulling her downwards.

"Yes. Even though he's not a citizen, I am sure that even non-citizens can be added. Especially if they are close kin."

"Okay, who do I talk to?"

Stephanie did not have a specific name, nor was she acquainted with anyone at the state's Health and Human Services Department. Yet she did know where their office was, as well as their hours. She also helped Carla plot the correct public transportation schedule to get there, having more experience using buses and metro lines. The day she went was the same day that George went into surgery. Carla was worried about paying before it was too late, but Stephanie assured her that the surgery can come first. They will figure out how to pay for it later, added the doctor. Mercies notwithstanding, payment still had to come soon.

Personnel at the HHS office were nice. The secretary smiled a lot and socialized some with Carla. The place had generic yet soothing music piped into the waiting room. It was a far calmer setting than the space for waiting within the hospital. Then again, the actual trappings of ease may have been more psychological. Carla had little angst over this outing, with credible confidence that she was going to get things squared with the insurance issue. There had already been some phone calls between the two parties, with the woman on the other line assuring her that it was likely going to be an easy process. The door opened to one of the private offices at the place and she was beckoned in by name. After a couple of minutes of conversation, all went sour and bleak.

"What do you mean months?" she asked in outrage. "I was told over the phone that this was going to be an easy fix."

"I am sorry, Miss, um, al-Hassan," began the thirty-something man behind the desk, "but the person you talked to probably didn't see the complexities of your situation."

"I was told it wouldn't matter that he was not a citizen."

"And it doesn't," replied the man in a mildly defensive tone. "However, there are other issues. Bureaucratic matters and getting Washington's approval. Things like that. If all goes well, it should be done no later than August."

"I don't have until August," she said, struggling to maintain her composure. "My grandfather's surgery was today. I only have a matter of days before I need to pay for it and the care he gets after that."

"Listen," he said in a compassionate tone. "I am sorry you are going through this. Tell you what; I will make some phone calls and see what I can learn. I will have someone get in touch with you shortly. Okay?"

"Okay," she said, unsure of the promise.

"Is there anything else I help you with today?"

"No, nothing else."

"Then please give me a number I can reach you at."

"Sure. Of course."

Carla saw her own way out. She did not stay any longer than she had to. Waiting for the bus, she felt misery flowing through her. Memories, memories of her grandfather looking after her, spoiling her, reading the newspaper to her, taking her to church each Sunday, and so much else. He put so much effort into raising her. Her memories of him outnumbered the memories of her parents. She devoted most of her energy to stopping tears, her posture slouched with her long black hair shielding her face on either side. Finally, the bus came and attention was devoted to getting up and going home.

She barely ate her dinner as the sun descended below the skyline. Talking to no one since the meeting at the HHS office, she meandered about her apartment. It was technically his apartment, leased in his name. Though for that evening, it was hers. All hers and all alone. She was given a faint jolt of hopeful energy when the phone rang and Stephanie confirmed that the surgery was a success. He was sleeping comfortably following the procedure and was scheduled to leave the hospital within the next week. The joy was weakened as the issue of payment remained a specter wallowing about the air. She tried watching television, but nothing engrossed her attention.

And then the phone rang again. She assumed it was Stephanie calling once more, perchance forgetting to note some comment. The ringing and the pushing of the cell phone button to begin the conversation happened too quickly for her to wonder about other possibilities. "Yeah?" she asked informally, having forgotten to check the number on the small screen of the mobile device.

"Hello, can I speak to Carla al-Hassan?" The voice was that of an older man, who she would later know only as Cato.

"This is she."

"Hello there. I am a businessman who is looking to recruit some new clients to make excellent commissions. If you want to make thousands of dollars in a single day, I can help."

"Really?" she excitedly exclaimed.

"Yes."

"How did you get this number?"

"Random telemarketing machine, to be honest."

"Okay," said Carla. "I would like to know more."

"Great! Then please meet me tomorrow evening at 8:00 PM at the Hopewell Bar on Downtown Main Street. There will be others in attendance. Casual dress is acceptable."

"So tomorrow, 8 PM, at the Hopewell Bar?"

"Correct."

"Thank you very much. I will be there."

"Excellent. Have a good evening."

"Take care."

***

Hopewell Bar was a scarce place. Once a hub of warm glowing social activity and drunken revelry, during the economic recession it lost business. So much was its decline that eventually it was reduced to being open solely for special events. Still, when it was operational, the service was good and the décor elegant. Political functions, social club outings, Bar Mitzvahs, Quinceañeras, and birthday parties were known to transpire with fond memories and ample photos uploaded to social media.

That evening, all looked dark. Carla viewed the building from across the street. A burnt out street lamp did not help things, making it look even more wickedly clandestine. It was the right address and minutes before the right time. She did not want to cross the street and enter the closed facility. Nothing seemed benevolent about this matter. Then again, alternatives were absent from her world. The fear of what existed within that closed bar was smaller than the fear of having to go to the hospital without the necessary funds. With a nervous breath, she said a quick prayer and went across the street.

As she got closer, she saw other people at the dark first floor. One of them had arms folded and appeared to be security. The other person was smaller and looked to be more diplomatic in his demeanor. Talking some with a couple of others, Carla saw their forms disappear within the lightless interior. Finally getting close to the entrance, she got a better look at the man in a black T-shirt and jeans and boots, a stern faced man. Intimidation enveloped her, but with only her grandfather in mind she kept walking. Soon the older man saw her coming and beckoned her in.

"Good evening, my dear," he said, wearing a well-tailored pinstriped suit. "Can I get your name please?"

"Carla al-Hassan."

"Excellent," he remarked. "We talked on the phone the other day. My name is Cato. You are even more beautiful than I imagined."

"Thank you," she smiled, adding further merit to his claim.

"Just go straight forward and you will see a door that has lighting behind it. Enter the room and go down the staircase. The others are waiting."

"Okay," she said, encouraged to feel like maybe, just maybe this was not some lurid scam. The verdict was yet to be decided. Her eyes had to adjust when she opened the portal to the basement, but the adjustment was quick and the descent down the flight of stairs came without problem.

The basement lacked the elegance of the first floor. No carpets, no vinyl, no bright colors of any kind. There were simple metal chairs, most folded up and leaning against the wall. A few wooden tables were present, all of which were holding up several boxes, presumably of supplies, spare glasses, and cleaning products. It looked like a social gathering minus the refreshments. Carla counted sixteen among those gathered in the basement. The environment was lax, even warming. Carla retained some concern over the objective fact that the basement level had only one entrance.

"Good evening, everyone," projected the voice of Cato from the stairs. "Please gather around, gather around." He corralled them verbally and peacefully to pay attention to him as he walked about the room and made his way to a large wooden crate at the far end of the basement. He stood upon the sturdy cubic container, all heads turning to face him. Remaining on the ground standing stoically was a tall, muscle-bound man with arms folded. He had a sidearm in a holster and wore black pants with black boots. Tan skin and short black hair, he looked like a Marine. "Welcome everyone to this special recruitment meeting. Welcome to a new and glorious future." Two other muscular men, smaller compared to the man beside Cato, nevertheless showcased a similar posture and presence. One was to the right of the group of visitors while the other stood on the bottom step of the stairs.

"By now you are all probably wondering why you are here. You each have your own reasons, your own needs. And we are here to provide you with the necessary means to meet those needs. In return for such sustenance, we ask only that you do our bidding every so often for our superior. For those wondering, wonder no more. My superior and now your superior is none other than Cicero."

There was a pause in his remarks. Cato knew that the name ushered forth whispers, infamy, curiosity, and some panic. He wanted it to come out immediately rather than fester, to be released at this early stage instead of being built up and released in some harmful way. Carla was among the surprised. She did not follow the news religiously, but she was aware that a terrorist named Cicero was masterminding several political assassinations. Her grandfather said it reminded him of the old country.

"By coming here tonight, you have effectively joined the Cicero Organization. An organization that serves the public and the people in a way that no other entity can fulfill. We are the controlled and purposed violence that maintains civic order. We are the people who help to justify various public policy efforts in order to ultimately create a more prosperous city, society, and, hopefully, country. Without us, people will stray away from healthy progress and good political decision making. With us, they are incentivized to pick wisely, based upon the most instinctual reason known to modern and premodern man: carnal destruction. All of you are going to help sustain a better world."

"Hold on, you guys are terrorists!" protested a young man with reddish hair and skinny build. He looked to be around Carla's age, no older. Cato simply smiled at the utterance of the word and then continued.

"George Washington was a terrorist. Malcolm X was a terrorist. Gandhi was a terrorist. Whenever someone actively pursues a cause to upend certain things, they always get labeled with that same simplistic word. If that is how you understand us, fine. We are all terrorists. But our terror is filled with virtue, morality. We do not blow up political adversaries or snipe off an activist here or there for the fun of it. We do it because it is necessary, necessary to create a better political discourse."

"By any other name," he grumbled to himself as Cato continued. Few expressed any other open concern for their situation.

"Now then, what will henceforth ensue will be a relationship between the Organization and you, its members. First of all, you all be trained in the art of virtuous terror. You will learn to fire guns, stab with knives, hand-to-hand combat, explosives, and other similar tactics. You will learn from the best, as your chief trainer and second in command of the organization, Livy, will be your guide." The tall muscular man to the side of Cato nodded, identifying himself. Cato continued: "You will each get official documents for your employers if you are currently employed stating that you are going to be on jury duty for the next couple of weeks. These are authentic documents, which you will collect at the end of this meeting. Before then, you must bind yourself to us in a way that guarantees your undying loyalty."

At that moment, the man who was before standing to the right of the sixteen recruits walked towards one of the tables. He took a box that was placed on top of several other items and opened it. He went about the people, handing them each a single packet, one inch in diameter, that had an odd looking bright green substance within it. "What my associate is passing out is something that you must take. It is not poison. At least, not as long as you keep consuming it in small dosages which we will provide. It has no other ill effects. It will not mess up your mind, it will not cause cancer. But, go too long without it and you will perish. Such is the trust we will establish together." While most of them went ahead and opened the packets, allowing the tooth-paste tasting substance into their body, the thin red-haired young man again spoke his dissent to Cato, holding the packet with his right hand.

"And if we refuse to take this garbage?" he asked critically. Cato looked at Livy and nodded. In a moment of a moment Livy drew forth a Glock handgun, aimed it at the red-haired dissident, and pulled the trigger, sending a bullet between the eyes. Carla screamed in horror, the blood splashing on two people standing next to her. Others screamed as well, with most of them trying to make their way to the exit, which was blocked by a guard. As panic and shouts continued sporadically, Cato talked over them, his arms outstretched with palms facing downwards to his audience while fingers were splayed.

"Everyone! Everyone! Calm down, all is well. All is well," he said, his tone and reassurance believable enough that the others began to listen. "Consider this the very first part of your training. The key lessons are numerous. Now you have learned the importance of doing what we tell you. Now you have learned what happens when you disobey." The group listened more, focused on Cato as Livy robotically returned to his original disposition with arms folded. Cato jumped down from the crate and beckoned everyone to return to the corpse, whose eyes remained opened and from which a small pool of blood was slowly expanding upon the hard basement floor. "Take a good look at this man. Go ahead, stare and stare more. By the time we fashion you, this will frighten you no longer. You will not be so fazed when someone once living is killed. You will be desensitized to this sight and sights similar. You will be trained to be as Livy is: calculated, efficient, able to take a human life in an instant without a moment of hesitation or moments of remorse."

They were too shaken to talk; many looked at the body not because of a want but of a fear, a fear that if shown uncommitted they would be shot next. Carla kept looking, not wanting to be seen as weak or frail. It was a matter of will, it was a matter of being more powerful than scared. She hardened her mentality for the first time that night, disconnecting from the realm of emotion and feeling. She had to do this, she reminded herself of that. The substance was consumed and the corpse was viewed. The tension was broken when Cato clapped his hands together and directed everyone away from the body.

"Now then, by now you are probably beginning to doubt your decision to come here. To counter such a false sentiment, we have one more thing for each of you," said Cato, nodding to the same man who handed out the green substance packets that the remaining fifteen people consumed. The guard took a large brief case and placed it on the crate that Cato had previously stood upon. He opened the case to reveal a grand amount of paper money. Bundled, counted genuine legal tender. "Just for coming tonight, each of you will receive ten thousand dollars to use for whatever you may. Each of you will get the amount along with the jury duty papers. Each of these things are legal and legitimate. Nothing counterfeit here. All is real. Welcome to the Cicero Organization."

***

Training came quickly. Maybe it was slow when it took place, maybe the demands and the rigors felt like an eternity when they were unfolding. In her mental projection of her history, they went fast. Exercise, fitness, combat, shooting, stabbing, kicking. All was drilling, practice, gradually moving upwards to be a better and better warrior for the mysterious cause. Carla was oft complimented for her abilities, her stamina, and her conviction. She excelled in the grappling and the wrestling. She quickly showed herself capable of accurate aim with all sorts of firearms. Before these days she had never even handled a paintball gun.

They were conditioning the whole time. Each day she and the others were given the green substance. Cato called it the "emerald commitment" while Livy called it the "loyalty oath." There was fraternization amongst the fifteen recruits. People ate wherever they wanted to, as the Hopewell Bar was within a few blocks of many restaurants both of high-end cuisine and fast food. Most of the time she ate with Tiffany, with whom she befriended early in the training program. Things were changing. Looking back, she realized that few of them were still in contact with her. Carla was unable to recall the precise fates of most of them. However, there was one whose fate she remembered. Indeed, that harsh memory was a distinctive among the collage of happenings in those days.

The room was small, about ten-by-ten. There was a single lightbulb hanging from the ceiling to give the entire space illumination. It was protected by a dark rusty grill. It was a dreary disgusting-looking chamber. The walls were corroding and mildew abounded in each corner, carving a rough triangular feature darker than the rest of the space. The floor was discolored and bare. Pockets of rust and mildew, as well as damp puddles pervaded within the dilapidated interior. Carla wondered if any man-made space in all the world appeared more abandoned and rejected than this one. Perchance the impressed vision of that rotting place served as a subliminal inspiration for eventually finding work as a maid.

It was a haunting place. No windows, only two doors. Carla entered one and faced the other. She peered about the place, spotting a single camera attached to the wall, a small red light confirming it was in operation. Cato and Livy were watching, hidden in a much better maintained quarter that included a couple of guards and a control board for the camera and the light. She knew why she was there. She had prepared for it. Wearing a tight-fitting shirt and pants that could have been used for a yoga session, her right hand lightly gripped a knife with an eight-inch blade. Her ebony hair was tied back into a pony tail and her eyes fixed upon the opposite door as it screeched when opened.

They had conditioned her along with the others. A hefty dosage of graphically violent entertainment, of increasing brutality added to the combat training. They were commanded to be near and then touch and then stab human corpses, requisitioned from the nearest morgue. Initial sessions involved killing animals, starting with cats and then dogs. Yet as the door creaked away it revealed the new target: a human being. Another one of the female recruits, this one with brown hair and blue eyes. She was younger than Carla and looked it. Her face appeared childlike, though she was developed enough in the chest that one could deduce at least a postpubescent individual.

She turned to close the door, the shutting coming with a profound thud. A stoic face turning to angered determination, she also held an eight-inch blade in her right hand. Nerves tore within Carla. For some reason, this seemed unreal. She started to grasp that she was about to engage in a duel to the death. Glancing briefly away from her opponent, she suddenly realized that a few patches on the ground she presumed to be rust were actually dried blood. For the time, they stood. It was part of the ritual. A few minutes of standing in silence before the fight was to begin. Feel the environment, it decaying core. Sense the life before you, the person you must kill to survive. They waited, with nerves assaulting them from within and a percolating layer of sweat from without.

"Ladies," a voice echoed through the small space. "When I give the command, you two will determine who lives." It was Cato. His elegant highbrow dialect was corrupted by the sound system's layer of fuzzy interference. Nevertheless, he was fully coherent. "Three ... two ... one ... begin!" With that, the lone lightbulb in the confined room went out with a faint zinging noise. Carla thrusted some only to miss the enemy. Quickly she backed into one of the damp corners, swiping her right hand from side to side as a force field against her foe. The left hand was also stretched out, blindly moving about to feel the opponent before she felt back. Moments passed with only heavy breathing.

Carla's eyes were starting to adjust to the dark. Meanwhile in the room where Cato and Livy were present, infrared gave them a perfect view of all that was taking place. They saw both women taking defensive positions in opposite corners. Cato pushed a button and then the lightbulb turned on for a second before turning off again. The move was intentional, messing with the eyes of the combatants. Carla got a brief view of her enemy, seeing her similarly crouched into the opposing corner.

Both women took the brief visual aid and went for the attack, swiping away at each other while also jumping back. Their poorly placed thrusts and their overcautious ducking and retracting made for another bloodless encounter as both moved away from the center of the room and back into opposite corners. The chaos was heightened as the lightbulb again went on and off. Carla saw her opponent and again went for the attack, crouching down as came at her. There was a scream, then another, but it was fear and frustration, not a wound. Carla almost felt the blade, feeling the brief movement of air between the knife and her torso. In a panic, she rushed backwards and hit the wall, causing her to voice a quick groan from the impact. The light came and went for a second again, with her opponent rushing at her in a furious scream muzzled by clinching teeth.

Carla rushed to her right, hearing her enemy swipe her blade some, only to grunt in frustration at hitting only wall. Carla was in another corner, her right hand retracted a little while her left hand groped about the blackness in an attempt to locate her enemy. It seemed like a pointless method, as the other woman was surely waiting for the light to give her a quick image of the one she must kill. Then, a moment before the lightbulb turned on and off yet again, Carla felt on the very tip of her left index finger the cold fine edge of the blade. Then the primal attack occurred, with the angered growling a giveaway to her opponent's charge. Carla again avoided contact, the other recruit landing into the wall.

The light came on and Carla saw the back of her enemy, whose brown hair was in a similar ponytail to her own. It was planned in an instant, a millisecond of decision, an impulse to violence that Cicero and his Organization longed to have in their troops. She had not yet turned around, her knife-wielding arm was swaying as though she was about to face the center of the room. She was going to adopt the defensive posture both implemented when possible. No, not this time. Carla was not going to let her keep this mistake and survive. With a loud, desperate breath, Carla charged at the back, gripping the knife intensely with her right arm positioned in an acute angle. As the dark descended once again upon the small enclosed space the first blow landed into the woman's right shoulder blade.

A high-pitched wail came from the opponent, the sound of a blade dropping a mere afterthought as Carla lifted her hand upwards, the pain doubled upon her foe as the blade ripped out of the shoulder blade. A split second and Carla delivered another blow to the back, this time hitting closer to the spinal column. Another scream of agony, more blood gushing out as the room remained cloaked in oblivion. Another stab, then another, and then another. There was little aim, there was little precision. Only desperation and fear. Carla wanted to stop as the screams became more pitiful. She was feeling liquid splash upon herself, undoubtedly the blood from the growing number of punctures.

Her right hand became wet and when the light flashed quickly again she saw the upper third of her arm layered in splashes of bright red as the opponent's screams were decreasing and her frame collapsed to the wretched, disgusting floor. Carla descended with the foe, delivering three more furious random stabs before withdrawing in panic at what she was doing. Breathing hard, she kept reversing her steps until her back touched the wall. Carla's left hand held her right elbow as she bent over in disbelief at what she had just done. The light came on again, but this time remained in use.

Carla saw her handiwork. Blood was gushing from the back of her opponent in multiple places. The white shirt the woman was wearing was dyed red in all but a few places, the blood streaming down onto the flooring. Her head was invisible as the thick brown hair was somehow liberated from its ponytail and thus was freely flung about in a thick cluster. After a couple of moments, Carla's breathing returned to normal. Her sweat felt cold now, her body temperature lowering.

"My compliments, Carla," said Cato through the sound system. "You have done well in this important test." A faint moan interrupted Cato's words. Carla returned to alert, her knife-wielding hand stretching outward. The guttural utterances were emanating from the body. Movement was taking place in the limbs. It was sluggish and soon Carla relaxed once again, seeing no threat to the profusely bleeding adversary. "Your job is not completed, Carla. Complete it now." Carla was too afraid to disobey, fearing both a vengeful enemy before her or a bullet to the brain courtesy Livy.

Her young enemy was slowly getting up, painful grunts abounding as she struggled to balance on the upper halves of her arms. She likely would have perished from the wounds already received, as the knife had burrowed deep into a few organs. With her left hand, Carla took hold of the thick brown mane of her enemy, who uttered a long groan of terror as Carla yanked it upward, propelling her to be on her knees. Before her arms could flail in resistance, Carla sliced her throat and then, using the hair as leverage, threw her back to the ground. A woman with a frozen heart stood over the other recruit, watching the former foe convulse like a fish thrown out of a pond. Eventually, the convulsing ended.

CARLA

***

Three weeks since her grandfather's surgery and all seemed to be going well. Carla decided early on to keep all her activities outside of her family's knowledge. It was like being a superhero, with her secret identity and alter ego barriers erected. To celebrate George's release from the hospital, she treated him to a high quality restaurant dinner. This was, of course, after getting the green light from Dr. Stephanie. The outing was nice and promising, with her grandfather being a gentleman who held the door open for her and pushed her chair in as she sat at their table. She bought new clothes for herself and her beloved kin and shrewdly kept several thousand of the dollars she was getting on a regular basis in a savings account for her grandfather. For some reason, she felt that for all his health issues he was going to need that savings account instead.

Her time with the Cicero Organization was also going well. Carla was raised well and set up with a moral code influenced by western society, Middle Eastern hospitality, religiously strict instruction, the Ten Commandments, and the Golden Rule. This worldview of obedience and kindness, charity and individualism, was mostly left behind whenever she was obligated to enter the domain of the Cicero Organization. She had to compartmentalize, or else she would have been unable to slit the throat of that recruit. Only a skeletal framework of her normal morality entered the Hopewell Bar or the Eagle Factory.

She was at the latter facility for an extended stay. Her grandfather was told that she was going on a vacation with some friends from school. It seemed plausible enough, as she had only recently quit going to community college. Her individual quarters for the time were comfortable. A well-made bed, clean floors and walls, television, wireless Internet, and three meals a day. However, Carla was told in advance that there was going to be a rigorous test to take place at the factory. Cato came to her on the second day of her time at the living quarters to inform her of what was going to happen.

"Are you enjoying your time here?"

"Yes, I am," replied Carla. "Even the training seems easier."

"There is a reason for that."

"What would that be?"

"The test."

"What test?"

"We are going to show you why you can never betray us," said Cato with a sinister undertone to his voice. Carla was perplexed, but not for long. "When I leave this room the door behind me will be locked. You will still get regular meals, Internet, cable, and what not. We will subtract only one thing."

"You mean …"

"Yes," he said with a smile. "This will not be a pleasant time for you. But it will be very, very educational." He left the room and closed the door. Carla heard the noise of the bolting of the door. She did not know how to feel about this, but within a couple of hours she felt it. It started as a gnawing headache, something one gets when hungry or experiencing a brain freeze. Within several minutes, it got worse, migraine quality. By the following day, it was piercing and spreading, as her chest and limbs were also becoming unbearable. She hoped laying down would help ameliorate it. Only faintly and that was in vain as the pain got worse and worse, to the point that fists were being clutched.

"Make it stop," she uttered aloud. "Make it stop." It was getting worse. Carla never knew that it was possible for such intense physical anguish to rise to such heights. Her vision decreased as her pain got to the point of blinding her. "Please … make it stop. Stop, please!" Time stood still, her body wracked by greater rushes of discomfort. She begged and begged, crawling into a fetal position on the bed. Her words became mere noises of pain, shouts whose semantic structure was gone but emotion obvious.

Then the door opened. She turned her head to face the man standing above her in a suit and tie. Cato looked indifferent. "Help …" she weakly muttered between shouts of intense sensation. Her arms gripped her sides, her toes curled and loosened just enough to curl once more. Cato took a packet from his pants pocket and bent down. He placed it in the hands of Carla who savagely threw it into her own mouth and chewed desperately, each bite a sting of pain vibrating throughout her body. The pain was still intense, crippling her on the bed, her hands now gripping the sheets she was lying upon. "Why won't it stop?" she shouted at Cato, now sitting at the foot of the bed. "Why won't it stop?"

"It takes about a half an hour," remarked Cato as though nothing significant was taking place. "At this point, the emerald commitment is entering your nervous system and has at the least halted the increase of pain you are presently feeling. Within a few minutes, you will start to gradually feel better."

"Why?" asked Carla, lines of tears from each duct. "Why did you do this?"

"Now you know what happens if for whatever reason you decide to leave us. We won't go after your family. No, we go after your very body. The pain accelerates the longer you go without the substance, beginning twenty-four hours after your last consumption."

"How long, how long does the pain last?"
"Four days."
"And then?"
Cato smiled. "And then you die."

***

It was a clear night. The sky projected many stars and a whole Moon despite the interference from city lights. A mild evening, the weather a little cool but not cold. Many of the pedestrians sauntering about with friends wore light jackets or sweatshirts. Some wore shorts with sandals or sneakers. This was the dividing line for the masses, as those who preferred warmth dressed more and those comfortable with the chill dressed less. The crowds were ebbing off, the hour getting late.

Cato and Carla stood in the short vacant space between a tavern and a closed beauty salon. The former was on its last call, a collective moan from most over the minor heartbreak of such an update. Lights were decreasing as more businesses were shutting down to rest until the morrow. The two were wide awake, with one wearing a jacket and underneath it business casual. The other wore the so-called Canadian tuxedo: jeans and jean jacket. They were worn, having been used plenty of times. The denim was fading and parts were thinned to the point of being a few white strings. For the work to come, Carla was not expected to wear clothing that she planned to wear again.

"The Moon lights you well," commented Cato. "It glows your left side just perfectly, as though casting a classical statue."

"Thank you," she responded, keeping her focus on the sidewalk. She was nervous, suppressing much angst.

"This will be both the easiest and hardest physical test you will take," explained Cato. "It will be easy because whomever you have to kill should not have the training nor the weaponry to mount a good resistance. It will be the hardest, because you will have to kill someone who is not a threat to you in any way. Indeed, you will be basically committing murder. I have explained this to you before, but I felt it best to explain again."

"Why?" she asked as another person walked past them on the sidewalk oblivious to their presence. "Why do I have to do this?"

"Because, my dear Carla," began Cato, a hand on her shoulder, "if you can kill someone for no reason without hesitation, then you can kill anyone Cicero wants you to kill." Another couple of people walked by. "Wait a couple minutes more. My source tells me there are only two people left besides the bartender."

"How do you know they are not together?"

"My source says otherwise. They sit on opposite ends of the place. No interactions."

"What happens if I fail?"

"Well, Carla," replied Cato as he removed his hand from her shoulder. "Unfortunately, if your target survives then you are out of the Organization and will have no more access to the emerald commitment."

Another person exited. The source inside the bar talked into his cufflink, which went to a receiver planted in the right ear of Cato. "The next one will come out shortly. He will have to go this way to get to his car. You are fortunate. My source describes him as being a bit on the small side. He might even be shorter than you." Carla's midsection felt horrible. Her stomach spurted acid intensely. She did not talk; she did not face Cato. She kept looking forward. She held the piano wire with both hands. "He is heading towards the door, get ready." Nodding, she got closer to where the alleyway and the sidewalk met.

She leaned against the brick wall of the tavern, the reflection of the Moon showing her face to the heavens. She raised her arms so that the wire was held in front of her face, her fingers shaking as they held it. Carla forced herself to keep her mouth closed, breathing ever harder through her nose. She heard the footsteps, he was coming closer. There was no halt or acceleration as he neared the alleyway. He was ignorant of her presence and of her internal anguish. As before and as again, she thought of her grandfather. She thought of him slowly dying of his ailments.

She blinked and upon the opening of her eyes there was the back of the man. She saw no face, no eyes to stare at her as she took that moment to lunge forward, her arms raised high above his head. In an instant, they came down and then backwards, the wire gripping tightly to the unprotected neck of the patron. No one saw her actions, retracting her arms and herself into the alley as the man failed to scream for help. His arms flailed about before desperately clawing at the wire that was cutting through his flesh.

In the sudden action, Carla lost her footing and fell to the ground, all the while maintaining the vice-like grip upon the wire to the point where her own fingers were turning a dark pink from the lack of circulation. The arms of the victim were hurling all about, going between the failed attempt to loosen the wire and the failed attempt to strike back at the unknown assailant. He made basic bestial sounds, grunts, and muted screams, unable to get the attention of the outside world.

Blood was flowing, the wire crushing his neck and opening a vibrant wound. The fluids flowed onto the jacket and jeans of Carla, but she held her grip. Gradually, the kicking of the legs and the chaos of the arms slowed to a halt. The noises of grunts and gurgling ceased and with a final breath, he resisted no more. Only her breathing was audible, her lips quivering as she loosened the wire and then threw it to the side of the alley. She pushed the body off herself as circulation returned to the tips of her digits. As he rolled to the cold paved floor she saw his face. The eyes and the mouth remained open, the latter producing its own crimson river. She did not know the man. He was not famous, though by the following evening his photo was going to be on the local news. It unnerved her in those moments. She began to feel very cold and very ashamed. She wanted to cry.

"Come on, come on," muttered Cato as though nothing of significance had transpired in front of him. He walked past her, putting his gloved hands on the body and lifting various valuables from the corpse. "How will you become a good assassin if you do not get to covering your tracks?" He took her by the arm and raised her up from her crouched pondering position. "Get some garbage and toss it on him." She obliged. By the time a trash man discovered the body the next day, all useful evidence was gone.

***

"So, it was pretty quick?" asked Tiffany. She and Carla were waiting on the first floor of the Hopewell Bar. They were sitting together at one of the small round tables located to the interior of the closed facility.

"It felt like forever."

"But pretty quick?"

"Cato timed it and said it all happened under a minute," acknowledged Carla. Her friend rolled her eyes.

"Girl let me tell you, you had it lucky."

"Lucky?"

"Yes. Your victim was small and went quick. Shoot, my guy was over six feet tall and five feet wide." The latter part of the description made Carla laugh aloud.

"Five whole feet?"

"Maybe six or seven."

They both laughed some.

"Six or seven. Okay."

"And he put up a fight, no joke. He slammed me into a couple walls, spun me around a bunch of times," she explained, placing her hand on her back. "It happened two nights ago and my spine still feels sore."

Carla could not believe she and another human being were laughing and giggling as they shared stories about how they brutally murdered innocent bystanders. She was not totally unaccustomed to such talk. As a child, relatives from the mother country talked of their time in the military and her grandfather did describe some of the more graphic experiences he had at Hamah. The relatives' stories always had a sense of humor about them. Then again, the relatives remained pro-Assad and unlike her grandfather they remained proud of their actions. They felt manly for doing what they did. If only those bravado-driven uncles and male cousins heard their adorable little kindred speaking now.

"So how did you get through it?"

"I just kept holding on, same as you."

"No I mean," began Carla in a more serious tone, "how did you get through it?"

"Well," softly replied Tiffany. "My father was abusive. And by the time I was old enough to fight back, he left my mom and I. So, whenever I am about to get into a fight, I just think of him slapping me around and everything is okay."

"Carla al-Hassan?" asked a guard who came up the stairs.

"Yes," she said.

"Cato will see you now."

Carla nodded and followed the guard down the rickety wooden steps. She had ventured up and down them multiple times. Sometimes she wondered if they were able to support an adult or if at some point soon they will give way. Tonight was not that point. As she entered the basement level, she saw a few people standing around wearing dark hooded capes as though they were some modern gothic version of Robin Hood. Despite the dimly lit space and the hoods that obscure the upper part of their faces, she was familiar enough with those around her to recognize Cato and Livy.

Leaving the steps, she was beckoned by a welcoming hand gesture from Cato to take a seat at a wooden chair placed in front of a small wooden table. In the dim light, it appeared like an altar. Cato stood before it, his genteel smile seen through the lack of light. As she sat down and rested her arms upon the table, the cloaked men silently walked towards her. She was not particularly scared at this point, even with the unusually loud closure of the door at the top of the stairs. They formed a circle, with her in the middle.

"Carla al-Hassan, I offer you my congratulations," began Cato. "You have successfully completed your training and are now a full member of the Cicero Organization. I know that we have been fairly clandestine in our intentions, but this is necessary. We cannot reveal our full intentions until one is fully initiated and bound to us. As I have explained before, so I explain again that we have no true political loyalty but rather do the bidding of Cicero, which can mean going after the liberals one election or the conservatives the next. Both wings are as vast branches that periodically need to be pruned. You will be one of the pruners and in my humble opinion, you can become the best." Livy flinched a little at the assessment. His face was obscured not only by the dark and the hood, but also his height and the fact that all in the room were centering their gazes upon the seated Carla. "Now then, undoubtedly you have questions. You are free to ask what you want and I will do my utmost to answer satisfactorily." She hesitated at first, looking about the stoic cloaked men. Cato prompted her. "Go on, do not be frightened. Ask whatever you want of me."

"How will you contact me when an assignment comes up?"

"We have your cell phone number. That shall suffice. Our messages will begin as being written in numbers. The code is easy to break and is meant to be so. After that, the message will come either via phone call or text message. It will tell you when and where to meet either myself or Livy. Full details will be given from there."

"How will you keep my substance supply regular?"

"Tonight, when you leave you will take a month's supply with you. The next time we meet, you will get another month's supply. That is even if we meet again in less than a month. Remember, only one is needed at a time."

"What if more than a month goes by?"

"Then you will receive the substance in the mail via package."

"I know you want me to kill, to rob, and to lie for the benefit of the Organization. Are there any other moral laws I must break?"

"No," stated Cato. "Whatever positions you have on alcohol or dress code, or sexual ethics can remain intact. Any other questions?"

"Yes, one more," said Carla, feeling safe amongst the circle. "Who is Cicero?"

Not a second passed after she completed the query that Cato slapped her across the face with the back of his hand. The impact threw her back into the chair and forced her to face the left side of the room. It was not so much the fury behind the blow as it was the unexpected nature of Cato's reaction. With fingers touching the sore cheek she slowly turned to face the older gentleman with a shocked expression. He stood still and composed as before. With a sinister looking smile he spoke.

"Ask me again."

Carla was conditioned to obey authority, especially the visible authority before her who commanded a certain action. Again, she queried, this time with some pause. "Who is Cicero?" Immediately after the question was spoken again Carla received a strong blow to the side that caused her to moan in pain and bend over in her chair. Eyes closed in response to the pain and then opened to see a stoic circle yet again. Cato nodded at Livy who stepped forward and put a handgun to her head. The loud clicking of the hammer alerted Carla to the weapon's presence and made her tense. Meanwhile, a calm and composed Cato stood before her, a serious and demonic expression.

"Ask me again."

Carla was no imbecile and nervously shook her head east to west and then west to east. The gun was still pointed at her head.

"Ask me again," he repeated firmly, as though withholding a great amount of rage. Carla nervously shook her head again, her breathing becoming deep. "Ask me!" he shouted, causing her to blink and shake her head many times. "Ask me."

"No!" she screamed.

"Exactly!" he replied, with Livy withdrawing the gun and the circle dispersing. "Your first assignment will be next week."

And there she was, taken through the depths and back to live a life of darkness. The pain was gone, the substance taking its full effect. She stayed at her place on the floor of the bedroom, her back against the bed. The tide of memories receded with the misery and returned to its chambers within the vast internal realm of the unconscious. Her right hand touched her forehead and traveled backwards, brushing through her long hair. Giddo was calling from the living room. He wanted her to see what the forecast was for tomorrow since she was going to be out for a while after work. She confirmed her presence and promised to be there shortly. Life returned to the present, the bland, bland present.

IV

The Exeter Hotel was one of the most elegant and stylish buildings in the city. Three floors tall, it was situated in the downtown area, having been there since the early twentieth century. This was the hotel where celebrities, foreign dignitaries, elected officials, and presidential candidates stayed when visiting. The vile elements of society even respected it, as the Cicero Organization prohibited its members from committing their acts of terror within five blocks of the landmark.

In one of its spacious meeting halls a political charity function was taking place. It was an elite gathering, where every attendee not connected to a media outlet was required to pay $2,000 for a seat. They were expected to wear formal attire, with the men donning black suits and white bowties while the women wore flowing dresses and high heels. There was a little deviation from this code, with some women wearing monochromatic pantsuits and some men wearing black ties instead.

The agenda was a pleasurable one. Guests waited outside the ballroom in a hallway that included velvet carpeting and white columns carved into the walls. Once things were ready, the well-dressed invitees entered through one of three pairs of double-doors, which included security and a person to verify their tickets. They enjoyed refreshments while they waited, water or wine being their options. Inside the ballroom, many directed their gaze upwards to the impressive detailed carvings on the ceiling. Large chandeliers provided light for the space, reflecting off the legion of spotless glasses placed before hundreds of chairs at dozens of circular tables. There was a stage at the far end.

Servers provided the opening appetizers, which included drink orders as well as bread and butter and a choice of four different kinds of salads. Over the course of a half hour, the tables were filled almost to capacity. At one end of the stage, near the doors that the waiters and waitresses were using to service the large crowd, a table was reserved for press. Six of the eight seated there had laptops and all of them had some kind of recorder for the event. They were focused less on reporting at that point and more on rummaging for food; they were not promised a meal for their time at the fundraiser.

Mayor Mary Bhatia and Governor Claire Voxner were both there, as they belonged to the same party. Attorney General Kyle Brown and District Attorney James Colbert were absent, as they belonged to the other party. Bhatia, Voxner, and their respective husbands were seated at a round table adjacent to the stage. When their meal was completed, they walked onto the stage along with a few party leaders. Around 7:00 PM they began the formal programming, which consisted of introductory remarks from Bhatia, a few speeches from party leadership, and then a sending off.

"Good evening everyone," began Bhatia. "My name is Mary Bhatia, I am the mayor of this fair city and I welcome you to this wonderful, marvelous fundraiser." She paused while the audience applauded. "It is amazing to see such great support for the cause and I think I can speak on behalf of everyone on stage that I am thrilled at the sheer number of donations that have poured in over the past couple months. While the elections are not for another year, to see such support means a lot." Some more applause, this time a little less intense. This was not because the audience was disagreeable, but rather many did not want to feverishly applaud at absolutely every optimistic talking point.

After making her initial introductory comments, Bhatia shifted to the people sharing the stage with her. She described each of them with glowing descriptions and the occasional light joke. All in good humor as Bhatia knew everyone else on that stage, having grown up watching politics from a personal perspective. A couple of party leaders, as well as Governor Voxner, were several years older than Bhatia. Voxner remembered better days for politics in the city and the state at large. When Voxner first began campaigning for seats, attack ads were less common and less personal. The violence at rallies was also rarer, to say nothing of the occasional participants turning up dead. Bhatia was nearing the end of her comments when someone from outside barged into the ballroom.

"Capitalist pigs!" shouted the mildly obese bearded man wearing a T-shirt, worn jeans, and sandals. The shirt included the statement "DEATH TO THE TWO PARTY SYSTEM!" in thick black letters and had a red fist pointed upwards.

Despite lacking the microphone equipment of those on stage, his voice traveled across most of the vast room in quick time and was audible to all but those elder attendees whose hearing had passed its peak. The closer to the stage, the harder it was to make out the exact words that the man was shouting. He dashed by the security folks, somehow getting in without a pricey ticket. Coherent or not, most, including all on stage, recognized the verbose heckler as Rafael Sanchez-Vargas.

"You're all the same! The same elitist crap that's been bringing the state to the dumps!" he continued as a hundred concerned conversations bustled about the dozens of round tables. Sanchez-Vargas was moving towards the stage in a straight line, accruing much verbal resistance as scores began to boo and heckle him back.

"Security! Remove that man!" shouted Bhatia through the microphone. "Get him out of here now!" A few men in uniform arrived and pursued Sanchez-Vargas as he continued towards the stage. He was still about fifty feet away from the row of speakers when he turned and saw the security coming closer.

"You can't shut me up! You scumbags can't shut me up!" he said repeatedly as security took hold of the activist by the arms and shoulders. Jeering drowned out his ravings as Sanchez-Vargas offered little resistance to the personnel leading him out of the ballroom. Boos were supplanted with cheers, sounds of acclamation for uniformed men who took the radical out of the midst of the rich party investors.

"Thank you, thank you," added Bhatia in relief. "Ladies and gentlemen, let us give the security an applause, for without them this enjoyable evening would be impossible." The crowds applauded even more. While the establishment felt they had prevailed, the damage was completed as all but one of the press exited the ballroom to follow Sanchez-Vargas to try and get his perspective for their ledes.

***

Josiah Sharp's occupation was more secretive since he agreed to be the lead investigator for the ongoing Cicero Organization affair. In public statements the Justice Department was implying that they had abandoned the investigation into the shadowy entity and its myriad of criminal acts. Some news articles from citywide publications pondered aloud if Cicero had been victorious. After all, city officials were quick to dismiss the Organization as a source of various brutal incidents and rarely mentioned them in public. No one had been named as the replacement for Myles Talbert and it was admitted that most of the evidence against the Organization died with him.

Sharp's official story was that he was overseeing the inquiry into the death of Talbert as an isolated incident. When interviewed by media he spoke only of the effort to catch the killer of Talbert and not the effort to take down a terrorist group. Sharp was adept at dodging questions on whether or not the Talbert case was connected to a grand criminal investigation. Sharp did the classic midway stance of neither confirming nor denying their claims. Behind the veneer of ambiguity was an absolutist mentality that centered on taking down Cicero for this and other offenses spanning several years.

Sharp was seated at his desk beside the large window. On either side, he read the two Bible verses, one from each Testament, doing so with the quick glance. While the intrigue was greater at his workplace so was the boredom. To allow him to focus on this most important of cases, his superiors agreed to cut down on his overall workload. This meant he had more leisure time at his desk than before. While waiting for the latest information to come his way or for a contact to return comment, he became quite talented at those classic computer games included with every purchased machine.

"Josiah?" asked the familiar voice of District Attorney James Colbert. He was standing before the employee, drawing his attention away from a chess game with a computer opponent. "My office now." Josiah nodded and followed Colbert across the floor to his more private space. As with previous meetings on this matter, Josiah was sure to close the door behind him as he entered the office. He looked about the professional space and its increasingly familiar trappings. His eyes then caught sight of the unfamiliar, the two thick stacks of papers that were found side-by-side on Colbert's desk.

"So, they got back to us?"

"That they did," replied James as the two men sat down opposite each other at the District Attorney's desk. "Everything our beloved feds were able or willing to send our way can be found amongst these stacks."

"I see."

"They were even kind enough to give us two of each."

Five years earlier agents from the Federal Bureau of Investigation came to the state in response to a peak level of election season violence in which eleven volunteers were murdered and another thirty were seriously wounded by unknown parties. It was nearly double the election year before that. Investigators quickly linked the various killings and beatings, as all but one of the fatalities worked for the same campaign ticket. Agents took over from state detectives, annexing their evidence and conducting the inquiry from there. The increased presence of federal authority had some impact, as the violent incidents declined. However, the campaign with the victims was so bruised by the experience that weeks before the election the candidate dropped out of the race, fearing more bloodshed come November.

For a year, the FBI kept scouring the crime scenes, each fiber or piece of lead gathered, each autopsy performed and known associates of the decedents. Interviews and surveillance uprooted some possibilities, but nothing was cemented with an indictment, let alone an arrest. After the November elections were held without incident, the FBI began to pull out. Some declared victory, as a relative calm descended upon the political climate of the state. Others were more skeptical, seeing the FBI as being in retreat. Talbert had contacts with the Bureau and they aided his investigation.

The two men sifted through the papers, the photos, and the notes jotted or typed by the agents who had been probing the state's underbelly for their research. One of the few positives was that certain minor criminals were apprehended on unrelated charges and sent away for short sentences. "This looks like a possibility," observed Colbert as Josiah looked up at the mugshot that caught the district attorney's interest.

"Anthony Albioni," factually stated James. "A smalltime arms dealer who was known to profit from both sides of any given overseas conflict."

"I see," commented Josiah as his superior placed his copy of the mugshot back into his packet of items. Sharp looked at his own information on the suspect. "It says here that they suspected him of supplying many of the explosive devices to the Cicero Organization. They drew a parallel to his business of selling explosives to assorted militias abroad."

"They couldn't quite piece together a good enough case, however," added Colbert. "They searched his office and his home and found nothing to link him. No ledgers, no receipts, nothing of that kind."

"He probably got rid of the necessary stuff before they showed up."

"That was the weird part," replied Colbert. "The FBI had gotten their warrants quickly and in secret. While two of their agents detained Albioni at a police station others went through his things. Still, nothing."

"You think someone on the inside gave him advanced warning? A sort of, wolf in sheep's clothing, if you may?"

"Most likely. Remember, we are keeping your involvement on this matter confidential for a reason. The fewer people who know about this, the better."

"Then it looks like it might be best if I contact him in an unofficial capacity, so that way even fewer know what is going on."

"You sure you want to do that?" asked Colbert, staring at Josiah with unease. "I mean, he is not the kind of guy to be cooperative. Even when federal shields were goading him to talk, he was a stubborn prick."

"Well, I would like to believe that I could use some simple moral suasion to get him to cooperate and then from there get some official information."

"Moral suasion?" laughed Colbert. "The man's a black market arms dealer. We got him to serve four years' hard time for his actions."

"True, but he also served in both Gulf Wars. Furthermore, the bank records the FBI found showed that he donated a portion of his ill-gotten gains to help wounded veterans."

"Let me talk with the others about your plan. If they give it the thumbs up, then do your best. Otherwise, we will have to look into other options."

"Fair enough."

***

Once again, Carla al-Hassan lost the race against the alarm clock. She did not recall the dream she had, just that sudden fast-forward from the night before to the loud buzzing of the morning. Her face grimaced and her body moved under the covers. Without opening her eyes, she located the snooze button and pushed down. Getting to a seated position, she stretched and slowly opened her dark brown eyes to the mundane surroundings of her apartment bedroom. Tossing aside the sheets with her right hand, she pushed herself out of the bed and onto her bare feet.

Walking slowly across the room, she got to the closet where she quickly located one of her three sets of all-white clothes for work. Taking the clothes by the hanger, she gathered a pair of white socks and light-colored underwear. Most of the shades were light enough to be invisible when put under the pairing of an undershirt and a collared shirt. When Carla was given the job, and told what type of clothes to wear, she spent one day testing them out to make sure her unmentionables did not appear. She almost forgot the undershirt as she went to the bathroom to shower. She hung the work clothes on a hook near the top of the bathroom door. Several minutes later she was clean and ready for work.

Gathering various things into a purse, which was slung upon her left shoulder, she quietly opened the door of her grandfather's bedroom. The moving barrier creaked a little bit as it was pulled away from the archway. However, he remained blissfully asleep, his chest rising slowly under the sheet. For the first couple of months that George was wheelchair bound, Carla helped him get ready for the day. It required both people to be awake at an early hour so that Carla had time to get to work. Things changed as George began to exercise his upper body and when they had a railing and seat installed in his shower to help him do such things by himself. George was determined to be as self-sufficient as possible in his circumstances. Mouthing the phrase "bye, Giddo," Carla gently closed the door and slowly turned the knob to have it latch. She then exited the apartment.

A bus stop was just a block from her apartment complex. It was one of the advertised perks of the building she and her grandfather ended up moving into. Carla had the weekday morning schedule for the buses pretty well charted, with their timing generally being no more than a minute or two off. She struggled with the weekend and holiday timetables though, especially when weather conditions prompted the public transportation powers that be to decree a reduced schedule.

Thankfully, that morning was normal. She walked to the stop, which had a bench about eight feet long and fiberglass walls on three of its sides with a black awning at the top. There was no one else present at the stop. This was also average. From time to time she was graced with the presence of another one or two people. No communication, no socializing. Just waiting for the bus and awkwardly avoiding eye contact. Her place was located a few stops after the beginning of the route, which aided her in getting whatever seat she liked. She had a personal preference for the window side.

Looking to her left, she saw the rumbling vehicle pressing towards her, its large windows like big eyes, its rearview mirrors looking like antennae. Across the top portion of the front was an LED sign that provided the name of the line, which she knew by heart. On either side of the frontal identification yellow lights flashed to show that the large craft was about to dock at the side of the road. It slowed to a halt in front of Carla, curving inwards into the part of the street labeled "BUS STOP." With a beeping noise, the side entrance opposite the driver knelt and the thin door folded back to allow entry.

"Good morning, Max," she said to the driver with a smile while she took out her fare card and swiped it to get a better deal than if she had used paper money or coinage.

"Morning, Carla," he pleasantly replied. "As usual, you are looking stunning today."

"Thanks, Max," smiled Carla once more as she put away her card within her purse and found a seat with a window view. Max and Carla had known each other for a few years, going back to when Max was reassigned to do the route that included her stop. Their socializing was mostly basic, rarely going in-depth. Carla did know that Max had an adult son who also worked for the bus company. She found this out one morning when he was a passenger in uniform learning some of the basics by observation. According to Max, he was a quick study and was doing the route that had stops in the suburbs. He believed his son had the potential to rise through the ranks.

The stops went as normal. Within ten minutes of being picked up, the bus had come to the stop Carla used to help escape the fallout from the car bombing she committed the month before. It was common for her to use that stop. This was not only for nefarious reasons but also because there was a breakfast-themed restaurant located there which she often ate at before going off to work. When she and her grandfather moved to the area, it was the very first restaurant they went to and she had held it in high regard since. Though her trips there were not daily, they were enough that she knew some of the staffers by name and had a level of socializing comparable to that with Max.

About thirty minutes later the former factory where the maid service was based came into view. Although a few people were at the stop ahead, Carla pulled on the thin yellow wire above her on instinct. The very first time she took the bus to work she failed to be vigilant and found herself at the waterfront. She had to wait ten minutes for another bus to come and send her to the right stop. That day, her first day, she was very late and very embarrassed. Fortunately, her boss was merciful and only punished her by rightfully clocking her in later, prompting a smaller payout by the end of the day. Since then, only the occasional obligation from her other employment caused her to be tardy.

"Have a good day!" she said to the driver as she descended the three steps between the bus's floor and the sidewalk outside.

"You too, Carla," replied Max with his usual big smile. Carla made her way past the five people patiently standing in line outside of the knelt entrance. Taking advantage of the low traffic she immediately crossed the street and was at the former factory ahead of most of her coworkers. Breakfast was provided, the banal but always desired triumvirate of donuts, coffee, and orange juice. Her bosses were there and welcomed her cordially. They were personable and typically approachable people.

Gradually the other cleaners arrived, trickling through the large open entrance on the side facing away from the street. Many took buses from other routes. Most walked, as the factory was only a handful of blocks away from a large Latino neighborhood. Called "Pequeña San Salvador", it manifested during the 1980s when large numbers of refugees from El Salvador's civil war made their way to the United States. Concepción's family was one of them, bringing her to the States when she was four. One of the reasons she and Carla were friends was due to the similar refugee experiences.

"Buenos dias, Concepción," said Carla to her friend as she neared her.

"Buenos dias, Carla," replied Concepción. "Como estas?"

"Estoy bien. Y tu?"

"Bien, claro."

"How is, I mean, como esta Renaldo?"

Concepción laughed some. "Renaldo esta bien. Turns out it was just a minor bug."

"That's a relief."

The small talk dissipated as their boss rallied the workers together for the morning assignments. Carla and Concepción were teamed together with a few others. Miguel was the van driver this time. They gathered up the necessary cleaning products and utilities and packed up the van. By the end of the hour the factory was again mostly vacant, with all but three of their vans going about their planned routes. Two of those three were in reserve while the third needed some repairs that the assistant manager saw to scheduling. Looking about the van, Carla noticed what she often saw.

"Concepción, I have a somewhat serious question," said Carla while the other maids chatted with each other in Español.

"Somewhat serious?"

"Is there a law in El Salvador that says only men can get licenses? Because it seems like we are always passengers."

Concepción laughed. "Claro no, mi amiga. My sister has a license."

"Double-checking," smiled Carla. "Maybe the law only applies to maid services, correct?" Concepción smiled rather than verbally responding. A few minutes later, the van stopped and they filed out of the back to begin cleaning the first house on the agenda for that day. They did three houses that morning. During the lunch hour, Carla watched the local news to see about the latest developments in the investigation of her most recent atrocity. Nothing new, the government spokesman said. She smiled some as she finished her lunch and heard that little attention was being given to Cicero.

Rather, much of the noon hour focus was on Rafael Sanchez-Vargas and his latest obstructions at a political party fundraiser. The local news outlet was able to get an interview with him the next day, the mild-mannered talking head throwing questions at the hotheaded activist. Carla did not have an opinion of the man. Her coworkers loved him, as Sanchez-Vargas often rallied on behalf of immigrants' rights and of course was basically one of their own, having immigrant parents from Costa Rica. While entertained by the spectacle of political extremism and debate, Carla was not one for that world. The horrid experiences of dissidents in the home country and some of the things done to kinfolk or friends who dared speak out instilled within her an inherent neutrality. If anything, when Cato told her that the Cicero Organization showed no favoritism towards any specific political party she felt a bizarre sense of relief at having needed to join them.

Then her smart phone buzzed. She felt the vibration in her right pants pocket. Taking out the device she read the message: "6338 28 25539 633 46 653 8696 … More Details to Come." A text message was sent after that offering more specific information, including that Tiffany was to be at the meeting. Carla replied, confirming via text message that she was able to be present.

***

"Okay. Do you want anything else?"

"Haven't I ordered enough?"

"Pardon?"

"No, that is all," clarified Anthony Albioni, slouched into his recliner with the television placed on mute.

"Alrighty then," replied the perky voice on the other end of the line. It was a young person whose temperament annoyed the struggling arms dealer. "So, it's one medium-sized two-topping pizza, one topping pepperoni and one topping green peppers, one order of breadsticks with marinara sauce on the side, and one two-liter soda. Is that order correct?"

"Right on the nose," replied Albioni with a lethargically sarcastic tone.

"Swell! Your total will be $19.86. Your order should arrive in about thirty minutes. Can I help you with anything else?"

"No that's all."

"Alright, awesome. Thank you for calling us and hope you have a wonderful evening!"

Albioni hung up without saying good-bye. He rarely said good-bye. Shifting in his recliner, he turned the volume back on via the remote. It was some program or another, one he sometimes watched but had no faithfulness towards. It was noise and light, which gave a sense of normalcy and company in a time of darkness and solitude. Not that he was much for socializing, as he lived alone and rarely left his second story apartment. A pudgy fellow, his beer belly was attempting to break through the border between his shirt and his pants. This was one of the few evenings that he did not drink beer.

Albioni's living quarters were humble. About 450 square feet and three rooms plus a closet. He remembered having better before his brief prison sentence. He also had more social engagements and parties, more friends, or maybe so-called friends, surrounding him with affection, attention, and pleas for cash. Once out of prison he was forced to restart his enterprises. He tried legal arms sales but found that tougher, with potential clients refusing to do business with what they dubbed a "low life." Were it not for his military pension, homelessness would have been his lot.

And so, he drank away many of his nights or spent them indulging in junk food. He rarely exercised and perpetually kept a week-old beard upon his face. His few spurts of hope came with the occasional small order for his work or his effective middle-management of various covert deals for powers and would-be powers abroad. Sometimes he did work for domestic villains, something that added to his drinking and self-pity. His usual antisocial glumness was broken suddenly when the phone rang. Albioni was unused to receiving calls, especially after normal business hours. As he got to a proper posture and picked up the phone he assumed that the call was the pizza place confirming his address.

"What is it?"

"Mr. Anthony Albioni?"

"Speaking," he impatiently spoke.

"Yes, good. This is Assistant District Attorney Josiah Sharp. I've called you a few times during the day and left some messages about you calling me back. Did you get them?"

"I never listen to my messages," frankly replied Albioni.

"Oh. Well, anyway, I am investigating the murder of Myles Talbert. The explosive that took his life bears a strong resemblance to the ones you used to sell."

"You accusing me of something?" asked Albioni, his energy awoken and his anger pronounced. "Because if you are, you damn well better have something more than conjecture."

"Nothing official, I assure you. But forensics tells me that the bomb was remote controlled, made with components manufactured in the US, and, most notably, had a calculator pad which one enters a code activating the device. When the FBI investigated you years back, they found those very kinds of bombs in your possession. It only makes sense therefore that I cover my bases, so to speak. After all, as the Good Book puts it, like a dog returns to his vomit, so a fool returns to his folly."

"Tell me why I shouldn't hang up?"

"Because you're not a fool, Tony. If you don't mind me calling you Tony."

"Mr. Albioni is better."

"Well, Mr. Albioni, you are not a fool. You know better. And if you have done something wrong, you are at best an accessory to murder."

"What do you want?"

"I want you to help me bring the killers of Talbert to justice. If you tell us what you know, I promise probation instead of prison."

"The FBI never promised me that," a grudge-filled Albioni said.

"Well, I'm not the FBI."

"Touché."

"Besides," continued Josiah. "I have read your record. I know the service you gave to this country in both Gulf Wars. I know that you've done much to look after fellow veterans who came out of those conflicts far worse off. And I have a hard time believing that someone who so actively worked to stop terrorism half a world away would be happy with seeing it a few blocks from his home."

"No prison, you say?"

"Yes. Only probation, with community service attached. A community service, I might add, that can be fulfilled by volunteering at any given veterans hospital."

Albioni was not typically one for engaging in discernment processes before making a decision. Generally, he went with gut instinct or whatever worked before, and ended the matter at that. His automatic response would have been to swear at the attorney on the other end of the line, slam the receiver down, and go back to watching TV. Yet he felt a little different; he felt that this suit might be a little different from the federal suits.

"Let me think about it, okay?"

"Okay," replied a pleasantly surprised Josiah. He was also expecting a sudden disconnection from an annoyed Albioni. "How about I give you my number and you can call either later tonight or tomorrow evening between 6 and 9 PM?"

"Let me get a pen and some paper."

"Okay, sure."

A white van was parked in a small back road that went between two apartment buildings located across the street from where Albioni lived. The taller of the two structures had a room on the third floor that was rented by an unknown party who seldom made appearances. The small unit had a bed that had not been slept in for months and an empty, unplugged refrigerator. Only the bathroom was recently used and that was because Carla al-Hassan just finished using it. After washing her hands, she exited the tiled restroom. She did not use the light in the bathroom, nor did she turn on any of the other lights in the apartment. Having been there several minutes, her eyes already adjusted to the lack of luminance.

It was a cooler evening than the past few days, caused by the rainfall earlier on. Street lights still reflected the glistening puddles located at various parts of the paved ground. Carla wore a light jacket on her way to the small unit, as well as jeans and a short-sleeved T-shirt. She also brought her blue duffle bag that had the white straps. Once inside of the dark apartment she removed the jacket, fearing the longer sleeves might interfere with her aim. Carefully placing her duffle bag on the wooden floor of the small living room, she unzipped it and took out the pieces of the rifle.

Trained well, she quickly and efficiently put together the components including the scope and the silencer. Her only light source was the outside world, the evening electrics that prevented total blackness and yet hindered sight of the celestial host. Per the unnamed researcher's description, there was a small table in the corner. Carla repositioned the wooden furniture piece so that it was a few inches from the lone window. Opening the clear portal to the outside, Carla was welcomed by a faint wind and the droning noises of the city. She pulled the two legs near the end of the muzzle outward, planting them upon the table surface. Rifle loaded, eye peering through the scope, she found the second story window.

Down below, Tiffany was pacing about the streets. She saw the window open, but did not see the end of the muzzle with silencer affixed. She looked intently, awaiting confirmation that Carla was ready for the mission. Arms folded as the seconds passed, she soon saw a smart phone through the window, made visible because its flashlight option was turned on, the lone beam emanating from the vesper unit. Tiffany sent a blank text message to Carla's phone, the exclusive purpose being to make the beeping noise associated with receiving a text and thus confirming sight of the signal.

Carla did not want to look at the screen, fearing that the sudden inclusion of a bright screen before her eyes might mess with her adjustment to the dark and overall focus on the window on the second floor. She knew which window to target. The apartment itself was rented by the Cicero Organization for this very purpose, in case this very scenario was to play out. Albioni never took the substance nor was even aware of it. His obedience therefore lacked the fear of a four-day writhing death. People like him were still kept under control, even if by one unshakable punishment.

Tiffany walked across the street after a wave of cars went by. A couple of blocks away the next fleet of vehicles patiently waited before a pair of red traffic lights. Looking to and fro to verify that no one else was nearby, she threw a few small rubber balls at the window, drawing the attention of the inhabitant. Without confirming her success, she crossed the street once more. After doing so, the next cluster of cars sped by on their way to various destinations. If it did not work, Tiffany's backup plan was to honk the horn of the white van. Meanwhile, she hastily entered the vehicle and turned on the engine.

Carla waited but not for long. Through the scope, she saw a shadow begin to manifest behind the curtains. She slowed her breathing, calmed her nerves, and stared deep into the scoped view of the target. Attentive and narrowed in her focus, she saw the shadow reach for the side of one of the curtains. Pulling it back, he bent over a bit to peer outside and see if he could tell what hit his window pane. Before his head was able to turn both ways to view the span of the city street below, Carla depressed the trigger, sending a muted bullet that went through the open window, across the street, through the glass, into and then out of the cranium of Albioni. It was a perfect shot.

Carefully putting down the rifle, she rushed into action. Carla closed the window and latched it shut. She quickly unscrewed the parts of the sniper rifle and then carefully but speedily placed each piece into the duffle bag. The small table was moved back to the side of the room and the light jacket was put back on. White strap slung along her left shoulder, she opened the door behind her and then locked it right after closing it. Going unnoticed by the underpopulated tenant community, she made her way to the stairs and bolted down three flights, her right hand holding onto the railing.

Using a back door, she exited the building, making a left to be on the small road between the two buildings. A place struck by evening, she nevertheless saw the caboose of the white van. The pipe at the bottom right side of the vehicle was billowing smoke as the engine moaned. She opened the unlocked back door and threw her duffle bag into the space, with the heavy luggage thudding as it landed beside a smaller black bag owned by Tiffany. Pulling herself into the seat-less space she greeted Tiffany, who was behind the wheel. Back door shut, Tiffany pulled into traffic without incident, none of the other travelers the wiser as to what had just happened. Fewer than ten minutes later, a pizza delivery car turned onto the street and parked on the side of the road with hazards blinking. The young man driving the brightly colored compact took out the packaged order and walked to one of the pairs of double doors located on the first floor.

***

Having both been with the Cicero Organization for several years, Carla and Tiffany both knew how to get to one of the dozen or so alleyways or abandoned buildings where transactions took place. Both had been to the Eagle Factory several times, occasionally staying for a couple of days on end for business, training, or even leisure. So, it did not require much instruction by their superior to tell them where to go following the completion of a task. Several minutes after Carla picked off her target, Tiffany made a left turn into the parking lot of a warehouse whose exclusive user was the Organization.

The van was parked alongside a few other vehicles of varying kinds. Exiting the van Carla was a bit amused by the parallels she was drawing between the warehouse and the former factory that her maid service was headquartered in. She and Tiffany walked side-by-side. Carla carried her blue duffle bag and her friend carried a smaller black bag. Before them was a hooded man, imposing in stature. Tiffany's expression turned irksome as she realized it was Livy standing in front of them. The two women stopped five feet in front of their superior, who smiled at Tiffany before speaking.

"No news reports yet, but then again we did not want this one to be public," noted Livy. "So, if anything, this is good. Do you have the rifle?" Without speaking, Carla placed her duffle bag on the hard, cold floor of the warehouse and unzipped it, revealing the pieces of the rifle including scope and silencer. Livy nodded. "Place them on the floor." She obliged. After that, Livy took a bag located beside him and opened it to reveal several bundles of paper currency. "Here is $6,000 for you, Carla." In stoic business manner, Carla held out her hand and it was filled with four bundles of big bills. She placed the payment into her duffle bag while Livy turned to Tiffany. "And here is $4,000 for you, Tiffany."

"Less for me."

"You did not pull the trigger," countered Livy, with Tiffany nodding in concession. "Besides, if you want more, you'll need to talk a little sweeter to me."

"My payment?"

Livy gave a wry smile at the response, digging out the remainder of the cash from the bag. He handed it to her, brandishing a fiendish smile as his hand inevitably touched hers while he gave her the money. Tiffany looked at him with an unimpressed expression. The amount secured, Tiffany placed the bundles into her smaller bag. Both women zipped up their bags and almost in unison slung them around their respective shoulders. Without further communication or a salute of any kind, the two women turned away and departed the presence of their tall, muscular superior. They kept silent until they exited the side door of the warehouse, which was to the left of the entrance Tiffany drove through.

"I hate it when its Livy," commented Tiffany, hesitant to project her voice just in case he was within hearing range.

"I am sure he means well," said Carla, immediately skeptical of her words.

"Yeah right," replied Tiffany as the two got onto the sidewalk on their way to the nearest bus stop, which was four blocks away. "He is a creeper and that is that."

"You're probably correct."

"Besides, he reminds me of my father and that …"

"Is not a good thing."

"Exactly!" exclaimed Tiffany. "Girl, you know the script."

"Well if he tries to make a move, I promise I'll do what I can to help you stop him."

"Thanks," said Tiffany, giving Carla a glancing pat on the back. "By the way, my phone is in my bag. What time is it?"

Carla looked at her watch, which she often wore on operations given that, unlike her phone, it did not make noise. "A few minutes after eight."

"Then the night is young," replied Tiffany, with Carla's eyes rolling. "And you have off tomorrow. Why don't we hit the clubs?"

"Oh, Tiffany," smiled Carla. "You always want to go out."

"And you never want to go out. It's a good balance."

"But my grandfather."

"Oh, please with the grandfather stuff," declared Tiffany. "Knowing him he's probably busy romancing your landlady."

Carla laughed. "Yeah, he probably is."

"How about we meet outside the Hopewell Bar in an hour? Sound good?"

"Uh … sure, why not?"

"Exactly," confidently replied Tiffany as the two made it to the bench and only waited a couple of minutes before the next bus arrived.

***

For the first time in several weeks, people other than the murdered arms dealer were inside his apartment. There were two uniformed police officers standing guard within the space, one at the door and the other at the window where the bullet entered. A third man, dressed in plain clothes with a lanyard around his neck, had a small bag of equipment placed on the recliner near the corpse. Wearing light blue gloves to hinder his disruption of the crime scene, he was taking photos and notes.

While he did so another man not in uniform arrived. Wearing a black tie, black slacks, and a dark red shirt and gray jacket, he was stopped at the doorway by the patrol officer standing guard. In response to the request for proper identification, the man showed the officer his badge. The policeman stepped aside and the detective made his way to the living room where the investigator was snapping photos. Hearing the man behind him, he halted his activity and introduced himself.

"Good evening," he said, camera in hand.

"Detective Frank Cooper, homicide," stoically replied the man who entered the apartment moments earlier. A deep voice and broad shoulders, he looked tough enough to walk a beat. "So, what do we got?"

"The deceased is named Anthony Albioni. Age 46, he lives alone in this very apartment. About an hour ago, he made a large order to a pizza place. The pizza man got to the apartment, knocked on the door several times, and then had the front desk bring someone up to open it. And that is when they discovered this."

"So a pretty small time frame of death, correct?"

"Very much so," affirmed the man with the camera. "And a fairly obvious cause of death." He pointed to the body, whose head was visible. A prominent wound was upon the forehead, slightly closer to the left eye than to the right. Under the body was a wide yet shallow pool of blood that stained the carpeting. His eyes were still open, as though still looking for the cause of the noise. "Death was most certainly instantaneous. The bullet was lodged about two inches into the floor."

"That's a high-powered weapon," commented Cooper, who was studying the body as it lay motionless before the pair of investigators. His gaze stopped when he saw the right hand holding onto a piece of scratch paper. The plain clothes man took a couple more photos until interrupted by the detective. "Do you have another pair of gloves? I think I found something of interest."

"Of course," he replied, going over to the recliner, searching through his things, and then taking out a pair of the disposable items.

"Have you photographed the right hand?"

"I will do that now," he smiled as he bent over and captured the image while Cooper pulled the light blue gloves over each hand. The man got out of the way while Cooper knelt and carefully removed the paper from the cold fingers. Albioni's death grip was not strong. Rising to a straight posture, Cooper turned the paper around to see a hand-written phone number on one side. Giving it a curious look, he took hold of the landline phone near the recliner and dialed the number.

"Hello?" asked a voice on the other line after two rings.

"Who is this?" asked Cooper.

"My name is Josiah Sharp. I am an assistant district attorney," said the confused-sounding person. "And who am I speaking to?"

"Detective Frank Cooper of the Seventh Precinct. I was wondering if you could meet me at the apartment of one Anthony Albioni."

"Is he dead?"

"Afraid so."

"I'll be there shortly."

Photos completed, the two ununiformed men went about collecting evidence from the living room. The piece of paper was placed in a bag and the body was moved slightly to get to the bullet. With some effort, the projectile was removed from the floor and placed in another transparent bag. A coroner team came at the same time as Josiah did, each showing some identification before the guard at the door. Josiah looked with pity at the body as the two people from the coroner's office went to carefully placing the body on a stretcher and covering it. Josiah then approached the detective standing over the morbid operation, drawing his attention as he walked towards him.

"Hello, are you Detective Cooper?"

"I am."

"Assistant District Attorney Josiah Sharp. We talked over the phone earlier," said Josiah, who offered his hand. Cooper took a few moments as he had to remove the glove on his right hand. Josiah sighed a deep breath as the team took away the body, leaving only the pool of blood and the two bullet holes in the glass and the floor. He shook his head. "The Lord giveth and the Lord taketh away."

"Mind if I ask you why the deceased was holding a piece of paper with your phone number on it when he died?"

"I called him earlier about a possible lead regarding the murder of Myles Talbert. He may have had a small role in it. He was open to testifying. He was supposed to call me back either tomorrow or tonight."

"I guess someone did not want that to happen," replied Cooper. "So what do you think, Assistant DA? Was this a hit?"

"It would make sense," said Josiah as he walked around the crime scene, analyzing the broken window and drying red puddle. "He had plenty of nefarious acquaintances. Whoever did it clearly was a professional. And somehow, someway, they knew that I was talking to him about this case. And that is what doesn't make sense."

"How come?"

"We at the Justice Department have been very cautious about this case for obvious reasons. Or maybe just one reason," he said with a faint quick smile. "Either way, this is troubling for the investigation. Any further questions, detective?"

"Not at the moment," responded Cooper. "Can you give me some contact information so I can reach you? I might find something pertinent to your case."

"Of course. I will give you my work number and my work email. I should be in the office all day tomorrow. Do you have a pen and some paper?"

"I do," interjected one of the plain clothes men as he was packing up his things. He walked over to the two men and handed Josiah his pen. He also tore a piece of paper off his note pad, which had several cursive comments on other pages. Josiah used the moderately hard surface of the pad to write on.

"Thanks," he said to the man.

"No problem," he replied while Josiah handed Cooper the paper.

"Thank you, Mr. Sharp," said Cooper. "Have a good evening."

"I do not believe that is possible now."

V

It was yet another abandoned factory. The company that once operated the space saw a better opportunity in the Deep South. They reveled in the fact that placing their jobs in that part of the country meant they got to pay smaller wages for the same amount of work and with little hassle from organized labor. Over the course of two days the business moved their equipment and their machinery southward. 1,500 workers found themselves waiting in the unemployment lines with that departure.

The shell remained for the community's usage. Making the best of a rough situation, the building became a meeting hall where gatherings of a diverse lot were held. Rooms that once stored raw materials for the assembly line stored an army of metal folding chairs and stage pieces, as well as lighting fixtures, microphones, and cameras. Security patrolled the old factory, with some of the elder personnel being the children of those who once manned the assembly line. They dived into cynical humor when recounting how each of their fathers told them with fullest certainty that someday they would work there.

Groups rented out the place for their performances and assemblies. For a time, a startup congregation met there on Sundays, though recently they raised enough funds to buy their own church building. Local schools were known to use the large area for graduation ceremonies and concerts. Drama troupes, enthralled with the concept of "theatre-in-the-round", enjoyed the space and used it for their experimental performances. Prices varied depending on the group and type of venue. Schools paid almost nothing and religious groups generally received cheap rates as well. The highest rates were reserved for the spectacles most likely to incur extensive cleanup and repair costs.

One such expensive spectacle was taking place on that Saturday morning. A stage was set in the middle of the large vacant space. The trained eye could see on the massive floor faint imprints where the large machines that had generated industrial might used to be. Few paid these ghostly markings any mind as they entered the open space. On the stage was a podium and four American flags, one to a corner. Guard rails surrounded the stage, giving some distance between the speakers and the audience. Security in its stone expression and black suits with sunglasses added an organic barrier.

As more and more came through the entrances a growing rumbling from the scores of different conversations filled the air. Having passed a quick security check, they were rapidly reducing the number of open seats. They varied in their fashion, with some wearing business casual while others wore basic t-shirt and jeans. The weather was warm enough for short sleeves and short shorts. The audience skewed older and male. There were veterans, former factory workers, campaign volunteers, and others.

Near the stage a sound system began to blare out a hodge-podge of feel good music, country western, and light Rock-n-Roll. There was some hooting and hollering, the enthusiasm of the audience growing alongside its numbers. Some shouted patriotic chants, others party catchphrases. A few Gadsden flags waved in the crowd, generating more passion from the committed souls present. It was the party that included among its registered members Attorney General Kyle Brown and District Attorney James Colbert. The two elected officials were not present, as they both personally disapproved of such populism, even when it was for their benefit. Besides, elections were not for another year.

Party activists walked to the stage, the space having filled near to capacity. The sporadic chants got louder, the classic "USA! USA! USA!" getting the most repetition. Soon the music was cut off and one of the party leaders announced that the National Anthem was about to be sung. All who were able rose from their seats and placed hands over their hearts. The performance was decent, the high notes reached effortlessly by the hired singer. Even before the last few words were sung, cheers began from the audience. A 20-something dressed in formal clothing removed the microphone from the podium and addressed the audience, pacing along the corners of the stage as he spoke.

"I am so glad to see this level of passion for our party. Can I hear some of that passion?" said the man, who did a lot of door-knocking and phone calls for the party during campaign season. Shouts came from the audience in response. "Do you want to see the establishment collapse in on itself?"

"Yes!" shouted back the crowd.

"Are you sick of politics as usual from those on the other side?"

"Yes!"

"Then you are at the right place. We are here because we want to take our state back and eventually, our country. We are sick of seeing the same antipoverty programs again and again and again that never work. Did the unions bring back our factories?"

"No!" shouted many in the audience.

"Did the welfare programs give us jobs?"

"No!"

"Next year is an important election. I dare say it's the most important one we have before us. We need you," said the speaker, pointing at various people in the audience. "We need you, we need all of you, to go out there, knock on doors, make those phone calls, debate those protesters, and show them what our state needs to look like. And most of all, you need to vote. Because if you don't vote, you don't matter. Do you matter?"

"Yes!"

"Yes, you do. Yes, you do," continued the speaker. "And that is the message we are going to send to Mayor Bhatia and Governor Voxner." Each name elicited a chorus of boos from the crowd. "If you are sick of the failed economic policies of the Bhatia-Voxner Reich then fight for freedom, fight for our America. Can you do that?"

"Yes!" they shouted with greater passion.

"That's what I like to hear," continued the speaker. "I will have you know..." He was cut off by a disturbance at the back of the factory. Shouting, not the kind desired for a political rally, was heard in the background. Multiple voices, multiple agitators entered the place. Soon they recognized the heavyset man leading them onward. A grand roar of jeering was directed towards the unwanted guests.

"You are all useful idiots if you follow this guy," shouted Rafael Sanchez-Vargas, "he makes the rich, rich and keeps you poor and stupid." Sanchez-Vargas was the spearhead of the eight people whose interruption was creating an ever-growing aura of hostility. "These elitists feed off your ignorance. Don't be ignorant!" Soon the other seven people, teenagers and folks in their early twenties, made their own little chant of "Don't be stupid!" followed by five hand claps. "Don't be stupid!" Clap, clap, clap-clap, clap! "Don't be stupid!" Clap, clap, clap-clap, clap! "Don't be stupid!"

Vitriol kept spewing back at them from the audience. It was like a great gathering of killer bees had spotted a human target. Buzzing towards their unwelcomed guests, some figure from the larger hive struck first, landing a blow upon one of the young men standing beside Sanchez-Vargas. Another fist came, striking a glancing blow upon one of the other men in the ranks of the dissidents. A hot tempered lad, he did not take the blow with passivity and struck back, gut-punching the other fellow. Soon, more fist fights, a tackling of one of the two women with Sanchez-Vargas. The shouts and jeers got louder as about a dozen started exchanging hits and tackling people to the ground.

Security rushed to the scene, pulling apart the two hateful sides. A loud chant "Throw them out! Throw them out! Throw them out!" erupted in the former factory, led in part by the speaker whose corralling remarks were rudely disturbed by Sanchez-Vargas and his ideological peers. The lead disrupter raised up his hands as the security became more abrasive. "Okay, okay! I'm leaving, I'm leaving." He had limits, and knew that more fighting awaited elsewhere. Small wonder political groups had to pay the most money for renting out that space, a space that once hummed with mass production.

***

Carla al-Hassan was walking, at least mentally. It was a strange gloomy setting, the background all black with blobs of gray. There seemed to be trees, a forest all around the blackness. They appeared as Cypress trees, or maybe cedars like those in Lebanon. There was wind blowing, things brushing in reaction. Yet she felt nothing. No pain and no joy. She was just there, walking and walking more.

A pointless task, she ebbed and flowed in her urgency, looking at the houses and apartments all around her. They appeared suddenly, coming from the darkness and being a member of the darkness. She searched for the one she lived in and found only others. It was frustrating, it was desperate. Her grandfather was probably all alone. He needed her, she was sure of it. Was she running an errand? That must be it! Carla tried to make sense of the insensible, the flowing sub-consciousness.

Then a rush emerged around her. It started as a murky reddish cloud, but then it began to rise at her ankles. It was the crimson flow of liquid that could only be blood. She asked herself if this is blood. And she nodded to herself amidst the blackened background. It was rising, higher and higher. Now to her knees did it flow by, figures now gathering around her. Some were screaming, others coldly silent. Some got close and she saw to her horror that they were not of the living. Freakish smiles came upon them, the bullet holes and stab wounds she inflicted upon them opening and flowing into the rising deluge. Some were laughing, pointing at her with their rotting fingers.

They were getting closer; she was unable to run. She stood as they created an impenetrable wall all around her. She struggled to breathe while the crimson rose ever higher, her legs disappearing under its soup-like thickness. Her legs did not move. She tried running, walking, anything. No reaction, no feeling. The blood rose higher as more of the living corpses donated their scarlet fluids to the river. They shook rapidly as their limbs and long fingers stretched over her, grabbing her, causing her to fight. She tried beating them away. They gripped and yet Carla was still free to flail her arms in revolt.

She directed her gaze above and saw the blackness open up. Like a tear in a fabric it peeled away and bright terrifying light was before her. As the light pushed to the sides of the gaping hole in the sky, she saw the figure of Christ as a great painted icon. With His left hand, He held a gilded Bible and His right hand formed the sign of peace with His fingers. A large halo with the branches of a cross brightly shone behind His head, while His body was adorned with a robe of red and blue. She tried to go towards Him, away from the surging tide of blood that was now a couple inches below her breasts.

But she stayed, trapped amongst the undead creatures, intransient among the cruel deluge. She attempted to cry out for mercy, but her voice was strangely mute. The living bodies testified against her, their crooked digits pointing and nearly piercing her. It was becoming harder to breathe, her eyes kept looking in vain above for salvation. With the iconic image of the Savior and Judge of All Creation, she saw mortals looking down. Her grandfather with an expression of grieved pity. Her parents, already among the faithfully departed, arm in arm in disappointment. Things were spinning, the blackness was covering up the bright spot of the sky. She kept her silent screaming.

Then she awoke in gasps of air, coated with a thin layer of sweat. It was the land of the living, the world of Earth. The digital clock by her side told her it was 8:23 AM. She was too rattled to sleep more and the morning was getting old. A few more deep breaths and she was ready to begin her preparations for the day. It was a recurring nightmare. She first experienced it a few weeks after she was initiated into the Cicero Organization. With each fatality added to her past the nightmare seemed to become more intense. It was as though her subconscious was keeping a tally of her sins, reminding her of each charge she faced once she exited the carnal life and found herself naked before the Judgment Seat.

Rationalization followed while she showered and changed for the weekend. Surely, she was not as culpable as the others. She had no choice, unlike those above her. The option of leading a civilized life were taken from her long before she killed her first victim. And her first victim, well she was trying to kill her so it's not that bad. Right? The effort to self-convince continued as she checked on her grandfather. He was out of his bed and showering in his modified tub. He was all the reason she needed. He was worth it. He was her plea in the courts of eternity. What merciful God would deprive her of paradise over this? Surely looking after one's elders is just, even if done unjustly.

The self-imposed argument began to die down as she prepared the cherry turnovers for breakfast. She decided to have them even after such a graphic dream. For a time, Carla struggled to eat items like cherry turnovers and other things with reddish filling. The breaded outer crust resembled human flesh a bit too much and her experiences of extreme brutality coupled the two images together in her mind. However, after a few years she was able to separate the juxtaposed pictures. As she took the turnovers out of the oven, the memories of such a parallel remained but lacked potency.

"Would you say grace, Carla?"

"Sure," she nodded. The two crossed themselves, going the Orthodox route of up-down-right-left, and then Carla began. "Dear Father, bless this meal to our use. In Christ's Name, Amen." The two crossed themselves again and began to eat. Steam rose from the turnovers with each fork and knife puncture. Blowing on the morsels was required. Drinking the cold glasses of orange juice aided the cooling process. It was a couple of minutes before either of the two al-Hassans spoke again.

"So how was last night?"

"It went well," replied Carla between bites. "Tiffany and I met up with some of her friends and we saw a movie."

"That's nice," said George, who took a bite before continuing. "Were there any nice young men in this group?"

"No Giddo, just us girls," smiled Carla. "So more of your type of company."

George laughed some. "Now, Carla, I am in a bit of a relationship now. I am not, how you would say, on the hunt."

"You mean you and our landlord are getting serious?"

"Some, yes," responded George. "Elnora is a nice lady. And she has a fondness for handsome, exotic men."

"I see."

"Apparently, her late husband was from Bulgaria."

"That's a little far from Syria, isn't it?"

"When its exotic, distance is relative."

"So, when are you sending out the wedding invitations?" joked Carla.

"Not yet," lightly replied George. "Anyhow, tomorrow after church she and I are going to have supper together."

"Don't worry, Giddo," she commented. "I will take a couple twenties from your wallet and go to the shopping mall, as usual."

He laughed. "Glad you know the system. I don't just tell you this to keep you updated. I, well I want you to know something else."

"Yes?"

"I might mess up a little as I explain this, but I just wanted to say this. You know, I cannot think of a better time or place, so now will do. Elnora and I, we are getting close. And she is good at being bossy, like you." Carla smiled, which encouraged George to continue. "I am saying that you should not feel that you need to sacrifice your social life just for me."

"Giddo—"

"No, no, no, let me finish. You are a nice woman. I would say you might be the only woman I've ever known who was as beautiful on the inside as you are on the outside. Any man would be blessed to have you as a wife. And I simply want you to know, I am okay with you having a life. Outside of me, I say. If you wanted to, for example, maybe a little extreme, but if you wanted to leave now, I would be okay with that. All I would want is for you to keep in touch, maybe send a postcard. And of course, invite me to the wedding."

"What wedding?"

"Whatever one may happen, wherever you may go." Carla smiled in amusement and in understanding. Done with her breakfast, she got up, approached her grandfather, and kissed him on the cheek. She then took her glass, plate, and utensils to the dishwasher and her used napkins to the trash.

***

Capitol hill was mostly quiet that afternoon. Small numbers of denizens walked and played on the greenery surrounding the pillared landscape. Birds chirped as they flew amongst the bushes and trees, tourists took their photos, and families dined at the vast collection of restaurants in the old town portion of the city. Traffic was minimal and no crossing guards were necessary for pedestrian safety.

Josiah Sharp was not feeling well. He was not stricken by some peculiar illness nor were allergies impacting his respiratory system. No fever nor nausea per se, just a general sense of dread. He did not want to update those four superiors on that day. He did not want to tell them anything, anymore. There was a ring of trust that evaporated the moment that Detective Frank Cooper called him earlier that week.

Not known for his paranoia, Sharp struggled to find an explanation that did not conclude that one of the four was working for the Cicero Organization. Yet what other conclusion could be reached?

Walking down the marbled corridor, his thoughts kept betraying his concern. Did he want to show them the folders of information? They were tucked under his arm, five thin manila folders that contained photos and a report on the murder of Anthony Albioni. Giving them even more information seemed counterproductive. Or did he remember that he was obligated to discuss with them these matters? Was there not a requirement to talk of this and other issues? Sharp decided that he had to keep his confident stride to the windowless room ahead of him, its entrance flanked by security.

Showing his identification meant holding up his lanyard. A careful look over and the security nodded him in. Sharp opened the door himself and then closed it gently behind him. He sat as before on one side of the lone table in the room while seated before him were, from left to right, Mayor Mary Bhatia, Governor Claire Voxner, Attorney General Kyle Brown and District Attorney James Colbert. There was a slightly longer distance between the placement of Voxner's seat and Brown's seat. A possible indicator of some of the harsh political rhetoric already out there in advance of the election.

"Good afternoon, Mayor, Governor, Attorney General, and District Attorney," formally spoke Sharp, who distributed the folders. His apprehensiveness was noticeable. "As you are undoubtedly already aware, a possible witness for my case was killed a couple days ago." He placed his folder on the bare table in front of himself and opened it, spreading out the photos and written notes as the four superiors did likewise. "The coroner's report notes that it was a sniper round that took him out. One shot leading to one kill. Given the trajectory, the fatal bullet was fired from a third story window across the street."

"Amazing," said Mayor Bhatia. "Cicero's reach seems boundless."

"That is my concern," replied Sharp. "And why I asked that all of you meet with me here on a weekend."

"Concern?" asked Governor Voxner.

"Yes, Governor," said Sharp, now trying to tread softly with his words. "I hate to say it, I very much do. And this is not a condemnation with certainty. What I am trying to say, without causing too much upheaval, is that—"

"One of us is working for Cicero," flatly stated Colbert. "That is what you are trying to say, correct?"

"Unfortunately, yes." There was some whispery conversation amongst the four superiors after Sharp's comment. Feeling left out of the conversation, Sharp spoke up. "It was the only conclusion I could reach given the situation. The only people who knew that I was reaching out to Albioni are the people in this room. Therefore, someone here has to have told the Cicero Organization about my plans."

"Now, Mr. Sharp," cautioned Bhatia. "I am a little skeptical of this conclusion. When I said that Cicero has a wide reach, what I meant was he might have the ability to bug an office or tap a phone."

"She has a point, I must admit," chimed in Brown. "And you know that pains me to say that." She smiled annoyingly at her cohort at his comment, then redirected her attention to Sharp.

"How about this," suggested Bhatia. "I can have a couple folks from my security detail investigate your office and see if they find anything."

"Anything?"

"You know, listening devices, bugs, that type of thing," added Bhatia. "If nothing else, I am sure it will give everyone some peace of mind."

"Sounds fair," said Sharp, who felt more relaxed. "Maybe this whole thing is getting to me a bit. My apologies for being so, I guess, accusatory."

"It is understandable," said Brown. "We told you from the onset that this was going to be a stressful and dangerous case."

"Yes, sir."

"And you have handled yourself well, despite the circumstances."

"Yes, sir. I guess I am not used to having someone connected to my case get killed."

"Unfortunately, he might not be the last."

"Yes," conceded Sharp.

"Tell you what," began Brown. "With the District Attorney's blessing, how about we give you the week off this coming week."

"Sir?"

"You know, just to recharge your batteries. You have time after all. Cicero is most active during election seasons, the next one not being for another several months," continued Brown, the other three superiors nodding in agreement.

"There is that."

"Besides," added Colbert, "maybe getting you away from the office will help you clear your mind from other distractions. Bring some inspiration."

"That sounds plausible."

"Good," said Colbert. "Then I agree with the Attorney General and give you permission."

"You sure I have enough vacation time to cover this?"

"Josiah," said Colbert with annoyed amusement, "you haven't taken a personal holiday in over eight months. Trust me, you have plenty of vacation time."

"Well okay," bashfully acknowledged Josiah.

"Is there anything else we need to discuss?" inquired Voxner. "I ask because I have another function I need to attend today."

"I think that about covers everything," commented Brown.

"One more thing," interjected Bhatia as everyone was starting to leave. "I know this is a little informal, but I feel that it might do you well." She opened her purse and took out a small envelope and handed it to Sharp. "This is an extra ticket to next month's Summer Ball. My husband will be on an extended work trip that month, so I am going alone. I would not even bother going were it not a de facto obligation of the office. But I thought I might as well give you my extra ticket."

"I am honored," sincerely replied Sharp. "When is it again?"

***

As the sunlight drifted away from the skies the countless lights of the city appeared. Thousands and thousands dotted the dark environment, casting all manner of color and radiance upon the night life. Down town and old town were especially active, their hubs of social activity overflowing with music, dancing, chatter, smoking, vaping, pool, and alcohol. Groups of young adults and older adults walked along the streets, enjoying the evenings' affairs and legal vices. They were largely oblivious to life's challenges and labors, for such was not the time for these things. They were also oblivious to a clandestine meeting taking place at one of the many former industrial centers.

The Eagle Factory was populated also. Seventeen lower ranked members, flunkies by and large, guarded the space. A dozen of them were on the first floor. The large space where once products were built had been sectioned off and formed into several different quarters. Like a distorted parody of a hotel, many of these spaces were rooms with their own keys and included a bedroom, bathroom, and various amenities and luxuries. There was still a main central plaza space between these various cells. However, it was far smaller and better dressed than its former incarnation.

Little evidence existed of the original purpose for the Eagle Factory. There were no machines and the internal spaces were refurbished and renovated. Only the outer frame of the structure resembled its former identity. To the passing eye of a driver, the facility appeared to be an abandoned industrial center. There was nothing much around the building, with vacant lots on three of its sides and a broken sidewalk next to the seldom used street. Even during the boom years, the edifice was on the economic and popular outskirts, with plans to build houses around it entertained, but never implemented.

The second floor was mostly ceremonial in nature. There was a large hallway with a red carpet path going from the elevator entrance to the main office room. On both sides of the broad scarlet road were statues of ancient Roman senators. Technically they were replicas, cheaper imitations of more expensive overseas pieces. Nevertheless, they presented a mystique of elegance for the space that never existed during its more utilitarian days. To the right of the elevator entrance were two alternative routes between the floors: a service elevator usually used by leadership and a stairway. These two routes were partially obscured by a narrow corridor that was sometimes used for storage. This vestibule area had two pairs of double doors, one in front of the service elevator and the other in front of the stairs. These two routes were on opposite ends of the long hallway.

Inside the main office room, there was more elegance. There were three replica statues, each one inhabiting a corner. The lower right hand corner had a statue of the historic Cicero, the upper right hand corner had a statue of the historic Livy, and the lower left hand had a statue of the historic Cato. In the upper left hand corner was a finely cut wooden desk and an office chair with bright red cushioning. This was where Cicero, apex of the Organization pyramid, sat and conducted business. Also in the room were Livy and Cato, executives of the terrorist group. Most of the wall was covered with book shelves filled with assorted works on politics, philosophy, and modern warfare. Beside the Livy statue was a dark green safe, which contained nearly all the paper treasury for the organization. In the final hours of the week, the Organization's leadership discussed various affairs.

There were six people present. All of them wore hooded cloaks of reddish brown. Hoods were placed over their heads and they sat in a circle, all save Cicero lacking a desk on which to place their things. Four of them, including Cato, were dressed in business attire while Livy remained in a sweatshirt and camo pants. Cicero's clothing was more classical, a white toga with a red line trim. The mysterious leader also wore a mask, which looked like the chiseled countenance of the ancient consul and philosopher. Even the eyes, which had faint porous punctures to allow for sight.

"And the weapons are being produced at the proper rate," recounted Cato from his notes. "When I visited the manufacturers, they were assembling more explosives and detonators, as well as assault weapons and of course the bullets for said assault weapons."

"How many explosives should be coming our way?"

"At least thirty, which should nearly double our stockpile."

"Good, good," smiled Livy. "I am glad they kept up production. When will they deliver them to home base?"

"In seven days."

"And they were not hesitant to help in light of our, shall I say, treatment of their associate?" asked one of the other hooded men sitting in the circle.

"If anything, they were encouraged to retain our business," replied Cato, with a couple of the hooded men laughing at the response.

"Is that the conclusion of your report?"

"Yes, Cicero."

"Then we have but one more item of business for this evening. We all know that the Justice Department is continuing its investigation into both the murder of Myles Talbert and our Organization. They have a new lead investigator, an assistant district attorney named Josiah Sharp. My question for you, gentlemen, is what is to be done about this new possible menace to our operations?"

"Kill him," immediately stated Livy.

"Now, now, Livy," said Cato, waving his hand at the younger leader. "Let's not get too aggressive in our efforts."

"We have the resources."

"And we should use them only as necessary," countered Cato. "Remember, our chief operations involve politics, not lawyers."

"Who's to say he will become a threat, anyway?" queried one of the others. "Does he seem all that dangerous?"

"He is a devout Christian with a strong righteous streak," stated Cicero. "A man of courage is also full of faith."

"Then order it and it shall be done."

"Hold on, Livy," objected one of the hooded men seated beside him. "He can have all the determination he desires. But he has nothing to work with."

"Nothing?"

"As I understand, Albioni was his best lead. And with Albioni dead, he now has nothing. He is at the starting point once more. Will it not take him some time to leave it?"

"Then let's kill him before he has a chance to recover from his setbacks."

"Listen, my violent friend," began Cato. "There are plenty of people out there who suspect or slightly oppose our efforts. If we try to kill them all, there would be hundreds of bodies in the streets. Ours is a surgical instrument, removing only the occasional cancerous cell. Not whole swathes of still healthy members of society."

"A healthy member?"

"Yes," interjected Cicero. "Sharp's other labors as an assistant district attorney are amicable in nature and, equally important, apolitical. This is why I seek your counsel in this problematic territory. This is not a mere matter of obviousness. Never forget, Livy, that he only employs his passion who can make no use of his reason."

"Then what is to be done?"

"Sirs," spoke Cato. "I think I have a middle space between my stance and the stance of our beloved friend and fellow Organization leader. I want the man to live and he wants the man to die. I believe him no threat and he believes him to be a great threat. Let us wait on this matter. Let us keep an eye on this Sharp figure. If his menace comes to naught, then we have no need to pursue further action. If he becomes a danger, then we can take the Livy option and assassinate him before he prevails."

"In public and in brutal fashion," commanded one of the other hooded men, garnering nods of approval from the others.

"Yes, public and brutal."

"Then it is agreed," said Cicero. "I shall have the man watched and his actions tracked. If he does wound us, we shall strike back in full fury."

VI

It was a different waiting room, albeit in the same hospital. There was little tension for this time and place. A greater presence was boredom as Carla al-Hassan waited for the checkup to conclude. She sat at a chair in the corner which bordered a small table. Upon the table surface was a collection of several magazines. To speed the feeling of time passage, she chatted with a couple friends via instant messaging. Thumbs punched away at the smart phone screen as she held the device sideways.

She informed her boss at the cleaning service that she needed to take her grandfather in for the appointment. Her boss was fairly lenient on medical leave or vacation time. This was not mere charity, but rather because outside of the permanent leadership no one there worked on salary. The more Carla worked, the more money she received. In that respect, her employment as a maid and her employment as a terrorist were identical. That and their headquarters both being housed in abandoned factories.

As such, she was wearing informal attire while she waited for the appointment with Stephanie to finish. It was blue jeans and a basic t-shirt. The upper garment was chosen a couple years ago, on a shopping trip because it was one of the few on the rack lacking a low cut neck. She brought with her a dark brown handbag that matched her shirt. It was bigger than her regular purse yet much smaller than her blue-and-white duffle bag. Her decision to bring it instead of the purse stemmed from two reasons: the dark brown handbag went with her outfit and it better served the transaction to come.

As she finished sending a message back to a friend, the door leading to the doctors' offices and examination rooms opened. Carla drew her attention away from mobile device to see George al-Hassan wheeling himself into the waiting room, with Dr. Stephanie Greenwald walking close behind. He smiled at her as she arose from the waiting room chair. She hugged him. "So, is everything alright?"

"Of course, it is," said George as though he lacked a history of medical emergencies. "I keep telling everyone the worst is behind me."

"I would like to hear it from another source," smiled Carla as she directed her attention to the professional. "How is he doing, Stephanie?"

"Your grandfather has a point, he is doing well," she replied. "However, he needs to stay on the medicines for at least another year."

"Okay," replied Carla as she made her way to the front desk. "So what do I owe the hospital?"

"Two thousand dollars," the receptionist dryly said. "So if you can tell me your grandfather's insurance, I'll be able to fill out the form."

"I'll have to pay in cash," responded Carla.

"You sure? I am not familiar with many people who do that."

"It's okay, Jill. That's how Ms. al-Hassan always pays unless she's the patient."

"Okay, Dr. Greenwald, but I was just saying I've never—"

The receptionist was cut off as Carla unzipped her handbag, and with a minor thud placed the bundle of one hundred twenties on the desk. The receptionist was surprised to see the amount of paper currency before her. Stephanie gave a faint smirk as her friend impressed her coworker with the sum put forth at once.

"You rob a bank?" asked the receptionist in jest.

"Not this time," remarked Carla in a combination of humor and factual accuracy.

"One moment and I'll print out your receipt." While the receptionist did so, Carla took a breath and turned her attention to Stephanie.

"Hey, Stephanie, um, is there a chance we can talk for a couple minutes in your office? It's a minor thing, but I would prefer to tell you about it in private."

"You're not pregnant, are you?" asked George as he wheeled around to see his granddaughter. Her unamused expression was his answer. "Just curious."

"Sure, Carla," said Stephanie. "My next appointment isn't for another hour, so I have some time on my hands."

"Good, thanks," said Carla as the receptionist handed her the printed receipt, the piece of paper faintly warm for having traveled through the expedient printer. She walked over to her grandfather and gave him the copy. "You don't mind waiting, do you?"

"Not at all," responded George in a light-hearted manner. "It's not as though I have not waited for you at the doctor's office before."

"Thanks," she said as she kissed him on the cheek. From there she followed Stephanie through the door to the offices and then to her office. It was a simple space with a hard white floor and a couple of chairs for guests. She had a messy desk with several types of papers in piles, as well as a couple of family photos. Her computer screen, slightly visible from where Carla was standing, showed Stephanie arm-in-arm with a man who looked to be around her age and not genetically related to her.

"So, what do you need to talk about?"

"Well," began Carla, some pause in her voice. "This is, like I said, between you and me. I don't want my grandfather to know about this."

"Of course."

"Well, um, okay good. It has taken me some time, a lot of time, to build up the courage to ask you this. I have a big favor to ask you."

"I am listening," said Stephanie as she sat down. "Would you like to sit?"

"No, that's okay."

"Okay. Whatever it is, I will not judge. I assure you that I have heard plenty since taking this job years ago. And if the patient wants it confidential, I keep it confidential."

"I am using drugs."

"What?" asked a surprised Stephanie. "You never struck me as the type. How long have you been using?"

"Eight years and a few months."

"What kind?"

"I don't know."

Stephanie's surprised expression transformed to confused. "How can you not know what kind of drugs you are on?"

"Because it's not the type of drugs you hear about. It's not cocaine, or marijuana, or heroin. Or, at the least, I don't think it is. And that's the favor." Carla reached into her handbag and took out a packet, the bright green substance changing shape as she pressed on the packaging with her thumb and index finger. "This is one of the things I have to take once a day or else I experience very painful withdrawal."

"Okay."

"Is there a way that you can have it analyzed? You know, maybe find a way to reverse its symptoms or something like that?"

"This is technically out of my field, but we do have a toxicologist on staff and he should be able to break down the components. I will send it his way. And don't worry, I won't tell him you gave it to me."

"Thank you so much."

"No problem, Carla."

***

It was a strange experience to not be required to turn off an alarm. For Josiah Sharp, Saturday mornings were the only time when this was the situation. Sunday through Friday something obligated him to awake at a certain time in the morning. Granted, he tended to beat the noisemaker. Nonetheless, it was a valuable backup plan. Getting ready that Wednesday, he was on day three of his exile from work. For the third day in a row, his completed fashion was a t-shirt and jeans.

Day one of the impromptu vacation involved enjoying various sites within the city. As an attorney, Josiah saw the rougher side of both the metropolis and human nature. Monday was meant to help restore a positive portrayal to his overall impression of the concrete jungle. So, he went through a couple of parks, took a tour of some historic buildings, and took several photos later posted to social media. As a city employee, he was blessed with discounted tickets for the tours. He concluded the evening by searching out more details on the Summer Ball, a state affair he knew very little about.

Tuesday was more utilitarian. He went to his local drycleaner during the day to bring in a few clothing items he had been meaning to get professionally cleaned. There was also a car repair trip, a minor issue with the muffler that he kept putting off. He was in and out within a few hours, picking up his cleaning on the way home. There was leisure time as well, him watching a few movies courtesy his cable provider's on-demand library. Josiah was a fan of the classics, films released years and decades before he was born. The newer stuff was more graphic on the violence and language. In his humble opinion, he got enough of that stuff from real life to not want it in his entertainment.

Wednesday morning was tougher. Barring holiday weekends, this was the longest time he had been away from work. His parents inculcated a sense of being useful. So his fundamental being was feeling a bit troubled by being away from his job for so much time. He had hard copies of both the FBI report from years ago on the Cicero Organization and the recent report on Anthony Albioni since he was murdered by an unknown assassin. Saying to himself *why not?*, Josiah sat down with the two collections of documents and began to look for a possible new lead. He went with the known associates and business partners first. It took him about five minutes before he encountered a strange association. Taking his smart phone in hand he punched the number for a superior and waited for him to pick up.

"Hello?"

"Hey, James, its Josiah."

"You know you're on vacation, right?"

"Oh, come on, you know me. The harvest is plenty but the workers are few."

"So, what is it?"

"I was wondering if you could contact Detective Frank Cooper. He is heading the investigation into the murder of Anthony Albioni."

"Why is that?"

"Well, I think I have a possible lead for him."

"Go on."

"Well, I was looking into the known associates for Albioni, both according to the FBI report from years back and the recent report filed following his death. And I think I found a common thread that is worth looking into."

"Okay."

"There is a company," began Josiah, as he handled the piece of paper listing its information. "They are called Saddler & Saddler. They are found in both reports. They have a phone number listed and nothing else."

"Did you look them up online?"

"Yeah and I found nothing."

"That does sound suspicious."

"So, could you have Detective Cooper call me?"

"Sure."

"Thanks."

"Oh, one more thing, Josiah."

"What's that?"

"Yesterday I heard back from the mayor. Apparently, her security team did find a few bugs in the meeting room and near your desk."

"Really?" asked a genuinely surprised Josiah.

"Yup. So, from now on we're going to be conducting more searches in advance of our update meetings. Sound good?"

"Yes, definitely."

"Anyway, take care."

"Good-bye."

The security's discovery of listening devices at the office allayed some of the fear Josiah had that he was unknowingly reporting to the enemy. However, he always kept a reserve of distrust for occasions such as these. For the next few minutes, Josiah reexamined the paperwork he had before him. He also tried again to search for the elusive business that Albioni was connected to while among the living. As he verified his earlier claims, his phone rang. He promptly picked it up.

"Hello?"

"This is Detective Frank Cooper."

"Yes, hello, Detective Cooper. You remember me from last week, correct?"

"Yes, Assistant DA Sharp."

"Correct. Anyway, as I told Colbert I think I have a lead for you. There was a company named Saddler & Saddler that Albioni was associated with. He did business with them both before and after his prison sentence."

"Okay."

"Can you check to see if he and Saddler & Saddler made any calls within the last, say, one or two months?"

"Yeah, I can do that."

"Thanks."

Josiah gave Cooper the number to look up. Another fifteen minutes passed by for Josiah while he waited. To escape the bonds of boredom, he went from his kitchen table to the living room, to a small table beside a plush, light-colored couch. The wooden table had two drawers, one of which was locked at all times and the other contained his Bible. Presented to him back in third grade during a church service led by his father, Josiah read from it each night and occasionally in times of long waits. As he made his way through the Psalms, his phone rang and again he was in contact with Cooper.

"Your hunch was right," he said, lifting the spirits of the attorney. "His mobile phone has numerous calls made between him and the number you gave. They seemed to have increased a lot over the past two weeks."

"You think they were working on some shipment or something?"

"Most likely."

"Is there any way you can trace the source of the number? You know, get a location spotted for them?"

"We are not that advanced," stoically replied Cooper. "But my precinct has some street contacts that might direct us somewhere. I'll spread the word and see what comes up. I'll call you later today."

"Okay good."

"Take care."

"Good-bye."

The next wait took longer than the other two combined. Hours in fact. Josiah ate lunch during the wait, his optimism waning some as the afternoon approached. Still, he was not that anxious. He knew that the type of information gathering that Cooper agreed to undertake was something that might take a goodly amount of legwork. Josiah opted for television watching to pass the time. His wondering mind focused little on the entertainment. Bringing an end to his waiting, the phone rang once again.

"It's Detective Cooper again."

"Hello again."

"You're in luck," said the man whose deep voice went up faintly. "One of our contacts told me plenty. He gave me a location and told me that they were prepping a lot of weapons for local usage."

"Interesting."

"And this is where things get more interesting. Apparently included in this shipment are some assault rifles and remote-controlled explosives."

"That sounds eerily familiar."

"He also told me that they are planning to move everything early Saturday morning."

"Sounds to me like we need to move fast."

"Way ahead of you," replied Cooper with some thrill undergirding his professional tone. "My captain is already calling in the specialists."

***

Josiah was back in business clothing as he was situated in a small gathering of law enforcers and Justice Department members, including his immediate superior, District Attorney James Colbert. They were on the fourth floor of the Justice Department building. Josiah's back was to his desk, with a computer that had been unused since the week before. Colbert was by his side, as was a lead officer for the special weapons and tactics teams placed around the warehouse. Josiah felt a bit intimidated by those around him, who were either more senior in their rank, more imposing physically due to muscle and armor, or a fusion of both. Yet they were there because of him.

Lights were on inside the Justice Department office building, with the curtains closed and radios on. They were mostly congregated around one table that included a transistor radio wherein the leadership could communicate with those in the field. There was a little light talk between the contemporaries earlier, however this was all silenced as the operation was about to begin. "Okay, team, what is your current situation?" asked Colbert.

"We are in position," responded Detective Frank Cooper in a voice slightly corrupted by static. "And our bugs are working."

"So, what are they saying?"

"Definitely an arms shipment. Here's the scary part," said Cooper stoically, "they keep mentioning that it is going to Cicero."

The very invocation of that name led to the people located in the Justice Department building to look at one another in surprise and concern. "Now we know it was a very good idea to bring in the SWAT teams," replied Colbert.

"Yes, sir."

"Have them move in," confidently ordered the chief of police, who was standing across the table from Colbert. "Let's destroy this cell."

"Yes, sir."

Cooper relayed the order to the leaders of the three teams of four SWAT members. They were an impressively outfitted lot, with Kevlar helmets and body armor, boots, gloves, automatic rifles, Glock handguns, flash grenades, and ballistic shields. Their items were all black, blending them into the darkness of the evening. Only the white letters "SWAT" on their chests and the fronts of their shields were readily visible. Each team had one man with a shield and Glock at the ready, another with flash grenade in hand, and the rest with automatics drawn and facing forward. Only their faces and for a few of them their wrists were exposed to the outside world. Otherwise they were covered in arms and armor.

They moved slowly and quietly, carefully placing each step as they tread upon the barren gravel ground surrounding the warehouse. Like so many industrial facilities, the warehouse had been abandoned several years ago. However, the few windows of the edifice had betrayed a warming glow of labor. The two specialists who drew close earlier in the evening to plant the listening devices peered through the small glass encased portals and beheld the small collection of men and women working on the munitions. They were joined by the gradually approaching teams.

Inside all was action. Crates were stacked to one side of the warehouse. The truck was not to appear for another 36 hours. Engineers meticulously fashioned the explosives, connecting the wires and the volatile components into a single device capable of taking out an unwanted person or persons within a small radius. Others finished piecing together the components of the assault rifles. Bullets were placed in large piles into certain crates, treated the least carefully of the three entities. There were twelve people, ten men and two women, dressed in plain clothes as they worked to complete the will of the Organization. There were no guards outside, no monitoring system to alert them of the approaching law enforcers. Exterior lights were kept off to literally keep others in the dark as to their actions. They were on schedule for the Saturday delivery.

One SWAT member approached the pedestrian entrance. On either side of the door were several members of two teams. Another team had taken positions at the windows, ready to provide covering fire for those entering the warehouse. He held a black battering ram, which had two handles, one for each gloved hand to grip. Aiming the ram at the door, he heaved the object backwards and then thrust the ram forward, delivering a heavy blow to the door that broke the latch securing it and sent it swinging inwards.

The noise prompted a halt to all the industrious activity within the warehouse and was immediately followed by disorienting flashes of light from the nonlethal grenades thrown through the opened door. With automatic rifles pointed forward, the heavily armored SWAT team members stormed the warehouse. Two of those rushing in had a Glock in one hand and held a ballistic shield in the other. Law enforcers shouted for the terrorists to raise their hands and surrender.

"Shots fired! Shots fired!" shouted Cooper over the intercom system, causing concern to flow throughout the minds of the men gathered at the Justice Department building. "SWAT is engaging the hostiles inside the warehouse."

In seconds' time, many of the people within the warehouse attempted to respond to SWAT with gunfire. Trained eyes neutralized them as they attempted to attack, each one getting several bullets to the chest. The shouted demands for capitulation got louder as the pointed rifles were turned to face the next resister and to fatally end their resistance. Soon six men and both women lay dead or dying on the cold, hard floor while the remaining four Cicero Organization members took cover behind several crates stacked on the opposite end of the warehouse. This smaller group returned fire, hitting the ballistic shields, the ground, and some of the armor two of the SWAT team members were wearing, but offering nothing serious in the casualty category.

"We have some of them pinned down, they are cornered," updated Cooper, granting some relief for those wondering how the firefight was transpiring.

The terrorists took turns firing into the opposing crates, ballistic shields, and windows where the SWAT gunfire was emanating from. As two unloaded their clips from their handguns or assault rifles, the other two loaded their firearms in preparation for their turn. Sheets of rapid fire from the SWAT team blasted numerous small holes within the protective crates, generating clouds of sawdust to mix with the smoke from the guns. It did not take the four remaining Cicero Organization members long to realize that SWAT team members were well placed at every exit for the warehouse.

Realizing the hopelessness of the situation, the four men, none of whom were older than thirty, looked at each other. With a sense of anger and disappointment, but not of fear or sadness, they agreed tacitly to turn their weapons upon themselves. SWAT members cautiously approaching the collection of bullet-ridden crates heard four more shots fired from behind the de facto barrier. Reaching the torn up wooden side of the crates, the SWAT team directed their sights and their weapons at those underneath the boxes. Rather than meeting additional resistance, they encountered four dead bodies.

"Cell has been neutralized," said Cooper through the partial static. "I repeat, the cell has been neutralized."

"Very good, detective," replied Colbert.

"Any casualties?" asked the SWAT head.

"A couple minor injuries, nothing serious."

"Excellent," said Josiah. "Thank you for doing this."

"And thank you for the tip, Assistant DA Sharp."

"I guess you both must mention each other in your reports," smiled Colbert, getting some laughs from those in the room as the danger became prologue.

***

Instrumental techno music played at a rapid pace while the multicolored lights flung themselves upon the dance floor. Beams of blue, green, red, and purple fell upon the gyrating bodies of scores of young adults. People were enjoying their beers, eating late night appetizers, dancing, grooving, attempting the pick-up, or drowning their miseries. The beats blared out in the shady interior of the club, normal vision obscured by the dim lights and the twirling hues. Plenty of conversation, voices largely successful in overcoming the layer of audio emanating from the multiple speakers. A few waitresses went about the stools and booths taking orders, mostly of a strong liquid nature. Bartenders mixed their drinks and chatted with the patrons, some of whom they had serviced for years.

The two friends were in a booth. One wore a short skirt, which had a matching lime green top. Her hair was puffed to an afro, several shades browner than her skin. Hoop earrings were worn along with a few bracelets of a similar design. She smiled a lot, a pleasant demeanor through the heavy eye shade. On the table in front of her was a completed light beer bottle and another that was two-thirds empty. Her acquaintance wore tight black pants and a light blue blouse. Looking more like an office worker, she had a watch on her left wrist and only basic makeup lining her eyes and adding rosiness to her pale cheeks. Hair was smooth and put in a thick pony tail. Her drink was a soda with ice. The establishment provided it as complimentary, falsely assuming that she was going to take advantage of the adult beverages for which money was earned.

"Listen, let me tell you what Bill told me. You remember Bill, right?" asked Tiffany as she had one hand on the light beer and another in the air somewhat directed towards Carla.

"Vaguely. Go on."

"Well, Bill used to tell me that he was better at shooting when he was shirtless."

"Shirtless," skeptically replied Carla.

"Yeah. Something about having less fabric in the way, or less inorganic stuff. Something like that. It makes one a better shot."

"So he says."

"Girl, listen to me. It works."

"Really?" asked a critical Carla, drinking some more of her soda through a straw while Tiffany continued her attempt at persuasion.

"Yes, really. Whenever I get a shooting assignment, I always wear one of my spaghetti-string shirts. I feel more, I don't know, liberated," Tiffany insisted. "You should try it. I promise you will never go back."

"My aim is just fine," replied Carla. "Unless you forget that Cicero chose me to pick off that arms dealer and you to get him to the window."

"Yeah your aim is good. But it can always improve."

"Spaghetti-string would not work for me."

"How come?"

"Because I am used to at least some of my arms being covered. If I found myself without that expectation, I would feel uncomfortable. Feeling uncomfortable would interfere with my concentration, which would interfere with my aim."

"Okay, okay," conceded Tiffany, who took another swig of her second beer. "If you say so, feel free to keep the status quo."

"Besides, Bill probably just claimed that so that he could imagine you shooting a gun with your top off," said Carla, prompting both to laugh.

"Oh no, no," clarified Tiffany. "Bill was never a perv. But I will tell you who is totally a perv and totally a creep."

"Who?" asked an intrigued Carla.

"Do you really have to ask?"

"Oh him."

"Yeah him. The big him. The Livy him."

"I know he tries to hit on you, but is it really that bad?"

"Girl, let me tell you, it hit a new low last night."

"Really? What happened?"

"Well, I was staying late at the Eagle, and so he and a few others, we all ate dinner together. We had some turkey sandwiches that were in the main fridge," explained Tiffany, having put the second light beer bottle beside the finished one while she moved both hands as she talked. "So, he and I ate with the others and then dinner was over and as I said my good-byes, he said." She took a breath, amazed at what she was about to say. "Do you know what he said to me?"

"No idea."

"Do you know?"

"I am waiting."

"He said to me ... and I quote," Tiffany deepened her vice to impersonate Livy, "I am glad you were here, because as my sandwich shows, I love dark meat."

Carla grimaced at the conclusion of the impersonation. "That is horrible," declared Carla.

"You bet it's horrible."

"Wow."

"Yes wow."

"Have you thought about, maybe sending a complaint or something?"

"Like to who? Cicero? Please, the big boss and Livy go back. They knew each other long before we showed up. Who do you think he'll side with?"

"Good point."

After that comment, both women took to drinking their drink. One was full of sugar and the other full of alcohol. Carla found it amusing that she and Tiffany talked so freely of their cruel occupation in a place like that club. It was not always this way. When they first socialized outside of work they did everything they could to avoid the subject. Eventually they realized that in the intoxicated distracted world of the night club few cared what they were saying. And even if someone overheard them, they could always claim they were kidding, or simply trying to get their attention. Looking around the crowded, dimly-lit room that periodically shined brightly in multicolored radiance, she saw her.

"Stephanie!" shouted Carla from the booth. "Hey Stephanie!" The second call got her attention, with Dr. Stephanie Greenwald approaching the booth with a big smile and a faint wave at Carla. "Fancy meeting you here."

"What a surprise! How are you doing, Carla?"

"Just fine," she replied, noting that Tiffany was seated there kindly waiting for an explanation. "By the way, this is my good friend Tiffany. Tiffany, this is Dr. Stephanie. She helps take care of my grandfather."

"Nice to meet you," said Tiffany as the two shook hands.

"Tiffany is a painter," explained Carla to a standing Stephanie.

"That's interesting," said Stephanie to Tiffany. "What sort of things do you paint?"

"Whatever gives me inspiration and whatever a rich person is willing to pay big bucks for," she answered with a smile. Stephanie laughed.

"So, what brings you here?" asked Carla to the doctor. "You never struck me as being the night club type."

"You're right, I am not," smiled Stephanie. "But my friends wanted another girls' night out, to celebrate the fact that this will be one of my last." Stephanie then showed the two seated women her occupied ring finger.

"Congratulations!"

"Thanks."

"When is the wedding?"

"September 13th."

"That exact?"

"It was my parents' wedding day. And it just happens to be his birthday. So, what could be more serendipitous, right?"

"Very true."

"Anyway, I need to get back to my party. Nice running into you Carla, nice meeting you Tiffany," she said with a wave and turned away after the two said their good-byes.

"She's seems really nice."

"Yes," began Carla. "You might owe your life to her someday."

"How come?"

"Well, earlier this week I finally built up the courage to tell her about the loyalty oath. She agreed to send it to a toxicologist. They might be able to find a way to reverse engineer it or something. You know, find a cure."

"Carla," Tiffany nervously said. "Why did you have to tell someone about this? If Cicero or Cato or Livy find out, you'll get a bullet to the brain."

"Listen, don't worry! I did not tell her where I got it from or Cicero or anything like that. I trust her. She assured me that she would not tell the toxicologist that she got it from me."

"Still. I feel like this is going to be bad."

"It's going to be great," said Carla as she put her right hand on Tiffany's left shoulder. "In a couple weeks, you might finally get a way to have Livy out of your life forever."

"We'll see."

"I will keep you posted."

"Thanks," said Tiffany, patting Carla's arm as she withdrew it back to the cold grip of the glass containing the soda, straw, and ice. "A couple weeks, you said?"

"At earliest, a couple. Might take longer of course."

"The sooner the better."

"Definitely." Then some pain entered the cerebrum of Carla. She looked at her wristwatch and realized that it had been more than 24 hours since the last time she ingested the substance. Looking up from the time piece, she saw that Tiffany seemed to be experiencing similar pains in the mind. "Speaking of which ..." Tiffany nodded and the two exited the booth, but not before each of them took a last swig of their drinks. After all, when they got back they had no plans to consume something unattended.

Grabbing their purses, they walked hastily through the mesh of patrons, dancers, talkers, tables, and busy waitresses to get to the ladies' restroom. Entering the tiled, mostly white interior of the bathroom, their ears mildly rang as they were finally given a barrier between them and the pounding music. They had the place to themselves, standing side-by-side in front of a long rectangular mirror that had four sinks before it. Unzipping their purses, they each quickly found a green packet. Carla immediately popped the packet into her mouth and chewed then swallowed while Tiffany tore the packet open.

"You know the package is edible, right?"

"I don't like the taste," replied Tiffany as she tore it open and then squeezed the green stuff into her mouth. The increasing pain began to taper off, but it was still another several minutes before it would go away. As though her shadowy profession had not done enough to intervene on her nightlife, Carla's text message alert went off as the two finished washing their hands. After drying herself, she looked at the screen. Her face straightened to seriousness that bordered on annoyance. The message began with "6338 28 843 32453 3228679." Tiffany was curious. "What is it?"

"Duty calls," replied Carla as she showed her the text message.

"Alright, safe travels," said Tiffany as the two embraced. "And don't worry, I'll pick up the tab."

"I would hope so," smiled Carla, "you were the only one who ordered anything that cost money."

***

Like any major city, taxis were a viable alternative to traveling in a privately-owned car or a route-restricted bus. Outside of the club, Carla was quick to hail a cab. She gave no specific address, but rather provided general instructions. The official story was that she wanted to be dropped off at the outskirts because she owned a place around there. Not an inquiring sort, the cabbie drove her from the heart of the nightlife, asking only for the occasional guidance on whether to turn or keep straight. The way to the Eagle Factory was basic, involving the usage of major roads and the highway. From the highway came the exit into what many locals called the boondocks. There were more vacant lots and abandoned industrial centers than there were houses or apartment complexes. Some of the mean-spirited folk referred to that area of the city as "Little Detroit."

"Could you stop here, please?" she asked the driver, pointing to a poorly lit stretch of sidewalk that was a few blocks away from her actual destination.

"Are you sure? Seems kind of dangerous."

"I'll be just fine."

"Fine," said the worried driver who nevertheless did what was asked and pulled over to have his front right tire touch the sidewalk.

"You can keep the change," said Carla as she handed him a couple twenties.

"Thank you, ma'am."

"Thanks for the ride," Carla said while opening the door and exiting the vehicle.

"No problem," he shouted back.

Door closed, Carla gave an extra wave and walked on, refusing to look at the cab any longer. Hint taken, the yellow vehicle went back into drive, turned off its hazards, and made a U-turn to get back to the highway and from there the downtown area where more customers were waiting to be transported. Carla walked at a brisk pace, knowing that the sooner she got to the Eagle Factory the happier her superiors would be. The journey went through about fifty feet of cracked squares and dying street lights. Her shoes caressed the lines of grass growing through the scars below her.

Veering right she entered a large vacant lot whose lighting was even poorer than the broken sidewalk. Large amounts of broken asphalt lay scattered on the gritty flattened terrain. Potholes were pervasive, made worse with every heavy rainfall or wintry freeze. A few lights at the old factory were on, allowing for easy visibility of the building and the three guards who patrolled it outside. These were not major lights though, providing no more than maybe thirty or forty feet of luminance for the sentries.

Carla walked calmly in a straight line aimed at the main entrance to the facility. It was a pair of double doors near the corner of one broadside and one narrower end. As expected, two of the guards saw her coming. One raised his assault rifle at her, a move that used to unnerve her. The other held his assault rifle at the waist with the muzzle facing the gravel. He raised his left hand, the palm shown to her face from about twenty feet away. Obliging, Carla ceased her progress to the front door and stood there.

"Name?" he projected.

"Carla al-Hassan."

"Password."

"SPQR."

"Password!"

"SPQR," she reiterated, knowing that she was expected to give it twice. With the second statement, the other guard slung his rifle back around his shoulder and returned to his walking around the exterior of the building.

"You may enter," said the sentry, who motioned with his hand for her to come forward. Carla nodded and kept walking. The guard then did as the other one and returned to his menial patrol of the exterior.

Opening the door, Carla found another three guards, two female and one male, lounging about the waiting room on the first floor. They were engaging in light conversation, their firearms not at the ready. They recognized her and said their hellos. According to procedure, one of them got up from her lax seating and followed Carla to the main elevator. Standing side-by-side as the gray doors pulled open, the two entered the lift. To expedite things, the guard pushed the button that closed the doors immediately. Less than a minute later they opened once more, this time after having moved up a level.

A more elegant interior than the one that was a floor below, Carla and the guard walked silently down the broad red carpet laid out between the two rows of classical statues. Each stern face looked forward with eyes of full alabaster, each stone cloak wrinkled and creased in a different way from the others. Their short-cut hair, chiseled facial lines and straight lips appeared martial in their discipline. A few had a right hand raised, a bent finger jutting upwards as though to make a point during some debate or soliloquy. They were as much Shakespearian characters as historical figures.

Before them were the two large wooden doors that separated the outside world from the office of the most dreaded terrorist organization in the entire state. To the left of the door was Cato and a couple of others. Far from professional, they were drinking a fine red wine and engaging in exchanges of petty chatter and pettier laughter. Cato quickly noticed Carla and the guard, standing in good order a few feet from the double doors. Collecting himself some while his peers continued to drink and talk, Cato approached the two. He was as usual in a well-made suit and tie. He smiled briefly.

"Nice to see you this evening, Carla," he began and then directed his attention to the guard. "You may return to the ground floor." She nodded and walked away.

"Well, let us now see Cicero."

"Yes," affirmed Carla, who had been in the room they were about to enter before. To her right was a service elevator, which was commonly used by Cicero to come and go from the facility. It was possibly the least elegant part of the second floor, at least as inelegant as the door to the stairway found closer to the main elevator and to the right of the entrance to Cicero's office. Cato knocked on the left door twice, waited a moment, and then pushed it open. As Carla and Cato entered she noticed that Livy was there and seemed to be finishing up a few not so civil words with his superior. It was a minor detail that went to the back of her mind and remained there until later that month.

Cato closed the door and stood behind Carla as she walked within a few feet of the desk where the masked Cicero was seated, a few fingers touching an old-fashioned rolodex. Livy stood with a displeasured look and arms folded. He was to the right of the new entrant, the safe being a few feet behind him. There was a pause in the air, prompting Carla's eyes to wonder to the book shelves to the rear and left of the seated Cicero. Her superior saw this brief abandonment of focus but did not mind it.

"Do you like my book collection?" asked Cicero, in a voice that seemed mechanized or even robotic.

"It is impressive," Carla responded, looking towards Cicero, but also down some as though feeling unworthy of beholding the mysterious leader. "There seems to be something different about it since I was last here."

"Truly," replied Cicero. "I have added a few more volumes of the *Discourses of Livy* by Niccolò Machiavelli. A room without books is like a body without a soul."

"Yes, Cicero."

"You did excellent work disposing of Myles Talbert."

"Thank you, Cicero," responded Carla, who bowed her head briefly each time she gave a response, which was less of an obligation and more of a tendency towards respect.

"He was a great danger to our efforts. He learned far too much about how we operate. Your removal of him from this mortal coil was most effective."

"Thank you, Cicero."

"As I understand, you were not properly compensated for your work. Cato told me that he was unable to provide you with the promised full payment."

Carla hesitated at first. "That is true, Cicero." There was a pause and then Cicero turned to face Livy, whose arms were still folded.

"Retrieve three thousand dollars from the treasury," commanded Cicero. As Livy was about to offer a word of dissent, Cicero firmly stated "now." Livy grudgingly nodded and then turned to the safe. Cicero returned attention to Carla. "I am cognizant of what most of your money goes to and for that I trust these funds will be spent benevolently."

"Thank you," briefly smiled Carla as she took the three bundles from an irritated yet restrained Livy. Placing them in her purse, she quickly returned to facing Cicero.

"You deserve it. Indeed, it is because of your uncanny talents for the art of death that I give you another very important assignment. This one involves history repeating itself, as another government agent draws a bit too close. Therefore, he must be eliminated lethally and publicly," said Cicero as the nefarious creature took out a folder full of information. "You may now approach my desk." Carla nodded and walked up to the desk, where she took the folder with the information on the newest target. Cicero continued to speak as Carla opened the folder to the first page, which included a printed out high definition screengrab of the target as found on a news channel video posted online.

"He is Assistant District Attorney Josiah Sharp. He took over the city's investigation into our Organization after Talbert was killed. I admit, I falsely judged him as incompetent. I assumed he could never garner the evidence that Talbert did. I finally assumed that after you took out his lead source of information that he would give up. But alas, I was mistaken and as a result he launched a crippling blow to our weapons manufacturing wing. He cannot be allowed to continue his investigation. Do you have any questions?"

"Where and when do you want me to kill him?" asked Carla as she closed the folder and tucked it under her arm.

"The first Friday of the month of June. He will be attending the Summer Ball on Capitol Hill. Research the facility, find a good place to have him taken out in front of all those important people."

"I will, Cicero."

"Wonderful," replied an enthused Cicero. "I have nothing further for you, so you may return home now."

"Thank you, Cicero."

VII

Capitol Hill was exceptionally beautiful that Saturday. Spring flowers bloomed in clusters scattered upon the grassy spaces separating the old town and downtown buildings from the sidewalks and streets. Trees stretched their branches, providing a vibrant natural contrast to the abundance of cement and asphalt. Pleasant outings by friends, family, and pets were occurring all over the place. At some of the fields children played soccer, tag, or touch football. Owners walked their dogs while parents monitored their kids.

The capitol building was open for business. While legislators and executives were not working that morning, the space was nonetheless filled with groups of tourists and sight-seers, curious locals and visitors alike. Uniformed guides led them through the ornate and imposing pillared edifice, allowing for photos but not video, and looking but not touching. She along with the others had to go through security, walking through the metal detectors and being patted down if anything went off. Her purse joined the other carry-ons that traveled along a dark gray conveyor belt through an x-ray machine and out the other end unharmed. On this occasion, she was unarmed.

Gathered with a group of strangers, Carla al-Hassan looked around the large space. The rotunda was grand, its ceiling well above the marble flooring. Corinthian columns were carved into the sides of the large room, which flowed into a major hallway. Carla was one of fourteen visitors in her group. They ranged from children to elderly, encompassing a few races and both sexes. A diverse cross-section of the general population, they were given basic instructions on how to act during the tour as well as a basic overview. The guide, a perky college student, had already conducted a couple of tours earlier that day.

"And so, without further ado, let us look into the world of state politics," said the guide as she motioned for the group to follow her. Half the time she walked she was turning to face her group and the other half she was looking forward. She stopped at the front of a parlor room whose door was open. Everyone crowded the entrance to get a good look at the chamber, which looked like a study. "This is the historic former parlor room. Built along with the main building in the 1920s, the room has long been used by legislative and executive leadership to broker deals and craft public policy. Many of the things you see on the TV when the legislature votes on bills that have gone through a lot of debate get rectified here. So this might be the most important room you see on the tour."

As the guide continued to describe things, namely the type and quality of furniture and architectural design, Carla took out her smart phone and grabbed some shots. She was not alone, as a few others belonging to the tour group did likewise. A couple of minutes later and the group continued to their next destination. It was one of the legislative offices, this time the office of the speaker. Unlike the parlor, the visitors were allowed to walk into the room, which had similar architecture and furniture pieces as the parlor. For her own amusement, Carla took a photo of the replica bust of Cicero. The expression on the stone face was the same stoic, distressed gaze that she saw at the Eagle Factory.

The tour continued, seeing other sites of note. They entered the large meeting area for the legislature, complete with its balconies for the public and the press. Their travels were delayed somewhat, as the guide for Carla's group was apparently faster than the guide ahead of them. They waited, but not too long, for the group ahead to clear out of the next stop. "While we wait, if any of you have any questions, I will do my best to answer them." One woman, clutching her son's hand, asked if the guide could point her to the nearest bathroom. The guide smiled and directed her with pointed finger to the proper necessary while voicing more specific details. By the end of the next stop, the mother and child successfully rejoined the group as they entered the area that most interested Carla.

"And here is the main ballroom," said the guide, who intentionally paused while the amazed visitors beheld the large open space. Palatial in its design, the area had Doric columns carved into all four sides, each of which had finely carved bouquets topping them. Expensive brightly-colored wallpaper covered the walls between the columns. Some of these wallpapered spaces had professionally-painted portraits of historical figures. Obvious ones like George Washington and Abraham Lincoln were among those honored, but also more local heroes and political figures from the past. "The most recent addition to the portraits of honored figures is that of Frederick Wilkinson. For those of you who do not know, he was a former three-term governor and the father of our current mayor, Mary Bhatia."

Carla took more photos in the ballroom than anywhere else in the tour. She took photos of the flat space, the entrances and the windows. The windows were the best part, as there were three large ones showing the street outside, as well as a couple of buildings on the opposite end of the road. As she took her photos, her intentions unknown to those around her, the guide continued to speak: "in addition to hosting many foreign dignitaries and several former presidents, the Formal Ballroom also serves as the location for the annual Summer Ball. Taking place on the first Friday of June since the 1950s, the Summer Ball brings together hundreds of politicians, public figures, notable locals, and businessmen. It is a formal event, with tickets starting at $1,200.00. So, start saving," said the guide, with some of the tour briefly grinning and a few of them laughing.

Twenty minutes later the tour was completed. While some of the group stayed to peruse the gift shop, Carla exited the building. There was a structure that took her interest while she was snapping photos of the ballroom and its large windows. After she descended the stairs from the public building, she veered left to get to the nearest pedestrian walkway. While more inclined to cut across the street where possible, in this circumstance she did not want to accrue unwanted attention from authorities.

Main Street Presbyterian Church was founded in the nineteenth century, the product of a wave of Scottish immigration to the city. Their building actually predated the more imposing capitol building across the street. Its exterior décor was similar, with four large columns supporting a simple gable and a basic church steeple at the top. Like the capitol building, it had a flight of stairs that led to the main entrance and, also like the capitol building, a few decades ago they installed a ramp for the wheelchair bound that snaked along the side of the stairs. Main Street Presbyterian had a parking lot on one side, though given the size of the congregation most worship attendees parked on the street.

Having gotten to the sidewalk following the trip across the street, Carla turned right to walk towards the sacred building. Purse slung over her left shoulder, she walked at a normal pace and was largely unnoticed by the public, even as she quickly and without warning turned left into the parking lot of the church. She saw that only two vehicles, a compact and a pickup truck, were parked there. In addition to the side entrance, Carla observed that attached to the long side of the church was a narrow stairway whose covering was about five feet below the roof line. Carla opted for that entrance.

Her right hand held one of the two railings as she sped up the stairs, her steps on the metal making loud thuds. Reaching the top landing she looked at the alleyway and the street before opening the unlocked door. Entering a humble stairway, she gently shut the door behind her. Walking a short distance, she then went to the door that led to the second floor. This portal included a rectangular window that gave Carla a good view into the hallway. All clear, she slowly opened the door, cautiously shutting it once she was in the hallway. Lights were on, but she was the only person around.

From there, she walked by children's art projects and photos from the most recent youth group mission trip to Latin America to try and locate the interior route to the bell tower. Turning a corner, she walked some more before finding another stairway. Also unlocked and unguarded, she used it to enter another wing of the church. Going by a bulletin board with photos of new members and printed congregational news, she finally found the entrance to the steeple. The sign saying it was a restricted area did not deter her, but the door being locked did. Then she heard their commotion.

"I'm telling you, this season is their season."

"Come on, Mike, you said the same thing last year."

The voices were coming from the opposite hallway. She never saw them, but rather doubled back, tracking their position from the echoes of their banter. Their sports debate was muffled as Carla placed more distance and physical barrier between herself and the duo of janitors. She sped by the kid's projects and the mission trip photos, but still made sure to show caution when opening and closing the two doors that led her outside. Again outdoors, but still at the head of the stairway, she reassessed her situation. After a few moments, she looked up to the steeple and then to the triangular roof.

Carla placed her purse along the side of the left railing, where the metal bars formed a corner. She reached for the awning at the top of the outdoor stairway and then placed her feet, one at a time, on the top of the railing. Balancing upon the thin rail, she carefully twirled herself around so that her body was hanging over the alleyway rather than the top of the stairs. The awning protecting the top of the stairs was flat-topped, making it easier for Carla to climb to its summit. Rolling as she got to the top of the awning, she discovered that the stair covering was indeed strong enough to maintain her weight.

Getting to a standing position, she viewed the street from the narrow confines of the alleyway. Things were becoming smaller. The angle from the top of the awning was not a good view of the Formal Ballroom, a fact Carla accepted even before she began her ascent. She turned her attention to the roof. She studied the wall, looking at the brickwork to spot any dents or holes she could use for the climb. Nothing. Having no better option and not wanting to stay on the awning any longer, she knelt and then jumped with arms raised high. On the first attempt, she successfully grabbed hold of the copper gutter.

The gutter moaned at the sudden increase of stress upon its frame, yet it held firm and allowed Carla to grip the corner of the roofing next. As she grabbed part of the shingled roof, her feet kicked against the brickwork, allowing her to thrust herself up to the slanted right side of the roofing. Soon she had all four limbs on the shingles. The roofing also held firm and the slant was not acute enough to risk her sliding off. Securely atop the church, Carla awkwardly walked forward towards the street side of Main Street Presbyterian. As she neared it, she changed her means of travel to crawling, not wanting a potential passerby to see her either on that day or on the evening of the Summer Ball.

Her pants and shirt became dirty as she crawled along the roof. Clearly a different outfit, one more for gritty work, was needed. She stopped a couple feet from the edge, the steeple with its one bronze-colored bell silently standing beside her. Looking ahead she had a perfect view of the Formal Ballroom. Unarmed, she made a pseudo-scope with her right hand, the fingers curving to form a tunnel for the eye. All three large windows were visible. Curtains were not going to be an issue, for none were present in the chamber. The tour guide explained that the original builders of the structure did that on purpose, as they wanted the public to see the elegance of their government.

Carla made the crawl back across the roof, rising some after several feet to walk. There were going to be other variables. Heavy rainfall would make the climb and travel across the roof risker. She needed to check the church schedule to see if the congregation was holding any events on that particular Friday. A crowd would make her choice of position a hard one. Still, it was a good potential spot. Carla slowly slid down the side of the roof, using the gutter once again to steady her climb down to the awning. Once on the awning, she took hold of the top and swung herself into the top space at the outdoor stairway. Her purse was still there and the two janitors were absent.

Fixing her hair after the physical activity, she took her purse, slung it over her left shoulder, and quickly descended the stairway, her right hand holding the railing. Just as she got down to the alleyway floor, she heard the door at the head of the stairs open, prompting her to walk faster. The two jolly janitors were still debating the upcoming season, unaware of any of Carla's activities. Later, while at a café with wireless internet, Carla used her smart phone to check the calendar for Main Street Presbyterian's website. To her relief, no events were scheduled for the first Friday in June. The lack of events was attributed to the expected traffic of the Summer Ball.

***

As the forecast accurately predicted, it began to rain as Carla returned to the apartment complex. Her journey from the canopy of precipitation was aided when one of her neighbors held the door open, saving her the time it would have taken to locate the proper key in her purse. A smile and a "thank you" and from there she walked to the elevator. Doors pulled open and a married couple who also lived on her floor exited. She had the lift to herself for the entirety of her journey up to the fourth level.

Walking down the hallway, she stopped before her apartment door. Carla unzipped her purse to search for the key. The key for the building lock and the key for the apartment door were identical in appearance until she plastered nail polish on one of them. She inserted the correct key into the lock. Door opened, she entered the space. "Hello, Giddo, I am back," she projected through the living room. Closing the door behind her, she took off her shoes and placed them by the entrance. There was no response to her initial announcement. "Giddo? Are you here?" asked the granddaughter.

Concern did not immediately enter her mind. After all, on her way out that morning George explained that he and the landlady were going to have an outing. Perchance they were still going about town, possibly one of the public parks. She knew that they often went there, with her walking and him rolling. A couple of times she ran into them, exchanging greetings and minor talk, yet knowing to keep such socializing brief. As an adult, she found it amusing that she was the third wheel for a grandparent.

"Giddo?" she asked again, remembering that usually such outings were over by the early afternoon. She heard movement in his bedroom. There was a tension that went through her. It was a tension that manifested from time to time ever since she joined the Cicero Organization. Cato once assured her that they were the only entity of their kind in the state, yet she always wondered if he was telling the truth. Maybe some other underground order wanted in on the action of Cicero.

She ignored the tension. Even if there was a rival force, they would go after more prominent Cicero Organization members. Approaching the bedroom door, she heard a little more shifting. Deciding that inaction would only prolong the dread, she gripped the knob and opened the door. Panic filled her innermost self when she looked down. George was on the floor on his side, his back facing her terrified countenance.

"Giddo!" she screamed as she descended to the floor in a hurry. Her hands touched his back and shoulder, prompting him to show signs of life. On his own accord, he turned onto his back, showing no wounds or visible scars. He seemed quite calm about the matter. He reacted with reserved nervousness at the sight of his fret-stricken granddaughter. "Giddo, what happened!?"

"It's okay, it's okay," he said, attempting to dismiss her fears. While she kept her hold on his shoulders he used his arms to lift his upper body up a little from the floor. "I just fell, that's all. I have only been here for ten or fifteen minutes. Twenty at most."

"What happened?"

"I fell, okay?" said an annoyed George. "I was going to take an afternoon nap and I thought I would try to walk to the bed. Just a couple steps. I actually did walk two steps before my legs gave out. That's all."

"You shouldn't be trying to walk when no one is around," declared Carla in a fusion of fear and anger. "What if I was gone for the weekend? What would you do then?"

"I would pick myself up," replied her grandfather as he got to a seated position on the floor. He then smiled. "But since you are here, care to help?"

After a moment, Carla nodded and gave a wry smile as she began to reposition her hold on her grandfather. Each hand went from the shoulders to the armpits. George's back was to the bed and since he was planning to rest there anyway, Carla decided that was the best place to bring him to. "Are you ready?"

"Always."

With a thrust of strength Carla was able to help lift the man onto the bed, with him seated on the edge. He slightly aided the effort, using his arms to push as Carla got him to the plateau surface of the made mattress. The task over with, Carla's emotion at the troubling first sight got the better of her and she hugged her grandfather with a good grip. He embraced her in return. As her mentality returned to normalcy, she loosened the hold and straightened her posture before speaking in a commanding manner.

"The next time you try this, make sure someone is here first."

"Even if it is someone who does not have the strength to lift me?" smiled George.

"Make sure someone is here next time."

"Alright, alright."

"Besides, they could always call someone if they cannot pull you up."

"That is true."

"Do you need anything else? Water, food?"

"I said I was only down there for a few minutes."

"You said as many as twenty."

"Either way, I am just fine," replied George, who pushed himself towards the interior of the bed and then spread himself out. "Now if you will excuse me, all this excitement has made me very tired."

"Have a good nap, Giddo."

"Thank you for the help, Carla. You are equally kind and beautiful."

She smiled as she closed the door, her last glimpse of him being the closure of his eyes and a little smirk upon his face. She took a deep breath, the ends of her fingers pressed against her forehead and right cheek. Another deep breath and she decided to go to the kitchen and get herself a soda. Task achieved, she made her way to the living room. She grabbed the remote, plopped down on the couch, and turned the device on, watching whatever looked mildly interesting. She decided to take this afternoon easy, as her evening was going to be much, much more eventful.

***

It was probably her least modest attire. The other potential candidates were the two evening dresses she kept in her closet. Their straps were pretty slim and they ended around the knee caps, showing a fair amount of skin. Then again, she always wore a light sweater with the dresses, covering her arms and most of the neck area. Her attire for that evening included a sleeveless black tank top that tightly fit on her upper body and a pair of gray sweat pants. Her hands were partially covered, specifically with fingerless gloves that matched her overall black-and-gray combination. Her long black hair was kept in order by a thick elastic holder that was the same color as her mane.

With intense force, she landed a sidekick to the red punching bag. The imprint of the collision was visible for a moment, but began to disappear as the bag attempted to return to its original morph. Before the bag succeeded, the side that was kicked seconds earlier was kicked again. And again. And several more times in quick succession. Carla maintained her balance well, having learned the art of hand-to-hand combat while under the tutelage of the Cicero Organization. The hefty object held firm, being suspended above the ground by one cable and kept stable by another that attached the bottom of the bag to the floor. Nevertheless, the kicks and then the punches that Carla delivered to the heavy sand-filled object did force it to move courtesy the blows.

Being a large building, the Eagle Factory had ample room for a gymnasium. It was located beside the temporary bedrooms and a break room that had seats for as many as thirty people. It was right below the main office where Cicero did business, perchance a symbolic gesture to how much physical aggression served as the foundation for the Organization's inner workings and external policy.

Carla was hardly alone at the place. Between a dozen and a score of people, mostly members in their twenties and thirties, were on the exercise equipment, battling punching bags, lifting, jogging on treadmills, squatting, jumping, or dueling in the boxing ring placed in the center of the large room. Despite its appellation, the ring was seldom used for something as sophisticated as boxing. Rather, brutish fights were performed there, combining punching, kicking, and wrestling. In rare instances, weapons were used, though they tended towards the unsharpened as it was merely practice.

A few jabs slammed into the upper portion of the red punching bag, causing a deep imprint that slowly disappeared. Carla had been at it for some time and was developing a layer of sweat. Breathing much through her mouth, she decided that the punching bag had had enough. She walked towards one of the multiple water coolers in the space and took a plastic cup. Pulling down on the tab, she saw the large bubbles ascend in the transparent drum before looking down to verify that she did not spill the liquid. Releasing her pressure on the tab, she quickly drank the pleasantly cold water. She repeated this process a second and a third time and then took a white towel from one of the nearby racks.

From there she joined Tiffany, who was seated before the boxing ring. Like Carla, Tiffany had recently completed some arduous exercise. She was wearing a similar tank top and sweatpants combination, though both items were hot pink. Tiffany's hair was placed in cornrows to keep it from getting in the way. The white towel she used to dry off the perspiration was slung over her left shoulder. Carla joined her friend, taking a seat beside her as they both saw Livy slam a man unto the surface. He was six feet tall, which still made him several inches shorter than the second-in-command.

"How's it going?"

"He never stood a chance," replied Tiffany as she kept her gaze upon the match. Livy, picked up the opponent just so he could scoop him up and throw him to the mat once again, the impact prompting both women to cringe.

"Anytime you want to give up, you can give up," shouted Livy at his opponent, briefly taking his attention off the man to smile at Tiffany, who in turn rolled her eyes.

"I'm just getting started," the opponent replied as he slowly got back to a standing position. Livy grinned.

"Don't say I didn't warn you," he said as the man tried to attack the imposing second-in-command, only to be grabbed by the neck and the chest and thrown to one of the ring corners, with him bouncing off the turnbuckles before landing on his stomach. As he struggled to get up, Livy took hold of him from behind, placing his arms around the unfortunate opponent's waist. With a heave, he threw the man over himself in a move professional wrestlers would call a German Suplex. Carla and Tiffany both cringed again as Livy repeated the move a few times and was about to do it again.

"Okay, okay! You win! You win!" said the man, prompting Livy to mercifully stop his physical barrage. He helped his opponent up to his feet, leaning him against the corner turnbuckles before patting him on the shoulder.

"That was for you, lovely," he shouted at Tiffany, who rolled her eyes once more.

"Say what you will about him, at least he's not weak," said Carla to Tiffany.

"He breaks the number one rule of any man I want to have a relationship with."

"He reminds you of your father?"

"Bingo." Livy did not hear the conversation but ignorantly smiled and waved at Tiffany, who patronized him by waving back. "There is some good news."

"What would that be?"

"You know how we just got eight new recruits in?"

"Yes?"

"Well, I've been seeing him eye one of the newbies. So, he might be moving on."

"Here's hoping."

"Don't need to tell me."

As the two friends chatted by the boxing ring, Cato entered the room. Judging by his formal attire, he was not there to lift weights. He went straight for the ring, quickly grabbing the attention of the hulking victor. Livy bent down some, leaning against the top rope while Cato spoke to him. After their brief conversation was completed, Livy clapped very loudly to draw the attention of the others in the gym. "Okay everyone, gather around the boxing ring." They obliged, walking at varying speeds to the area just outside of the ropes. "I know it's the dinner hour and Cato has agreed to pay for takeout. Susan, Riley—you two are the ones who will pick up the order, so go ahead and get to the showers. The rest of you, do as you want." As the two aforementioned people made their way to separate showers, the rest either went back to exercising or became lax and socialized with the others gathered around the ring. Livy himself went to the showers soon after, with Cato following him as they continued to discuss some business.

"You staying for dinner?"

"Do you think I have anything in the fridge at home?" asked Tiffany.

"Yeah, I guess starving artists don't, do they?"

"Maybe after next assignment."

"Or the next sale, right?"

"We'll see."

"Is it that bad?"

"Well, you know with the economy being what it is," commented Tiffany, "a lot of people are looking for groceries instead of paintings."

"They should know better," jokingly replied Carla, making Tiffany smile at her bad fortune. "I am going to shower and change for dinner. See you at the mess hall."

A little while later, most of those in the gymnasium had washed up and were in the break room. It had tables with attached stools like that which existed in an elementary school cafeteria. Riley and Susan returned fairly quickly, carrying a few orders of large pizzas divided into pepperoni and cheese, as well as a few two-liter sodas. Rather than hail a taxi the two had used one of the four compact cars at the site. The Cicero Organization kept a couple of vehicles at the Eagle Factory, parking them away from the road to obscure them from the occasional person driving by or in rarer instances walking by. Among them were two vans, which were used on certain operations.

By the time dinner arrived, some of those who were in the gym had left because of other plans or a lack of interest in fraternizing. They were not required to stay for dinner. Each table got a pepperoni and a cheese pizza respectively, as well as two of the two-liter sodas. There was no grace spoken aloud. Carla did cross herself before eating, as did some other fellow at another table. Livy, Carla, Cato, and Tiffany were at the same table and even at the same end. For a time, Tiffany had taken to sitting as far from Livy as possible, but with the belief that he was already looking to conquer a different woman on the staff, she felt more secure around him. For most of the evening, this security seemed true.

About an hour later, most of the food was eaten and nearly all the folks had left for the night. Some carpooled in while a few had to walk several blocks before they got to a seldom used bus stop. "Alright, y'all have a good night," said the man Livy defeated in combat. "And Livy? Someday I'll beat you."

"You and everyone else," he replied, the man smiling as he walked away, still sore from his beating. Carla and Tiffany were briefly out of the room, having both gone to the bathroom. Only Cato was present for the time.

"Good exercise, a good beat down, and a good feast," said Livy to Cato. "Now that is how a man should spend a Saturday night."

"Sounds good, for a young man at least," responded Cato.

"There is only one thing missing from it," said Livy, who smiled as Tiffany and Carla returned to the break room. "And here she is."

"Excuse me?"

"I was talking to Cato here about a good night. And I would say, I owe you a good night tonight," said Livy as he got up, his height and frame blocking the image of Cato who was seated beside him.

"Listen, Livy," began Tiffany. "I get that you want me, but I am not interested. It's not your fault, it's probably mine, but still."

"Cato, I think she's nervous," smiled Livy. "Oh, come on, you know I am just the kind of man you want in your life. Strong, commanding, and energetic."

Tiffany blurted out a laugh. "Energetic? Boy, you need to brush up on your romance skills. I said no and I mean no. No, last I checked, means no."

"How about this?" posited Livy. "I am in a good mood tonight. How about we settle this like two people skilled at fighting settle something."

"You want me to fight you?"

"Yes. But not just in any fight," continued Livy in a diplomatic tone of voice. "To make things fair, I think a first-blood fight will do best. That way, you don't have to pin me or knock me out or something like that. If you win, I take a cold shower and leave you alone forever. But when I win, you are mine."

"I am not fighting you, Livy."

"Come on!" he whined. "You cannot lose. If you draw first blood, I quit hitting on you. If I draw first blood, you will have the time of your life tonight."

"And other nights," chimed in Cato, who was otherwise trying to be above it all.

"Exactly," concurred Livy. "So let's do it."

"No means no."

"And what if I ordered you?" forcefully inquired Livy, causing Tiffany to draw back.

"I'll do it," interjected Carla, prompting the other three to look her way in surprise.

"What?"

"I said, I will do it. I will fight you in a first blood bout. If I win you leave her alone and if you win, well I guess you can have us both."

"Tiffany will do."

"Carla," said a concerned Tiffany, grabbing at her friend's arm. "You do not need to do this. I could always complain to Cicero."

"Like Cicero will take your side," confidently stated Livy. "And there ain't no place you can file a harassment suit, so yeah. It's either you do it or Carla does it."

"I said I would do it."

"Then it is settled," grinned Livy. "And Cato will be the judge."

"Keep me out of this," said Cato while looking down at the cafeteria table top.

"Come on, Cato. We need an impartial referee and you know that we are doing this with or without your help."

"Well, in that case," replied Cato. "Let us venture forth to the boxing ring and get this little matter over with."

***

Carla was back in her sweats. Her street clothes were again folded into her blue and white duffle bag, which was placed to the side of the ring. Tiffany stood there, too nervous to sit down. Cato was in the very middle of the ring, standing between the two combatants. Livy retained his blatant arrogance. As the three stood in the ring, Livy pulled his shirt off, revealing a ripped muscular physique. Tossing it to the side, he flexed a few poses as a reminder to his opponent of his indomitable frame.

"Now you strip," said Livy to Carla.

"No."

"Take your shirt off."

"It will not be necessary," interrupted Cato. "Having seen these first blood fights before, I can say with confidence that wearing a shirt makes no difference."

"If you say so," conceded Livy. "Besides, when I cut you first, this will make it all the more rewarding a victory."

"Come on, Carla! He talks a big talk, but he doesn't stand a chance!" shouted Tiffany from the sidelines.

"Alright then," said Cato. "The two combatants may approach and receive their weapons. Remember, the fight does not begin until I say so." The two obliged and walked towards the center of the ring. Standing within a few feet of each other, Carla was further reminded of how outclassed she was in the size department. Drawing near, Livy's head disappeared into a wall of chest. Cato presented an opened box with two daggers bearing eight-inch blades. The two foes selected the blade closest to them and then drew back to their corners. "Now that each person is at their respective corner, I will count to three. When I reach three, the fight begins and will continue until one is bleeding."

Carla was suppressing her nerves. She kept telling herself that she had the advantage. After all, there was more of him to strike at. Furthermore, he ate a lot of pizza and probably would not be as agile as he could be. Plus, he was very confident. Then again, he had every right to be confident. Livy trained Carla and Tiffany. He knew how to fight and to pound an enemy into dust. There was no bright spot to losing. To lose was to fail her friend, to possibly lose her virgin honor, and to bleed, maybe profusely.

"One ... two ... three!" said Cato, shouting the last number and rushing out of the ring as the two combatants closed in on each other.

"Come on, Carla! Give it to him!" shouted Tiffany, who decided to curb her cheers from there on in lest she accidentally distract her friend.

Neither person rushed the other. Both were in hunched positions, with one hand gripping the dagger and another stretched out to try and parry a possible blow. Even hunched over, Livy towered over Carla. He swung first, narrowly missing his target. For a man his size, he was fast. His first attempt did not leave him vulnerable as he immediately returned to that defensive posture. Cato studied both cautiously, looking for any indication of injury. Livy swung a few more times, the blade going to and fro but missing Carla each time. He kept smiling, like he had already won.

Carla went for his left hand, which Livy had outstretched as a way to try and parry her attack. He withdrew it in time and then delivered a kick with his right leg into her midsection, hurling Carla back into the ropes. Livy went in, though with caution. The leniency of the caution was such that she was able to roll out of the way. It hurt to breathe, as the kick made Carla's abdomen sore. She started to slowly back into a corner while Livy gradually got closer to his opponent.

"You know another positive to all this, Carla?" he asked. "By fighting you instead of Tiffany, I get the benefit of having damaged you instead of her. If she fought me, I might scar her so bad that I might not want her anymore." Carla swung at Livy and missed. He swung at her and sliced at her side.

"Stop the fight!" shouted Cato. "Combatants to your corners. I think it might be over."

Tiffany's heart sank while Livy walked with swagger to the opposite corner. He smiled at Tiffany outside the ring, winking at her as she looked away. Turning from outside the ring, he focused on the two people in the other corner. Cato checked on Carla, seeing that the dagger thrust struck her in the side where shirt covered skin. Examining the impact, he saw that the blade had only sliced the shirt, creating a three-inch opening. The skin underneath remained its fair quality. Livy's smile melted away as Cato looked up and then at Livy, shaking his head in the negative.

"No blood. Fight will continue," said Cato, who then made his way out of the boxing ring once again.

"He was close, that's all. You got this!" shouted Tiffany with renewed hope. "Keep it going. You got this, Carla!"

The two combatants started to circle each other. The break from the action gave Carla time to heal up from the kick she received. Hunched over, the two started to close in. Livy was feigning thrusts, laughing at every bit of seriousness and nervousness befalling his foe. Then he went for her but missed. She was tempted to throw the weapon at him, possibly hit him and thus win the fight. But these were not the kind of daggers meant for throwing. And besides, what if he dodged it?

Livy came in again, swinging and narrowly missing Carla three more times. Carla then tried to strike back, with Livy struggling to dodge the attempts but still ultimately being successful in avoiding them. He backed into a corner and Carla went in to pursue. Yet the long thick legs of Livy were again a menace, as he kicked her in the gut, prompting her to fall to both knees. Then she saw it. A split second of weakness, a mere moment of time unlikely to appear ever again. The leg was coming back to kick her, rolling towards her gut to knock her down once again. This time she caught the leg and before Livy could respond jammed the dagger into the side of it, causing him to scream in anguish.

"Stop the fight! Stop the fight!" shouted Cato as he rushed into the ring. Carla rolled away from Livy, whose expression was all rage. Cato placed both hands on the chest of Livy, trying to keep him at bay, trying to calm the beast. To Livy's credit, he could have easily thrown the older gentleman to the side, but he kept enough sanity to forgo such an action. The inspection was brief, as the blood was quickly dripping from the pant leg. "Match is over! Match is over!" declared Cato, to the joy of Tiffany and Carla both. He then looked at the giant man, whose hands each gave a death grip to the top rope. "Damn, Livy. Why did you have to do something so stupid like this?"

Carla took no victory lap, but simply left the dagger in the boxing ring, rolled out from below the bottom rope, and exited the place alongside Tiffany. Cato meanwhile hastily got some medical supplies and saw to tending to the leg wound. Fortunately, Carla had missed any major veins or arteries. It was just a matter of applying pressure to the wound, washing it, wrapping it, and then Livy taking it easy for the next several days. All of this was doable, even as he seethed heavily from within.

VIII

Exeter Hotel once again provided the setting for a major formal political fundraiser. As rainfall cascaded onto the streets and sidewalks outside, within the large meeting hall all was pleasant and sociable. Suits with ties and dresses with heels were the norm for those at the circular tables. Dinner had already been eaten, with assorted speakers talking about the needs of the party as servers in properly tailored outfits came and silently took away the used dishes. Some of the plates still had a fair amount of food on them, but that universal symbol of a discarded napkin upon the tops of the contents informed the help that their service of removal was requested.

The proceedings were identical to the fundraiser from a couple weeks ago. The model setup the hotel operations crew used when preparing for the feast was identical to the one before, with its large collection of round tables and the stage for speakers. The speeches thanking the attendees for their generous donations were also similar. For the servers who were unfamiliar with the current political climate and whose English was not the best, it is possible they thought it was the same faction overseeing the fundraiser. Yet such was not so, as it was the party of Attorney General Kyle Brown and District Attorney James Colbert and not that of Mayor Mary Bhatia and Governor Claire Voxner. In keeping with this, Brown and Colbert were present while Bhatia and Voxner were not.

During the first several minutes, some of the attendees in the far back of the hall looked behind themselves. They wondered if Rafael Sanchez-Vargas or maybe some of his followers were going to try and storm the hall to shout at the people present. Out of about twenty official fundraisers and rallies overseen by both major parties, Sanchez-Vargas either alone or with a group had disrupted half of them. Of that number, a third of them resulted in physical violence between disrupter and disrupted. There had already been a dozen arrests made at these events, two of which were of Sanchez-Vargas himself. And yet, somehow, he was still considered a viable contender for next year's mayoral election.

"I would like to once again thank each of you for all your support, not just financially, but also your prayers and your many, many campaign efforts," continued the last speaker on the docket. "Remember, next year is going to be tough. We are facing a well-funded political machine that is not above using violence to keep its place of power. But we can beat them. We have beaten them before, and we can beat them again. Thank you all and God bless!" His concluding benediction received wide applause. It was also the queue for the servers to wheel out the desserts for the evening.

"Ah yes, the generic Sundae," observed Attorney General Brown, who was seated next to District Attorney Colbert. "Inoffensive, widely loved, and broadly consumed."

"So now Sundaes have become a model for political success?" asked Colbert as he indulged in the dessert.

"My mentor used to always liken a good campaign to a Sundae," replied Brown, who took a bite before continuing. "Sweet but cold, memorable but fleeting, and at times the source of much emotional contention."

"He should have written a book," continued Colbert.

"A child's guide to politics?" sarcastically inquired Brown, with both men briefly laughing at the thought. Colbert took a few more bites and then changed the topic.

"I am surprised that Sanchez did not show up. Is he still in jail?"

"No, no," responded Brown. "An aide of mine informed me just before we started that he was leading some blue collar workers rally in some nameless little town."

"And all this time I thought he was starting to like us."

"He's going to run again."

"Probably."

"No, definitely," somberly spoke Brown. "A friend of mine in the election commission confirmed to me that he recently submitted paperwork."

"Well that should be a source of joy, correct?" asked Colbert, having finished his dessert. "I mean, doesn't he usually take votes away from our friends on the other side?"

"Mostly. But that is not the point. Whenever Sanchez-Vargas runs, things always get more vitriolic and chaotic. The ads are always meaner, more personal."

"Personal attacks are the norm in politics."

"Yeah, but he takes it to another level."

"At least he doesn't take it to the level of Cicero," bluntly stated Colbert, putting his voice a little lower.

"Few ever do."

"I heard it's getting to the point where they might have to set up a 'political crimes' unit for our police department."

"I will throw you one worse," responded Brown as he put down his spoon in the empty dessert bowl. "I hear that similar groups are starting to sprout up in other states. Nothing as bad as we have, but disturbingly similar."

"I guess that makes Josiah's efforts even more important."

"Yes, it does."

"He is going to brief us tomorrow about another couple of raids. Not as impressive as the one from last week, but still something that helps wound the Organization."

"Hopefully, fatally."

"Hopefully."

***

Some called it the War Between the States. Others dubbed it the War of Northern Aggression. Generations ago some called it simply the Rebellion. Most commonly it was referred to as the American Civil War. Whatever the name, the refurbished basement room that Carla and Concepción were cleaning that morning was immersed in the theme of that nineteenth century conflict. Book shelves had various histories written by authors above and below the Mason-Dixon Line. Framed photos showed the home owner standing beside figures like Shelby Foote and Ed Bearss and Ken Burns.

Carla carefully removed the painted metal figurines of assorted Confederate and Union troops from the mantle. The owner had purchased them from a hobby store as bare objects, skillfully adding the painted details later. His work was exceptional as each soldier, though only a few inches tall, had finely crafted coloring right down to the eyes. Placing them on a small table she already dusted, Carla then went toward clearing off the thin layer of gray mites that developed along the platform. As she did her work, a replica portrait of General Robert E. Lee in full uniform hung above her.

"Carla?" asked Concepción, drawing her friend's attention. She was on the opposite side of the room, where fittingly enough a replica portrait of General Ulysses S. Grant in his full uniform stared in the direction of Lee. Carla turned to face her coworker who decided to have her practice her language skills. "Tengo una pregunta."

"Okay. Cuál es tu pregunta?" replied Carla with some American accent.

"Juegas ajedrez?"

"Um … como se dice 'ajedrez' en inglés?"

"Chess," Concepción responded.

"Oh okay. Poco. Por que estas interesado?"

"Because I removed all these chess pieces from the board when I dusted it and now I have no idea what pieces go where," she explained, prompting Carla to approach her and study the board. In keeping with the theme of the room, the checkered board was divided into blue and gray squares, with one army being in federal uniform and the other secessionist. "I do know that the smaller ones go in front of the bigger ones. But after that, no se nada."

"No worries, amiga," replied Carla, putting down her duster and taking pieces with both hands and accurately placing them on the field of battle, "I know where they go." To Concepción's relief, Carla quickly placed them on the squares they needed to be on and even adjusted a few of them so they were more centered. "My grandpa taught me. We used to play all the time until I kept beating him. That was when he surrendered."

"Are you good at this game?"

"Not really. I lose to everybody else."

"Ah," said Concepción as the two redirected their efforts to finishing up in the room. A few minutes later, the place was in good condition, with the various memorabilia about that quintessential American conflict back in their respective places. When the homeowner returned hours later, it was like only the dust and dirt were moved. With the work completed the two went up the firm wooden stairs to the main floor. There they found that the other maids had successfully finished their part of the assignment. As the two stood in the main hallway of the spacious suburban home, Concepción spoke up. "Tengo una pregunta nueva."

"Sí, cuál es tu pregunta?"

"You remember meeting my daughter once, right?"

"Sí, yo recuerdo," smiled Carla. "How's she doing?"

"Pretty well. She is in high school now."

"Really? She is growing up fast."

"Muy rapido, sí. Anyway, next year she is going to take Arabic for her language requirements."

"Okay," replied Carla, who had a good idea what Concepción was going to inquire about next.

"I was wondering. You're Arab, could you, you know, help her out? Like tutor and stuff?"

"Sorry, but I cannot be of much help."

"Really? Por que?"

"Well, to be honest, I do not know a lot of Arabic myself. Only a few words and phrases here and there."

"Really?" asked a surprised Concepción. "How come?"

"Well, I was basically raised by my grandfather. And he never taught me much other than a few basic words, like 'Salaam' and 'Shukran.' Yo se mas Español que Arabic."

"That's very strange."

"I know. It is weird and not common."

"Very uncommon. Pero, I know immigrants used to do that all the time. When I first came here I remember running into some Chicanos. Their grandparents were Mexican and spoke Spanish, but they didn't know the language or celebrate the holidays or anything," said Concepción, who started laughing some. "In fact, I used to think they were gringos pretending to be Mexican."

The hour was nearing noon. Since the cleaning took place, the house was more pristine than it was earlier that morning. Assignment completed, the maids ate together outside on a beautiful spring day. Sodas, sandwiches, and chips were on the menu, with the coworkers either sitting in the opened van or along the sidewalk. "You know," observed Carla as she and Concepción ate together, "now that I think of it, I have gotten a similar experience with people around here."

"People think you're white?"

"Yes, often," replied Carla. "You thought I was white when we first met, didn't you?"

"A little, yes."

"I remember this one job application I filled out in high school. They asked for my race and of course they did not list 'Arab' or 'Middle Easterner' as an option."

"So, what did you do?"

"Well, I went for what I thought was the most accurate and picked Asian."

Concepción laughed, almost spilling her soda.

"What? Its geographically true."

"Okay, okay," agreed Concepción as she regained her composure. "So what happened?"

"Well, I went into the interview and they refused to hire me."

"Por que?"

"They claimed I lied on my application," smiled Carla as both laughed at the thought.

"That was their loss."

"Thanks."

"So your grandfather never wanted you to learn your language or your culture or anything like that?"

"Nope."

"Still seems weird. I can't imagine growing up without somebody in my family telling me how I must be a proud Salvadoreña."

"I think it's because my grandfather had a bad experience with the Mother Country."

"Oh, come on," replied Concepción, "most of us come here because we had bad experiences back home."

"True, but his were really, well, disillusioning. You know what that means, right?"

"Disappointing?"

"Yes, exactly," said Carla. "I think he felt that it was not just some oppressors who were bad, it was everybody. The whole system, the whole nation. Everything. I think he wanted me to be more American than Syrian."

"I see. How is that going?"

"Bastante bien," said Carla who then said with a smile, "but if I am not careful, you're going to make me more El Salvadoran than American."

***

The room lacked windows. A sterile looking environment, it had a rectangular table in the middle of its space with four chairs on one side and one chair facing them. Seated in the four chairs, from left to right, were Mayor Mary Bhatia, Governor Claire Voxner, Attorney General Kyle Brown, and District Attorney James Colbert. Security stood silently outside the lone entrance. In advance of the meeting the same security searched the space for bugs, making sure that the enemy was not within hearing range.

None were found. The only instance when any were discovered had been soon after Josiah Sharp accused the panel of superiors of having a traitor among them. This matter made Josiah curious. He wondered why the Cicero Organization, which clearly benefitted from the bugs, did not try to replace them upon their loss. Then again, perchance it was a one-time success and that with the recent attacks on their efforts the Organization was attempting to stay away from hostile territory. These raids were the grand focus of that meeting, which was going on without incident or extra little ears.

"Then what happened?" asked Governor Voxner to Josiah.

"SWAT forces scaled the five flights of stairs without being detected. They located the office where the five Cicero Organization members were and where they had taken a good deal of stolen money," stoically described the assistant district attorney. "SWAT then broke down the door and engaged the Organization. After a firefight that lasted several minutes, all five members were deceased."

"A violent affair," commented Bhatia.

"Did SWAT kill all five?" asked Colbert.

"No," responded Josiah. "According to the team captain's report, two of them were killed after the door was broken down, but the other three apparently killed themselves."

"Suicides?"

"Yes, Governor. At that point the only way out of the room was a five-story drop onto hard concrete. As SWAT demanded their surrender, a few shots rang out behind the desks they were using for cover."

"And they were dead?"

"Yes."

"And then there was yesterday's raid," commented Colbert, with all five seated figures turning the pages in their respective folders to view the series of documents pertaining to that incident.

"Yes, sir."

"Care to walk us through this one also, Mr. Sharp?"

"Yes, Governor," began Sharp. "This was another minor outlet for the Organization that I was able to find when I examined the late Tony Albioni's contacts. As with the Saddler & Saddler business, this was another one of those mysterious names that popped up in both his initial FBI file and the state investigation file created after his demise."

"More phone records?"

"Yes, those again. Once again, they led to suspicious activity. With the help of Detective Frank Cooper, we were able to locate this setup at a former school."

"Which one?"

"Swainn Elementary," replied Josiah. "As you may recall, Swainn was closed following budget cuts around five or six years ago. Apparently, the cell in question took up shop at the abandoned building."

"Okay. Go on."

"Well, Det. Cooper led a mixed force of SWAT and police to the site. An unnamed source among the underground arms dealing community said that they were expecting a shipment there. Cooper's force arrived at the school building just as the weapons came in. There were ten people there altogether."

"Were they all members of the Organization?"

"No, it does not appear to be so."

"Explain, please."

"Well, Attorney General, the two men who came with the truck were private arms dealers, like Albioni. The FBI sent me their criminal records and known associations. This was their first time dealing with Cicero. By contrast, the other eight waiting for them were affiliated with the Organization. A couple of them were even directly connected to past acts that the Organization has taken credit for."

"Fair enough," nodded Brown. "Continue."

"Well, after they shook hands Cooper and his men moved in. A firefight ensued in which both arms dealers were killed."

"Who killed them?"

"The Cicero Organization did. They actually fired at the dealers before they fired at us," said Josiah, causing two of his superiors to look at him with discerning curiosity. "Law enforcement exchanged gunfire with the six Cicero members still alive following the initial strike. They doubled back to the school building, with Cooper sending in special teams to smoke them out, um, so to speak."

"And did they, as you put it, 'smoke them out'?" inquired Bhatia.

"Nope. All Cicero members remained in the school. A few attempted resistance and were killed by the special forces. The rest, once again, were found with what the folks at forensics believe were self-inflicted gunshot wounds to the head."

"No survivors?"

"None, Governor."

"Do they ever surrender?" asked Colbert with some bewilderment. Josiah remained silent while the more seasoned Voxner spoke up.

"Not that I am aware of. I have heard briefings about broken cells and cornered Cicero members for years now. Always the same story. None alive."

"Amazing," commented Colbert. "Even the Islamic terrorists occasionally turn themselves in. Have we basically concluded that the Cicero Organization is more fanatical than the likes of al Qaeda or ISIS?"

"Seems like it."

"But what is driving this fanaticism?" continued Colbert in his disbelieved query. "What could possibly lead these people, men and women, presumably of varying mental stabilities, to decide that killing themselves is better than getting arrested?"

"Still looking into it, sir."

"Well, hopefully we can get something figured out. As long as they keep refusing to cooperate, we can only do so much damage to the Organization."

"Least of all in finding out who runs that whole operation," added Brown. "The sooner we find that out, the better."

"Moving back to the specific raids," interjected Bhatia. "Mr. Sharp, any further developments of worth?"

"Well," began Josiah as he closed his folder, "I can say that we are definitely harming the Organization both in men and material. In addition to the roughly 30 members who have been killed or committed suicide, SWAT and the police have seized at least 5,000 rounds of ammunition, a hundred firearms of varying calibers, 200 explosive devices, and over $130,000 worth of currency."

"A job well done," optimistically noted Colbert.

"Thank you, sir," replied Josiah. "But I must stress that Det. Cooper deserves more acclamation. He is running most of the risks after all."

"Truly," stated Voxner. "I will be sure to honor him at the Summer Ball in a couple of weeks. If nothing else, it should further help your cover as being the actual head of this investigation."

"Yes, Governor."

***

An early rain had some of the artists nervous. That morning a front swept through the city, pouring down quite the tumultuous deluge. Large puddles abounded in every dip in the sidewalk and every pothole in the street. However, by midmorning the clouds dragged away and the sunshine beamed onto every uncovered spot. By lunchtime, evaporation cleared away the aqua impediments. With the afternoon came the setup and the arrival of the various artists, local folks of varying ages, races, and economic statuses.

As was customary, the event took place at the downtown public park. It had rolling hills of green with light gray lines of walkway wide enough to include both pedestrians and bicyclists. Their tents were placed in a row alongside the walkway nearest to the lake, which was roughly in the middle of the park. Each tent included a white pavilioned top with three ivory sides adding privacy and sometimes weather protection. A steel frame kept the tent structure stable as the artists and their work faced the direction of the walkway and the lake. The afternoon sun glimmered upon the watery surface.

Tiffany held her own in one of the tents. She had three paintings that were for sale on that day. The three were similar in their nature, with black stripes and eyes of varying sizes and glances scattered along the canvas. Each one had a different primary color combined with the stripes and detailed eyes. Some had splotches meant to symbolize bruises, with angry eyes staring at the viewer while the stripes seemed to point to the furious presence. To close friends Tiffany claimed that her upbringing influenced the intense imagery, focusing on her and her audience's rage upon the bruising features.

"Do you see something you like?" asked Tiffany to the silver-haired bespectacled man who was eyeing one of the pleasanter looking pieces.

He was staring at the one that was yellow and black. Its eyes were larger and kinder looking. The man smiled a bit at Tiffany, stroking his chin with his left hand while his right hand held his left elbow in support.

"I think I like this one," he responded in a proper voice. "How much is the piece?"

"$40.00 for the 24 by 36 inch or $65.00 for the 48 by 72."

"Hmmm," pondered the gentleman. "I think I will take a 24 by 36 one."

"Okay," immediately replied Tiffany. She turned away momentarily to search the dozens of paintings stacked behind her on a couple of tables placed there by the operations crew for the event. Each painting was encased in a thin white cardboard box, with each corner having some extra cardboard meant to prevent the rectangular painting from tossing back and forth within its packaging. After a couple of moments, she found the correct size and type of painting. She turned back to face the gentleman, who was standing there patiently in front of the table where business was to be conducted. Carefully placing the painting flat on the table, the gentleman opened his wallet and handed her two twenties.

"Anything else I can help you with?"

"That will be all, thank you."

"Have a good day."

"You, too," he said as he took the portrait under his right arm and walked away, going right down the walkway. On the table at the opened front of the tent there was a small dark pink pouch that was originally meant to hold pencils. Tiffany unzipped it and placed the gentleman's money in it. The two bills kept the seven other bills of different denominations company. An earlier customer paid with a fifty-dollar bill for one of Tiffany's $40 items. She was kind enough to let the artist keep the change. As Tiffany looked up she saw a familiar face studying the paintings on the side of the tent.

"Can I help you, miss?" said Tiffany in a feigned customer service impersonation.

"No, just looking," said Carla, feigning seriousness. The charade did not last and her serious facial expression melted to a smile. She turned away from the painting and towards her friend. "So how is business, Tiff?"

"Pretty good," replied Tiffany. "I've sold a few today, which is more than usual." Tiffany noticed that Carla was wearing all white and her hair was in a ponytail. "Did you come from work?"

"Yes. The line of houses I cleaned was near a bus route that I knew would take me here. And since you said you were going to have a tent, I thought I would stop by."

"Thanks for showing up," said Tiffany. "Feel free to buy anything."

"Okay, okay," said Carla, smiling as she looked about the three paintings. "Do you have names for these?"

"Of course."

"What's this one called?" asked Carla, pointing to the yellow and black piece of which the earlier person bought a copy.

"Fantastical."

"Really?" laughed Carla.

"Yes."

"Why 'Fantastical'?"

"Why not?"

"Fair enough," acknowledged Carl, who looked at the painting below it. This one was a light blue-and-black-striped masterpiece. She pointed at it while looking at the artist. "And this one?"

"Exuberance."

"Okay," giggled Carla. She looked down at the last. The red and black one with its angry eyes and painted bruises. "How about this one?"

"A Father's Love."

Carla blurted out a laugh, covering her mouth as though she had sneezed. "Wow. So, painting really is a therapeutic practice after all."

"Very," agreed Tiffany. "Which one do you want?"

"A part of me leans towards 'A Father's Love', but I think I have to go with 'Exuberance.' You got any in stock?"

"All day, every day," commented Tiffany. "Which size?"

"What are my options?"

"24 by 36 or 48 by 72."

"I will go with 24 by 36. I live in a small apartment, after all."

"Of course," smiled Tiffany, who turned and quickly found a copy of the requested painting and as with the previous transaction gently placed it on the table.

"Do you take credit?" jokingly asked Carla.

"Girl, do I look like a register?" replied Tiffany in faux annoyance.

"Okay, okay, here you go," replied Carla, who took out a couple twenties. "And here is an extra one to show that I support the arts."

"Donations are always accepted," said Tiffany, collecting the money and putting it in the dark pink pencil case. Her tone then softened. "So … have you heard anything from your doctor friend about the loyalty oath?"

"We last talked a few days ago," replied Carla, who leaned over the table to be closer to Tiffany. "She said the toxicologist at her hospital was looking into it."

"Keep me posted."

"Agreed."

"The sooner I can present my art on the French Riviera the better."

"Very true," said Carla as she took hold of the purchased painting. As she took a step back both her and Tiffany's phones went off. Carla's made a brief melody while Tiffany's buzzed loudly.

"Want a bet that we got the same message?" posited Tiffany, her annoyed expression being legitimate this time. Carla nodded as they each took out their mobile devices and with the pushing of buttons and the swiping of fingers confirmed the same. As typical, numbers began the text message. They needed to help offset the recent financial losses of the Cicero Organization. A bank was selected, minimal security expected. Both texted back confirming receipt of the message and acceptance of the mission.

"I guess the Riviera will have to wait."

"It will always be in my dreams."

"See you in a few hours."

"Bye."

***

Tiffany was better at breaking into and disabling circuit breakers, so she was the one working on the issue. Carla held the flashlight close, not wanting the beam to shoot too far out and thus alert the scarce eventide world of their presence. Picking the mild gray lock, Tiffany was able to jerk the little door open. The small yet important light source illumined the buttons and the red switch that Tiffany pulled down with a gloved hand. A small mechanical noise was heard within the building as all the items requiring power were put to slumber on that still spring night, enabling access without alarm.

Wanting to keep in practice, Carla took out her picklock equipment while Tiffany put hers away. The two were both wearing ski-masks and gloves as well as dark pants and long-sleeved shirts. Tiffany cut her hair short for the occasion, allowing the mask to fit over her head more easily. Carla settled for the usual hunchback appearance. She once tried a short hair look back in high school, hated it eternally, and never looked back. To her long hair was not a visual issue; the only time it made her look awkward was at a time when people were not supposed to see her in the first place.

A friendly click and the back alley door was opened. The two women were standing in a minor paved route used for deliveries both for that particular bank and the businesses to its right and left. They were all closed at that hour, none of them being bars or diners whose clientele sought a latter evening location to patronize. A lone security officer patrolled the area, but the research one of their peers made in advance of the robbery found that his rounds occurred once every 25 to 30 minutes. Carla kept track of the timing with her wrist watch as she opened the back door and the two entered.

They were greeted with a camera whose red light was off. It was perched high above them and angled downward towards the door. The two walked down the simple hallway, which quickly brought them to the main room of the facility. They cautiously entered the space, staying close to the back of the room as the front wall and the wall to their right was glass. Outside, a person walked by the bank oblivious to their presence within the darkened interior of the building. In front of them was the long row of teller stations, united by a single barrier that was four feet high. There were four stations, each with a computer and a landline telephone, as well as a register below the desk space and a small machine for bank cards.

Several feet behind this row of stations was a mostly enclosed space that included a chair and a desk, as well as a computer and landline phone. They speculated that some manger on duty or higher ranking official of some kind dwelt in that area, with its own four-foot high barrier between it and the customers. Looking around, their eyes adjusting quickly to the dark facility, they located the vault. Since the cameras were going to be off for the duration, both Carla and Tiffany removed their masks and tucked them in the same belts they were wearing that included the picklock equipment and, in case unexpected security showed up, handguns. Both had already taken their substances for the evening. They did so while waiting for the security man to leave the area. Carla swallowed hers without unwrapping it while Tiffany tore the packet open and, upon consuming the substance, tossed the wrapper aside. A car went by but once again did not notice the people inside. Another car was parked on the other side of the street, its four passengers getting out.

"My turn, right?"

"I did do the door," smiled Carla. "And you're faster."

"Challenge accepted," agreed Tiffany, who approached the closed vault and began to examine the imposing protector of funds. She directed her focus to the thick round door in front of her, taking out a listening device for the tumblers.

"Need some help?" asked Carla, holding the flashlight.

"Nah," replied Tiffany, keeping her staring gaze at the small numbers on the round lock. "I see them. Besides, someone outside might see us."

"True."

"Okay baby," she said to the door. "Open for mama."

The four who were in the parked car hastily crossed the street, not bothering to veer right to the nearest pedestrian crosswalk. Like Carla and Tiffany, they were in dark clothes that blended with the shadows. Unlike Carla and Tiffany three of them wore night vision goggles that gave them visions of shaded green. Three of them also carried assault rifles with silencers attached. The fourth was in business casual and armed with a Glock. Like his peers, he had gloves on. He walked with a slight limp.

"Okay, this isn't right," said Tiffany with concern. "Nothing is happening."

"Nothing is happening?"

"The door ain't talking to me."

"Why not?"

"Because it is on time delay," said Livy, whose voice boomed not only because of his strong projection but for the sudden surprise in which he interrupted the robbery. Carla and Tiffany jumped back some at the sounding of his presence, as he had successfully opened the locked front with little noise. To his left were two armed men and to his right, one. His one leg looked a little bulgy underneath the pants. It was a visual reminder of Carla's victory over him in that first blood match. "The vault will not open until 7:00 AM tomorrow morning. No matter what you do, it remains shut."

"Really?" replied an openly annoyed Tiffany. She and Carla both neared the four men, but Tiffany got closer and with greater irritation, passing by the teller stations to be within six feet of Livy. "Then there is no way we can rob it. What idiot did the research on this target?"

"I did," stoically responded Livy.

"Liv—"

Tiffany's statement was cut short as Livy raised his right hand with Glock and silencer firmly grasped and shot a single round that went through Tiffany's forehead and exited spent outside of her left occipital lobe. She fell to the ground. Carla screamed without making noise, her gaping mouth and widened eyes saying all necessary speech. The three assault rifles were raised and rounds were discharged. Carla ducked behind the teller stations as the rounds chewed up the mahogany and plastic structure. Fearful they were going to close in she fired a few rounds in response into the air. Meanwhile holes started to develop in the barrier, shining the faint glimmer of the street lights onto her panicked body. One of the holes near her head and arms were large enough to fit a muzzle through. Within a minute the firing ceased as the three reloaded.

Three empty clips were detached from their weapons and thoughtlessly tossed to the ground. Each man took out another clip, fresh and full of bullets. As they were attaching them back to the firearms, Carla saw a chance. Through the hole near to her line of sight, she pushed the muzzle of her handgun through the opening like it was a cannon on the portside of some eighteenth-century battleship. As the clicking of the newly applied clips was heard, Carla fired off a single round. It struck with a scream, shattering the kneecap of one of the three flunkies Livy brought with him to the bank. She saw his goggled face grimace as the other two finished reloading and fired.

His screams were partnered with the muted spurts of the rifles, taking away several small pieces of the teller stations. Carla got up and, while crouched low, desperately rushed to the nearest hallway. It was not the short one that led to the loading area, but rather the longer one that included access to three rooms. The first one, to her left, was that of a minor executive. The second one, farther along and to her right, was the bank manager's space. The third, which was near the dead end of the hallway and to the left, was the bathroom. Still crouched, with bullets flying overhead, she scampered into the manager's office. The firing halted once again as the two able-bodied men reloaded their rifles and the third remained on the floor, gripping his badly wounded leg with both hands.

"Can you walk, recruit?" asked Livy, hovering above him.

"No, I don't think so."

Livy aimed his Glock and fired it, perfectly placing the bullet between the goggled eyes of the young man. The two others were shocked at the action, even though they were recently made acquainted to Livy's murderous tendencies during their training. Still, to see him do such a thing so sudden. Livy looked at both men, his demeanor remaining without emotion. "Go into that hallway and find Carla. Kill her or I will do this to you." Obedient as a pair of young pups, they anxiously nodded and directed their attention to the dark hallway made into many degrees of green by their goggles.

Cautiously and with little noise they ventured past the row of attached desks, the teller station barrier made porous by their onslaught. Slightly bent and with rifles aimed, they studied each view of the world in front of them to verify that the enemy was not present. Careful step after careful step, the two made their way into the hallway. Meanwhile, Livy looked at his handiwork. Tiffany's eyes were still open, as though beholding the pearly gates. Above her eyes was a dark black hole about an inch in diameter. Below her frozen expression, a slowly-growing pool of blood and small pieces of cerebral tissue.

Inside of the bank manager's office, Carla pushed back the curtains to see a rectangular portion of the outside. To her dismay, the glass before her was a solid double-paned border. There was no lever or latch to undo and open it. She searched about the room, looking for an object strong enough to smash through the two thin layers of the window. The desk was to her left, but was too cumbersome for the task. There were a few framed items on the walls: a couple of diplomas, a portrait of the bank's founder, and some inspirational quote with a landscape shot. None of them were a good option.

In the hallway, the tense duo kept their weapons aimed onward, their index fingers touching their triggers. Pulses pounded as they got close to the first office. A moment of pause and then the two rapidly entered, one veering right and the other left. Looking in the dark room they found no hostile presence. With temporary relief, they gathered themselves and slowly headed outside of the space. Back in the hallway, they neared the bank manager's office, from which seemed to emanate a few rustling noises. At the faint echoes, they looked at each other and nodded as they returned their intense stares to the route ahead. They both got closer to the right side of the entrance, halting just before the ominous chamber. This was the place where their certainty and their angst forged as one.

Carla eyed the chair tucked into the desk when she heard their steps. Faint as they were, they emitted enough warning to pull her attention away from the possible means of breaking the window to the opened entrance from the hallway. Gripping her handgun with her right hand, she rushed to the wall adjacent to the left of the entryway. At that point, in those fleeting moments of peace, Carla and their enemies were only separated by a wall that was six inches wide. Adrenaline cooled her nerves as she aimed the gun forward, waiting for the enemy to arrive within the room.

Fearing the impatience of Livy, the duo swung into the space, with one veering left and the other veering right. They both rushed in from the right side of the hallway entrance, fearing that if one of them tried to reach the opposite side of the door they would have been spotted and taken out. As it were, Carla saw them both enter the room a split second before they encountered her. This was the difference between who lived and who died. With one shot discharged, Carla launched a bullet into the head of one of them through the right ear. It exited with a trail of blood behind it.

Instantly dead, the force of the shot threw the body leftward into the other man, throwing him to the left side of the room. In desperation Carla fired three more rounds, all of which were absorbed by the deceased opponent. A human shield if ever one, none of those shots impacted the body of the living foe. When she tried to fire a fourth shot, nothing happened but a click from her handgun. Frightened at the absence of ammunition and seeing her hostile company push the dead body off himself, Carla raced towards him as he fiddled with his assault rifle, tackling the man and pushing him back into the sturdy wall. She tried to wrestle away the rifle, only to have the man put up resistance.

Stronger than she, he gained the upper hand in the fight and pushed her to the opposite wall, where her back painfully impacted the portrait of the banks' founder, cracking the glass. Still gripping the rifle with both hands whilst her foe did likewise, she pushed back, getting some space between her back and the cracked framed portrait only to have him forcibly push her back into the picture again. This time the impact resulted in the portrait being knocked from the wall and crashing to the ground, the glass breaking into pieces of varying jagged sizes scattered upon the floor.

Four hands were still gripping the rifle, its deadly muzzle facing away from both of them as the goggled man forced them towards the middle of the room. With a grunt, he threw Carla, still stubbornly clinging to the rifle, into the window. The smacking slam into the window resulted in the shattering of the first pane of glass and the heavy cracking of the second pane. Small pieces of glass entered her hair and adhered to the back of her shirt as she kept hold of the rifle, gradually moving her right hand to where the clip was located. As the man threw her upon the top of the mostly cleared desk, Carla was able to get the clip removed, its payload falling upon the desk and then in the shuffle being knocked across the room beside the corpse of the other goggled man.

One bullet left in the rifle, the man she struggled with pulled back on the rifle, causing Carla to be at a sitting position on the desk. He quickly let one hand go of the rifle long enough to punch Carla to the side of head, helping a light purple bruise gradually develop. The blow led her to loosen her grip on the rifle. The man took the advantage and shoved her off the desk onto the ground a couple feet from the corpse. As he began to aim the rifle Carla again charged in desperation, tackling him just as he fired the one shot, causing him to miss and instead lodge the round into the wall near the doorway.

She punched the man multiple times, each strike to the face hurting her as the knuckles landed onto the goggles. Clutching the rifle with both hands, the man thrusted the broad side of the rifle forward, using it to successfully push Carla off of him. In a rage, he changed his grip on the rifle so that both hands were holding it close to the muzzle side and then swung it hard against her left thigh. The force was enough to bend the rifle and cause brutal pain for Carla who screamed at the hit before being push away to the ground beside the fallen portrait of the bank's founder.

His firearm useless, the man took an eight-inch blade that was tucked into a pocket on his right pants leg. Carla saw the blade, which resembled the type of weapon she had used to kill that one recruit during her training. She also saw him smile. He was confident, for his prey was on the ground wounded and unarmed. He went for the attack, but Carla accurately predicted his motion and grabbed the arm with the knife. In a judo-style move, she used his energy against him and hurled the assailant over her and into the wall. Groaning as he tried to gather himself, Carla saw one of the long jagged pieces of glass by the fallen portrait. It looked like a flattened icicle. Taking hold of it while still on her knees, she turned with it to face her rising opponent and drilled it into the bottom of his neck, inches from his shoulder. Blood shot out and resistance from him ceased as he collapsed to the floor.

Livy walked with a faint limp down the hallway. He took his time getting to the bank manager's office. From the hall, he heard the sounds of struggle, the hollers of pain and heavy visceral breathing. Then the gurgling noises of one badly hurt combatant. The tone seemed deeper, leading Livy to speculate that it must have been his subordinate rather than Carla. Detached emotionally from the struggle for life, Livy was only truly shaken when he heard a loud smashing noise and then sensed a slight wind from the office. That led him to raise his Glock and run into the chamber.

Carla did not look behind her, that would take too much time. She knew who was entering the room during that second. The last of the transparent border removed, Carla jumped out of the room and landed on her curved back, rolling forward and almost perfectly into a running status. Her dash from the bank was a rough one, as her left leg prompted a skip to her sprint. Still she rushed, leaving behind her firearm, her mask, and her dead friend. Her mind raced as fast as her body. Where to go? Where to hide? Home was not an option; they knew where her apartment was. They knew where she worked as well. There was one place, though. Maybe that place would work.

Livy looked around the office in muted disappointment. His attention was drawn to the gurgling noises from the recently recruited underling. Unable to form words, he looked intently at Livy while moving his muted lips. Blood was flowing from both the side of his neck and mouth. He did not have long. Yet Livy was one for bloodlust. Pointing his Glock at the helpless dying man, he depressed the trigger and fired another shot that perfectly planted itself between the two eyes. The gurgling stopped. The sole survivor, Livy put his gun back in his holster, removed his gloves, and shoved them into his right pants pocket while looking outside the broken window. He then walked away.

As he got to the front, he saw through the glass wall black-and-white cars speeding towards him with blue lights flashing. Coming to screeching halts, they had been summoned by a nearby walker who saw movement in the bank. Men in black uniforms and rounded caps drew forth handguns, using their vehicles as shelter. Detective Frank Cooper, the only one in plain clothes, shouted at the figure inside to come out with hands raised. Livy was collected, almost annoyed, as he exited through the front door.

"Put your hands above your head!" shouted Detective Cooper.

"No need to panic," replied Livy as he obliged the order. "If you check my left pants pocket you will see we are on the same side."

Cooper had one of the police officers verify Livy's claim. The young man approached the physically imposing figure before him and placed his hand into the pocket. He felt a wallet and pulled it out. Opening it, he saw a badge. "Yeah, he's telling the truth," shouted the man to Cooper. He then handed the badge back to Livy.

"Okay, you can put your hands down," replied a cooled detective who left his vehicle protection and approached Livy. "So, what happened?"

"I was on my way home when I saw a robbery in progress. Things got really bad and now there are a few dead folks inside."

"Sounds brutal," commented Cooper. "Any survivors?"

"Yes, one got away," replied Livy.

"Did you get a good look at him?"

"Her."

IX

Josiah Sharp was alone in the living room. He was sitting on a chair placed beside a blue couch that was seven feet long including arm rests. The chair itself was an auburn hue and had a lever on the side allowing for it to be reclined. As was his custom that time of evening, he was reading from his black leather-bound Bible. Given to him when a youth, the Bible's once prominent gold lettering had since faded. However, Josiah did not require a written title on the cover to know what book it was that he held. A skinny bright red bookmark hung over one of the pages. He was reading Psalm 22: "Many bulls surround me; strong bulls of Bashan encircle me. Roaring lions that tear their prey open their mouths wide against me. I am poured out like water, and all my bones are out of joint ..."

His concentration was broken as loud pounding echoed from the door. Someone was feverishly demanding entrance. Closing the Bible with the long red bookmark hanging out at the end, he placed it on his mantle by the chair. This mantle included two drawers, one where he placed the Bible and another which was locked at all times. Getting up, he briefly looked at the locked drawer before hearing a desperate female voice through the barrier. She did not sound particularly threatening. With a chivalrous demeanor, Josiah walked towards the door, undoing the bolt and then unlocking the door.

The pounding ceased with the movement of the door. There before him was a black haired young woman with a pleading face. Breathing hard as though having finished a marathon, she had used her left hand to pound the door while her right hand propped open the screen door. Josiah quickly observed that she had a bruise upon the side of her face. The knuckles on her right hand also appeared bruised. Hers was not a peaceful evening. She did not take long to explain her rationale.

"Please, can you let me in? Please? There are some men who are trying to kill me. I need to find a place to hide. Please, hurry," pleaded Carla, whose words were partly an act and partly drawn upon sincere trepidation. Josiah looked with pity and obliged, opening the door wider so that she could enter. "Thank you, thank you so much."

"No problem," replied Josiah as he closed the door and locked it once again. He kept his eyes upon the visitor. She looked around the comfy space, with the home owner noticing a faint limp in her stride.

"Is there a place I can hide? They were right behind me and could be here any minute!"

"Who is after you?"

"Please!" she nearly shouted. "I need some place where they cannot find me. I promise I'll explain everything when they are gone. Please."

"Alright, alright," replied Josiah. "The bathroom is a good place. You can hide there."

Carla nodded and went into the tiled space, which was only a few feet from where she was standing. Door closed, Josiah was left standing in the living room, trying to make sense of the situation. Earlier in his legal career he dealt with the occasional domestic violence victim, so he drew those parallels for the couple minutes between when Carla entered his bathroom and when another person knocked on the door. Until then, he calmly walked back to his chair and returned to reading from the Psalms.

Carla put her back to the closed white bathroom door and slowly slid downwards so that she was sitting on the cool tiled surface. Her breathing began to return to normal, but she was still tense. There was uncertainty as to whether Josiah Sharp was going to keep to the intended script when he discovered who was asking for her. Carla studied the interior of the bathroom. There were a couple of towels hung on the door, another draped over the bar that held the shower curtain in place. Toiletries were not visible, likely stored away behind the personal mirror she saw to her right. Josiah provided her with a good hiding space, as the only view into the room was a small narrow window with closed drapes. Then again, this also meant that there was no good escape. Carla's heart raced again as she heard the knocking and then the opening of the front door.

"Good evening, sir," said an imposing detective. Josiah had to alter his gaze upwards to see his face.

"Good evening, detectives," said Josiah, noting the other men with Livy and briefly nodding in recognition to seeing Frank Cooper amongst the small group. Cooper nodded in mutually understood recognition. "How can I help you?"

"About an hour ago there was a bank robbery. A suspect fled the scene but not before I got a good look at her," said Livy. "She is about 25 to 35 years of age, dark hair and dark eyes, light skin, about 5'5" or 5'6', maybe 130 pounds. Have you seen any woman in your neighborhood fitting that description?"

"Sorry, sir," began Josiah, carefully choosing his words. "But I have been reading this evening and have not been looking out the window."

"In case we need to follow up, can you give us some good contact information?"

"Det. Cooper should have that already," replied Josiah, prompting Livy to turn his large frame to look at Cooper, who nodded in the affirmative.

"Very well," said Livy. "You have a good night, sir."

"You also. Stay safe!"

As the law men walked away from the door, Josiah gently closed it and then locked it yet again. Bolting the door, he looked at the closed bathroom door. He became quite suspicious of the presence he had allowed to charm its way into his domicile. He then looked at that locked drawer near his chair. As he walked to the drawer, he decided to provide an update to the woman in hiding.

"They are gone now," he shouted as he took out the key for the drawer.

"Good. Thank you," replied the voice behind the door. "Do you mind that I go ahead and use the bathroom, since I'm in here?"

"Go ahead," replied Josiah, opening the drawer.

Carla got to a standing position, which had some struggle given how her legs were sore, especially the left one. She approached the sink, which had a clean mirror suspended above it. She got to look at herself for the first time since before the failed robbery. Using her right hand, she moved her face to one side to better view the purplish bruise left by the punch. She saw a couple of small sparkling items in her hair. Turning on the faucet, she splashed cold water upon her face and used a comb she spotted while waiting for the trouble to pass to brush her hair. Small specks of glass plummeted to the tiles as she began to cry. She wept for her friend, she wept for her broken world. Hands washed and more water to the face, she collected herself once again and exited the bathroom.

"Thanks again for helping…" Her voiced cut off when she saw her rescuer armed with a revolver, its muzzle aimed directly at her. His face was serious, his posture firm and well placed. She was too weary to run. Her situation was hopeless. Too close to duck behind something, too far to grab the weapon or charge him with any success. She raised both hands, her freshly washed palms visible.

"Stay right there," he advised firmly. "This may not be the most advanced firearm on earth, but it does the job at this range."

"Just stay calm."

"Why are you here?" he asked in determined anger.

"Just be calm."

"I asked, why are you here?"

"Listen, there were men who are after me. They want to kill me."

"'They' are the police. For some reason, I covered for you."

"And I am grateful," she said, trying to ameliorate the tense situation. Josiah was unfazed by the attempt, keeping the pistol firmly directed at the guest. "But they are not the police. They are terrorists."

"Stop lying," stated Josiah. "I talked with them. They showed me badges. I know one of the people who came to the door."

"Okay, maybe some of them are cops. But the huge one? The one that's really big and looks Hispanic?" Josiah gave her a look of faint surprise, conceding with his expression that he knew who she meant. "Yes, him. He's a bad man. He's a murderer. He killed my friend earlier tonight and he's trying to kill me."

"Look," said a calming Josiah, weapon still pointed at Carla. "This can all be very easily resolved with one phone call to the authorities."

"No, you can't do that. Please don't do that."

"As the Good Book puts it, there is nothing hidden that will not be revealed."

"Please, don't call the police. They can't be trusted."

"And I can trust you?" critically asked Josiah, who made his way a couple steps back to where a landline phone was located. Carla was racing for thoughts. She did not want to tell him everything. Everything might get her shot. Yet she had to say something, anything. So she took a deep breath and grudgingly spoke.

"Okay, okay. I did not come to your place by chance. I came here because I know who you are. You are Assistant District Attorney Josiah Sharp."

Josiah was unimpressed. "I have been on TV occasionally, quoted in the newspaper. A lot of people know who I am." He picked up the receiver and was about to dial the first number when Carla went further.

"And how many people know you are the lead investigator in the Cicero case?"

Josiah paused. Carla stared at him without blinking. His confidence ebbed and after a moment he consented to hanging up the phone. "How do you know that?"

"The same reason I know where you live. Cicero told me."

"You have met Cicero?"

"I work for him."

"You belong to the Organization?" asked Josiah with a raised voice and heightened excitement. The pistol was no longer aimed right at Carla, but was pointed at her general direction. She nodded. "And the detective I talked to?"

"His name is Livy."

"Livy, Livy ..." Josiah heard the name before. The effort to recount was successful. "He is one of the lieutenants of Cicero, correct?"

"Yes."

"Why does he want you dead?"

"It's a long story."

"How long?"

"Very," said an exhausted Carla, putting her hands down without incident. "And it is very late and I am very tired." Josiah began to think more during the moments of pause.

"If I let you hide here, will you agree to tell me all you know about Cicero and the Organization?"

"You mean, testify?"

"Maybe," replied Josiah. "I want to know what you know, first."

"And you will let me hide here?"

"Yes."

"Alright. I will do it," immediately replied Carla, too weary and too desperate to weigh alternate routes of survival. "I will need to make a couple calls. Can I sit down?"

"Sure," said Josiah, backing away from the furniture while Carla walked over to the couch and sat down. Taking out her mobile phone, she began to search for the saved number of the maid service. "You will put it on speaker phone." Carla conceded and did so. A few rings and the usual business message was left. After the laconic statement was over, the machine beeped and Carla spoke.

"Hey, there, its Carla. I know I am scheduled to come in tomorrow for the usual cleaning rounds, but something came up. I won't be able to make it. Really sorry, but this might take a few days. I promise to touch base again on Monday. Bye." She pushed a button and the call was ended. Josiah stood nearby, pistol still out. He looked perplexed, trying to think if her words could be some sort of code. Meanwhile, Carla found another saved number and pushed it to call. Once again, she placed it on speaker.

"Um, hello?" asked a groggy sounding George al-Hassan.

"Hey, Giddo, its Carla. How are you?"

"I was sleeping," said the voice on the other end. "Why, why are you calling me so late? Is everything okay?"

"Yes, Giddo. Nothing too big," lied Carla. "Just letting you know that I will be out of town for the next several days."

"Is this another work trip?"

"Yes," she maintained. "You know how it is, my boss wants our maid service to go all over the state, attend some business gatherings, clean tons of houses."

"Yes, yes, I get it," replied George. "When will you be back?"

"Not sure, but hopefully sometime next week. I'm, I'm staying at a coworker's house tonight so we can wake up extra early."

"Okay."

"Anyway, that's all," she said, her emotions starting to show outwardly to Josiah. "Sorry I had to wake you."

"No problem, Carla. I always love to hear from my favorite granddaughter."

"I am your only granddaughter," she said, laughing for the first time that night.

"True. Anyway, good night."

"Good night." She hung up and then faced Josiah.

"Giddo?"

"It means grandpa in Arabic."

"One last question."

"Yes?"

"Do you want to take the bed or the couch?"

"The couch will do."

"Then I will get some sheets and a pillow. Be right back," said Josiah. He went into his bedroom, located on the same floor. It was a small house, but it was his, after all. Tucking the pistol in between his pants and side, he opened one of the closets in his bedroom and found an extra pillow and a couple of sheets. Compiling the items into his arms, he walked towards the bedroom door, which was ajar. Before entering he looked at her. Attractive even amidst the trauma, she was starting to wither. Her elbows balanced on her legs while she sat on the couch. Her face showed a sincere wrestling with all that was taking place. If she was deceiving him, her efforts were among the best ever conceived. Pushing open the door, he placed the items on the couch and entrusted her with making it comfortable.

"Thank you. I mean that," she said as she got up to arrange the sheets and pillow. "Have a good night."

"Yes, you too," said Josiah as he left for his bedroom, closing the door and locking it just in case it really was all for show.

***

While on the outside the Eagle Factory seemed desolate, within its four cold walls was a buzz of action fused with frustration. On the second floor, within the main hallway, just outside of Cicero's office, Cato was in command. Dressed in a pinstriped suit with tie, he and a few subordinates surrounded a table with a few wine glasses and a couple bottles. Originally, they were having a minor social function; with the news from the field, they found themselves coordinating patrols and search parties. Once sitting upon a few plush chairs, they were now standing about the table. Cato was on the phone yet again, getting an update from two Organization members.

"Anything new? ... So she has not yet appeared ... Okay ... Any indication that anyone has entered the building? ... And you are sure that none of them were her?" asked Cato, his nervous peers looking on as they heard only half of the conversation on the smart phone. "Okay, understood ... How much longer? Until you are relieved, that's how much longer!" He angrily pushed the button on the screen that ended the call. Phone in one hand, he went for a glass of wine with the other, the glass shaking some as he lifted it to his lips and swallowed the entire contents like a shot glass. Unaware of anything better to do, he took the bottle nearest to himself and poured the glass full.

As Cato placed the bottle back on the table, a single bell rang behind him. Across the wide red carpet, near to the entrance of the main office, the doors shielding sight of the service elevator were pushed open. The three men including Cato turned their attention to the lone occupant, a stately muscular fellow who garnered timidity from the two acquaintances of Cato. As he walked out of the elevator with a slight limp, Cato showed little concern and even less hesitation in expressing his annoyance.

"You," he grumbled while Livy walked to the nearest seat and sat down upon it, his wounded leg dangling over one of the arm rests. "You stupid buffoon. Three new recruits dead. Their ammunition and rifles wasted. An expert hit-woman running around the city while half the Organization is trying to find her before the police do!"

"I killed one of them."

"Fifty percent success," flatly commented Cato, who took hold of his drink and again downed the entire contents in one swoop. His consternation continued. "In grade school, your success rate IS AN F!"

"I cannot help how poor the recruits were."

"Why didn't you do it? You were the one offended, whose honor was tarnished by both women. Why not lead from the front?"

"Tiffany was the one who truly bruised me," stoically replied Livy. "Carla being dead, by anyone's hand, is enough. Besides, with this damn wound I still have a few more days before I can stop taking it easy."

"Easy," said Cato, struggling to control his anger. He looked at the other two people about the rounded table and fermented liquids. "Be gone. Have a good evening." They obeyed without hesitation and said their good-byes before departing that night. Cato pulled one of the chairs closer to Livy and sat in it. "When I agreed to look the other way on this matter, I did so because you used that very word. Easy. This would be easy, you told me. Just send them on a bank robbery that you knew would be impossible to complete, attack them at their time of weakness, use the recruits to back you up, and then with them both deceased leave the sight and let someone discover their bodies. How did this 'easy' assignment become so very hard for you to complete?"

"Carla was harder to kill."

"Yes, yes, she was," agreed Cato in a calmer tone.

"We taught her well."

"And the Romans trained Spartacus."

"The old badge came in handy."

"By mistake."

"Mistake or not, it helps to have that thin blue line on our side."

"But only so much," cautioned Cato. "We cannot have Carla going to the authorities. She knows far too much about our Organization. Maybe even enough to take us down."

"Do not worry, my badge has surely scared her out of that route."

"Again though, the police can only help us so much."

"No worries," said Livy, "I only gave them limited, basic information on her appearance." Cato got up from his chair and approached the table where the glasses and bottles were situated. Picking a bottle, he began to pour himself yet another drink. "Does Cicero know about all this?" Cato waited to finish pouring his drink before answering.

"Not yet. I told him that you would be the best man to explain everything, in detail, when you got here. Cicero has been waiting for you. Do not make him wait any longer." Livy was disconcerted by the news and quickly rose from the chair.

"Then I will tell Cicero everything."

"Good," said Cato as he raised his latest drink. "If it helps, be sure to remind our leader that time is on our side. That may soften the blow. Maybe."

Livy wanted to respond in anger, but he knew that the meeting with Cicero was of greater import. Limping to the door, he slowly turned the knob and then opened the right door of the two large doors before closing it. Cato grinned sadistically as he sipped some of his wine, knowing that the hammer was falling upon the second in command rather than himself. Soon, however, he was back to business, as one of the Organization members called in with an update. Nothing special, nothing sighted; nevertheless, checking in as the night crossed the chronological border into predawn morning.

***

Carla was walking, walking though she did not feel the pounding of the pavement. There was little feeling, the world was all black and gray. Everything loomed with melancholy, guttural fear as she kept going forward into the constant darkness. Soon the black veil was lifted and there were clouds and sunshine before her. It was so close, even from a distance it felt pleasant. A great icon of Christ the King was at the center. It pulsed as though alive, a growing number of candles suspended around Him.

Yet as she kept walking, never seeming to get closer, the ground opened. It looked like flesh, puncture wounds shooting forth a red substance that seemed both cloud and liquid. Soon the punctures produced a great sea of crimson, its waves getting higher and higher. Carla struggled to stay within sight of the icon. The waves climbed so that at their crest she only saw the top third of the Christ image. Then lines of black, branches or arms, stretched around her. Like a cage, it enveloped her while the waves pushed against her body. She was suffocating, she was collapsing, she was drowning.

And then she awoke. Breathing hard and eyes widened, she gathered herself when she saw that her surrounding was the still and pleasant living room. Wearing the clothes from last night, she pushed away the two sheets with her legs and then got to a seated position on the couch, her feet touching the ground. She shook off the grogginess of the slumber, got up and walked towards the kitchen. It bordered the dining room, which had a medium-sized table with two chairs placed on opposite sides. Searching the counter and the fridge, she found the materials necessary to make scrambled eggs and toast. Seeing this as a possible show of gratitude, she decided to make enough for both of them.

Four white-shelled eggs were placed on the counter while four slices of white bread were taken from a long clear bag. She placed the four slices inside of the toaster oven located to the left of the refrigerator. Carla then directed her attention to cracking open the four eggs via tapping them on the corner of the countertop. Each one was cracked and then pulled open to allow the whites and yolks into a small bowl she took from one of the cabinets. She went to the fridge and found some milk, which had not yet reached its "sell by" date. Being unable to find a cast iron griddle, she went to the next best option. She poured some milk into the bowl. Then she placed a paper towel over the bowl and put it into the microwave. It was located to the left of the toaster, suspended above the counter. Before pushing the buttons, she went back to the toaster and turned the knob.

A ticking noise began while Carla pushed the buttons on the microwave to prepare for the cooking of the eggs. Each button beeped slightly. As a guestimate, she entered two minutes on high and then pressed start. The droning sound of the microwave accompanied the ticking of the toaster. Carla maintained a vigil over both the microwave and the toaster, making sure the latter did not burn the bread to an ashy crisp. After about 40 seconds on microwave, she opened the device and removed the paper towel. She had already located the utensils and thus had a spoon ready to stir the cooking eggs. Placing the paper towel covering back, she shut the microwave door and pressed the start button, allowing the eggs to cook some more before returning to check on the toaster.

The bread was starting to change color, a faint browning that was more expressed in the two back slices than the two nearer to the opening. After another thirty seconds, Carla checked on the eggs. They were getting more solidified, making the stirring more of a challenge. She decided to leave them in for the remainder of the time, just in case. Checking again on the toast, Carla saw that the browning was increasing. The back pieces were getting browner quicker. As she neared the time in which she would take them out, Carla heard what sounded like a shower turning on in the bedroom. This was a relief to her, as she hoped he would be up and about before too long.

The microwave was still droning on as Carla pushed the toaster knob leftward to get it to the end of its session sooner. With a ding, the toaster's work was done. The slices were moderately brown. Carla searched for and quickly found a couple of plates. With one of them grasped by her left hand, she pulled down the toaster oven door with her right hand. She pushed the slices onto the plate with the aid of a knife. Placing them on the counter, she was going to look for placemats, but the table already had a tablecloth stretched over its top. The microwave announced the completion of the eggs with a series of beeps. These sounds halted the moment Carla opened the microwave.

Placing both plates on the counter, she put two of the toast slices on the plate that initially was clear. Carefully removing the hot bowl from the microwave, she placed that item on the top of the toaster oven. With a fork, she divided up the scrambled eggs between the two plates, providing near equal servings. Bowl in the nearby sink, she took the two plates to the dining room, putting them in front of the respective chairs. She then found some napkins. Each plate got to its side a collection of napkins, a knife, and a fork. Carla heard the shower stop as she went back into the kitchen and opened the fridge, looking for and discovering a mostly full jug of orange juice. She poured the contents into two plastic glasses and then placed them at the table. The butter was the last thing added to the table, placed between the two plates, equidistant from the chairs. Shortly after everything was set for breakfast, the bedroom door was unlocked and opened. Josiah was already fully clothed, though now wearing a simple t-shirt and jeans instead of a dress shirt, tie, and slacks.

"Good morning," he said with surprise.

"Good morning," she said with a smile. He studied the table. "I thought it was the least I could do, since you're hiding me and all that."

"Thanks," he said with some amazement while the two of them sat down simultaneously at the table. Josiah placed his hands together and bowed his head.

"If you like, I could say grace for the both of us," posited Carla, bringing Josiah's attention towards her.

"Sure, okay."

Carla crossed herself and then closed her eyes before speaking. "Father bless the meal You have provided. In Jesus' name, amen."

"Amen," replied Josiah as Carla crossed herself again. "Orthodox?"

"Yes," smiled Carla. "How did you know?"

"Because you went up-down-right-left."

"That's correct," said Carla as she took a napkin and tucked it into her pants to protect her lap. She took a knife with one hand and a fork with another. Before she ate, she saw Josiah looking somewhat hesitant. Quickly figuring out the reason, she reached across the table and with her fork cut off a bite of the scrambled eggs. Stabbing the morsel with her fork, she brought it to herself and put it in her mouth, chewing with her lips closed and then clearly swallowing it. "You want me to try the toast next?"

"No, that won't be necessary," said Josiah, who started to eat what was brought before him. "'Kill and eat, Peter', as God commanded."

"That would be Acts chapter 10, correct?" asked Carla. "The story where St. Peter was told to welcome a Gentile and his family into the Church?"

"Correct," replied Josiah between bites. "And to think, so many Protestants believe the Orthodox don't read their Bibles."

"It's that or they mistake us for Catholics," smiled Carla. Both ate more of their breakfast before Carla spoke again. "So what happens today?"

"Well," began Josiah after he drank some of the orange juice. "Later this morning, once you're ready of course, I am going to interview you. This won't be a deposition or anything official like that. Very preliminary."

"Okay."

"I will still swear you in and it will be recorded. But it will not be admissible in court, since you technically haven't yet turned yourself in."

"Will this lead to Cicero and all them getting punished?"

"I hope so."

"I will get punished, also, won't I?"

"Most likely," said Josiah. "But do not fret. Unless you did some really bad stuff, you're at the worst, looking at a couple years in prison, maybe probation and community service."

Carla did not respond. Thankfully the lack of response could be justified through the process of eating breakfast. A few minutes later and both were nearly done. "Did you like the meal?" she asked.

"It was pretty good. The eggs tasted a little different."

"That's probably because I cooked them without butter."

"Interesting."

"I learned to do that for my grandfather, given his many health issues. The less butter and salt, the better."

"Sounds reasonable," said Josiah, using the nearest napkin to wipe his mouth. As both rose from the table, Josiah explained things. "Okay, so, in that room behind you, by the kitchen, you will find a closet with a bunch of women's clothes."

"Have I encountered your secret life?"

"Very funny. I have a sister who lives overseas and occasionally visits. She keeps a lot of stuff here so she can travel light. Anyway, there should be an unused spare toothbrush, toothpaste, and I think mouthwash also."

"Okay."

"That room used to be a bedroom, which is why it has its own full bathroom attached. Now I mostly use it for storage, so it should be a good place to film when you are ready."

"Okay," she said. "Thanks."

***

The good news was that Josiah's sister and Carla were nearly the same size. Searching through the closet, she found that the items were just about right. Any disparity between measurements was not sufficient to warrant discomfort. The bad news was that most of the shirts and dresses were quite immodest. Necklines were lower than what Carla was used to and three of the four dresses fell above the knees. Since the affair had an aura of formality, Carla went for the dress that landed close to the ankles. The straps holding the dress were skinny, but she was able to find a thin black sweater that complimented the outfit. There was a pair of flats that coordinated well with the dress.

While she waited for Josiah to get the camera ready, Carla thought about what she was doing. It seemed so peculiar that after years of loyally serving the Cicero Organization she would find herself helping to birth its destruction. Even stranger was how quickly it was all rent asunder. Was she really viewed as a traitor by Cicero? After all, she had heard nothing from either her leader or Cato for that matter. Perchance Livy was the traitor, having gone rogue in an effort to form his own faction. This might be some power struggle in which she and Tiffany were only collateral damage.

"Okay then, almost ready," commented Josiah, who had opted to wear a button-up collared shirt and necktie for the occasion. His bottom half was still jeans and sneakers. As he continued working on the camera, she started to wonder about him. Would it make a difference if she killed him now? What better peace offering than the corpse of their lead adversary? Then again, that might not be enough. She was already guaranteed to kill him early next month and Livy still sought her death. No, there was no point in killing him. There was no point in trying to make amends. A part of her always wanted to quit that entity. Now she finally had a way out for one part of her reliance. The other, that substance, was still an issue. At some point that day she had to leave the house, sneak into her apartment, and get the remaining supply. She still had another few weeks' worth.

"Okay, are you ready?"

"I think so, yes," replied Carla as she adjusted herself some, combing back some of her hair with her fingers. She sat in dignity, proper posture, with both hands clasped together on her lap. The camera light was on.

"This is Wednesday, May 17th, at about 9:00 AM Eastern Time. This is an interview recorded for the Cicero Organization investigation. The witness will be sworn in and answer questions regarding the nature of the Organization, her involvement, and other details," said Josiah off camera. He then approached the camera, holding his Bible. "Please put your hand on the Bible." Carla obliged. "Do you swear that what you are about to say is the truth, the whole truth, and nothing but the truth so help you God?"

"It is. Yes."

Josiah exited the video feed and sat in a chair put beside the camera and its various buttons including play, pause, record, and stop. Carla was not instructed as to what to look at while she spoke. During the brief moments of silence, she looked at the camera, her hands attempting to remain still as the right hand rested upon the left. When Josiah spoke and she replied, her gaze went towards him.

"Please state your name."

"Carla al-Hassan."

"Age?"

"29."

Josiah paused the recording. "Not to be that guy here, but just to double-check you are really 29, correct? And not just one of those, you know what I mean?"

"Yes," smiled Carla. "This is the first time I have been 29."

"Okay, just, like I said, double-checking," said Josiah, who then returned to his professional tone and pushed the record button. "Place of birth?"

"Damascus, Syria."

Josiah paused briefly as though for dramatic effect. "Are you now, or have you ever been, a member of the Cicero Organization?"

"Yes."

"How long were you a member of the Cicero Organization?"

"Eight years."

"In what capacity did you serve as a member of the Cicero Organization?"

"I carried out various duties as assigned."

"Can you explain what those duties were?"

"They were various duties, as I said. They included gathering research for certain targets, committing various robberies including the one last night, and finally ..." Carla trailed off a bit. She knew she was about to cross a line.

"Go on, Ms. al-Hassan. What else?" She became nervous. Then she channeled herself, deciding to mentally treat this as she would any mission commanded of her over the past eight years and some months. "Ms. al-Hassan. What else did you do for the Cicero Organization?"

"Targeted assassinations."

Josiah flinched. Perchance it was his chivalrous attitudes. Whenever he dealt with a case regarding a guilty female party, violence was rarely a part of their wrongdoing. Still, he had a job to do, thus he continued his inquiry. "Targeted assassinations?"

"Yes."

"Have you carried out these targeted assassinations before?"

"Yes."

"Who have you assassinated?"

"Many, many people," she said looking right at a clearly unnerved Josiah. "And I must add, that while I use the term 'targeted assassinations', many of them were just plain murder. The victim was not important enough to be labeled assassinated. Just killed. That might be a better term. I killed them."

"So then, who have you killed?"

"Like I said, many."

"How many?" asked Josiah, expecting a fairly low number.

"Over forty," coldly responded Carla, widening the eyes Josiah. He hemmed and hawed some before he continued.

"Um, why not, why not an exact number?"

"I do not keep track," replied Carla. "I am not proud of what I did. To help some, I know it is fewer than fifty."

"How do you know that?"

"I was told by one of the more senior Cicero Organization members that whenever an assassin reaches their fiftieth kill, they get a party held in their honor."

"A party," Josiah said to himself aloud. "You would think they were talking about selling cars rather than killing people." He returned to the task. "Okay then. So, it is right to say that over the past eight years you have killed somewhere between forty and fifty people?"

"Yes, that is correct."

"Who was your first victim?"

"A young woman. I do not remember her name. She was a fellow recruit and I killed her in training because I was ordered to do so. That one was technically self-defense, since she was ordered to kill me."

"How can you both be ordered to kill each other?"

"Cicero Organization recruiting mandates that near the end of training, half of the recruits must face the other half in one-on-one mortal combat. We were each given a knife and whoever survived went on to complete their training."

"Okay," said Josiah with a breath. "And the one after that?"

"I never met him. He was a random guy on the street that I was ordered to kill to help me get used to killing people."

"How did you kill him?"

"With piano wire. I do not know which killed him first, my choking him or the fact that the wire slit his throat. Either way, I did it and it was not in self-defense."

"Do you know the names of any of your victims?"

"Yes."

"Okay then," said Josiah, who was starting to adapt to the macabre conversation he found himself undertaking. "Let us start with that. Name one of the people that you killed."

"Myles Talbert," she said with a firm composure as Josiah flinched again in disbelief. He paused before speaking again.

"How—how did you kill him?"

"With a remote-controlled explosive device I placed under his car. I triggered it near a crowded intersection."

"Were you caught on camera?" asked Josiah, still maintaining some disbelief.

"No. There was only one working camera in the street outside the parking garage. In advance of the assassination, I timed the camera's movements so that I could know how long I had to cross the street and enter the garage."

"That makes sense," conceded Josiah, with a heightened sense of seriousness when he realized that his former superior's murderer was in the same room as he, and had even slept in the room adjacent to his bedroom. "Who else?"

"Anthony Albioni."

"How did you kill him?"

"I sniped him. That is, I shot him from an open window on the third floor of a building across the street from his apartment. A fellow Cicero Organization member threw something at his window to draw his attention, and then when he appeared I shot him. One shot, one kill. We then escaped in a white van."

"That sounds correct," said Josiah, recalling that the details she gave fit the diagnosis of the forensics expert. "Are you currently assigned to kill anyone?"

"Yes."

"Who have you been ordered to kill?" inquired Josiah, expecting her to say someone like the governor or the mayor.

"You," she said swiftly. Josiah jumped out of his chair and nearly hit the camera when he heard her say it. He regained his wits quickly enough to push the pause button. Carla remained seated, moving little.

"And you made me breakfast?"

"There was nothing in your breakfast to poison you."

"How do I know that?"

Carla sighed and rolled her eyes. "How does the Cicero Organization kill public figures who stand in its way?"

Josiah thought a moment and then became less tense. "They do it in public, so that many witnesses can see it. The essence of terror."

"Correct," responded Carla.

"So, when were you supposed to kill me?"

"At the—"

"Actually, hold on," interjected Josiah, who repositioned his chair and sat down by the camera. "Let us get this on the record." He pushed the record button once again. "To confirm, you were assigned to kill me, Assistant District Attorney Josiah Sharp, correct?"

"Yes."

"Where and when were you scheduled to assassinate me, that is one Josiah Sharp?"

"I was to assassinate you at the Summer Ball held June 2nd at the Formal Ballroom at the Capitol Building."

"How were you planning to do it?"

"I was going to scale the roof of the church across the street and shoot you while you danced in the ballroom."

"Good thing I am a wallflower," Josiah commented to himself, though within hearing distance of his witness. She cracked a faint smile at the remark. "Are you currently affiliated with the Cicero Organization?"

"I do not know."

"Please explain."

"Last night, I and a friend of mine, a fellow member, we were ordered to rob a bank. When we got there, we were tricked by one of my superiors. He goes by the name Livy. He, he killed my friend, and then he tried to kill me. He brought with him three men, I think they were recent recruits. I killed at least two of them, I think. One for sure, because I shot him in the head. Another maybe. I did stab him in the neck, but I do not know if he lived. I only know that I escaped and came here for refuge."

The interview continued for another two hours. They had a five-minute break midway through at Carla's request, as she needed to use the bathroom. They broke for lunch about an hour after that. During that time, Carla provided numerous details about her many other robberies and assassinations. She described the payment system, the alleyway meetings, and personage of Cato. She admitted to having met Cicero multiple times, but to the heartbreak of Josiah she did not know the figure's true identity. There was still much she kept from him, but as she saw it the worst was already spoken.

***

"Can you tell me more about the Eagle Factory?" asked Josiah to an increasingly weary Carla. Lunch had gone without incident, with Josiah eating quickly so he could work some on the earlier recording. By early afternoon, she was back in front of the camera, sitting as though posing for a portrait.

"It is the headquarters for the Cicero Organization."

"What is at this headquarters?"

"Many things. On the outside, it looks like one of the many abandoned factories. And that is purposeful. It camouflages them. On the inside, it is very different. There is a lobby, several living quarters, and a large exercise room. And that is just the first floor."

"What about the second floor?"

"There is the main hallway, a long route from one end of the factory to the main office."

"Who is at the main office?"

"Cicero."

"Have you been inside the main office?"

"Yes."

"Can you describe it?"

"I can."

"Please do so."

"Well, there are a couple Romanesque statues and lots of books. Mostly on political theory, philosophy, things like that. There is a safe, we call it the treasury. It is where the money, at least most of it, is stored."

"And the safe?" asked Josiah. "Is the safe accessible to anyone?"

"Anyone with the combination. It is not time delay."

"Go on. What else?"

"There is the desk of Cicero, where he sits and conducts business. On the desk is a rolodex. You know, a traditional paper one. It includes contact information for all the members of the Organization. It may also have other people's contact info."

"What other people?"

"It's speculation. I admit that. But I have heard from those who have seen it, that it includes people from businesses, groups, maybe political parties."

"Everything, basically," said Josiah to himself. "So, you have met Cicero in person?"

"Yes."

"Who is Cicero?"

"I do not know."

Josiah paused the recorder in amazement. "How can you not know? You just finished saying you have met before."

"He wears a mask. And the way he talks, it sounds distorted, almost robotic. I haven't even seen Cicero get up from his desk. For all I know he's paralyzed."

"Okay, okay," said Josiah as he wiped his dry face with his hand. Carla shifted in her seat as Josiah returned himself to professionalism and pressed the record button again. "Going back to the Eagle Factory, do you know where it is located?"

"Yes."

"Good," said Josiah with relief. "Can you show it to me on a map of the area?"

"Yes."

Josiah left the video playing as got up and looked into a box of things. Sifting through the random contents, he found about a dozen maps of the state, the city, and the nation. He picked the one that included the city and its surrounding area. Carla waited patiently for Josiah to return. The assistant district attorney got in front of the camera briefly with the unfolded map. Placing it in front of her he asked for the location. After looking briefly for the correct street, she located it and put her finger on it. Confirming orally the location for the camera, he returned to the camera's side.

"May I ask a question?"

"Sure," said Josiah as the recording continued.

"Now that you know where the Eagle Factory is, can't you order some strike of some kind on it? You know, SWAT or National Guard?" Josiah decided to turn off the recorder, confusing Carla. "Did I ask something wrong?"

"No, no, in a more perfect world it would be a good idea," noted Josiah. "However, you and I both know someone loyal to Cicero is inside the system. I cannot take the chance that I inform Cicero by mistake when I inform my superiors." Josiah then had a moment of inspiration and turned on the recorder. "Hold on. You work for Cicero. Surely you must know who it is. Who is the mole?"

"I don't know."

"Dammit," said Josiah, who felt greatly frustrated. "You don't who the mole is, you don't know who Cicero is, and you don't know the real names of Cato or Livy. This is getting tiresome."

"Listen, Josiah, I am telling you everything I possibly can. In the Organization, you don't ask questions you don't need answers to. Near the end of my training, Cato told me I could ask any question I wanted to. I asked him who Cicero was and proceeded to get a beating from other members. If they don't want you to know something, they make it very clear. When I was told to take out Albioni, all I heard was that we learned it from our source in the Justice Department. Nothing more. And since I didn't need to know who it was to do my job, I was smart enough to not ask."

"You know," said Josiah, his ire ebbing away. "We've been at this all day. You deserve a break."

"Thank you," calmly replied Carla as she got up. "I'll admit; this dress is a little tight, which might be adding to my anger."

"Well," smiled Josiah. "For what it's worth, you wear it better than my sister does."

Carla smiled as Josiah turned his attention to getting the chip with the film footage on it to his laptop. "I plan to change into something more casual. Could you close the door?"

"Sure, no problem," said Josiah as he exited the room and shut the door behind him. Alone in the room, Carla went into the closet and searched among the leisurely fashion items within the space.

Josiah powered up his laptop. Plugged into the wall via an outlet, the lower half of the thin black technological machine rested on his legs. He could have placed himself and the machine in the dining room, but the chairs not being particularly comfortable for long term sitting he opted for the living room. The chip was inserted into the side of the laptop, three quarters of it hanging out by design. He downloaded the video files, adding it to the earlier one. From there he emailed himself the video as an attachment. That way, even if somehow his laptop and the chip were destroyed, the file lived on.

"How do I look?" she asked as Josiah just finished sending the email. Josiah turned to see Carla standing with a faint smile in tight jeans and a black t-shirt.

"Stunning as always."

"Thanks."

"Anyhow, I think we have done a lot for today. Tomorrow I am looking forward to learning more about the operations of the Organization."

"I will do what I can to help."

"Good," said Josiah. "Anyhow, um, I guess in the meantime feel free to make yourself at home, watch some television, you know."

"Yeah, I know," she replied as she sat down on the couch.

"I'll be right back," said Josiah, carefully placing his laptop on the carpeted floor near the outlet he used for juicing the machine.

Carla found the remote and turned on the television. She surfed through the channels before finding a sitcom she watched from time to time. Her mind was focused less on the jokes and more on her evening. She needed to get back to her apartment somehow. It was nearing the twenty-four-hour mark since she last took the substance. There were ways to get into her apartment complex without being noticed. As a veteran robber and assassin, she could think of ways to go in unnoticed, grab her supply, and then return to Josiah's house. How would she explain her sudden appearance to George? She told him she was going to be gone for days. Maybe say something came up? As she wrestled with how to lie to her family, her smart phone started making noise.

"Josiah," she shouted into the kitchen. He appeared immediately. "Cato is calling me."

"Put it on speaker."

She nodded and then pushed speaker before pushing the answer button. Her surprise at his call was complete. Usually they used text messages. Then again, this whole situation was not typical. "Hello Cato?"

"Yes, Carla. It is I."

"Thank God, oh how I thank Him," she said with relief. "I am so glad you called me. Livy went berserk. He killed Tiffany and he tried to kill me. I've been on the run ever since. Can you please help me?"

"Why?"

"Because I ... wait, what do you mean why?"

"Oh, my poor dear. Do you really think that I am going to help you?"

"But, Cato. After all these years?"

"I have known Livy longer. And if he wants to kill two women who offended his honor, one romantically and the other professionally, then who am I to judge?"

"But, Cato," she pleaded in sincerity. "It's not right."

"Right?" Cato laughed. "You want to lecture me about right? After all the evil you have done in this world, you now are offended by the idea that you can be wronged. Fantastic."

"So there is nothing I can do to return to you in good grace?"

"Nope," he said frankly.

"What about my assignment? Who will kill Sharp?" she asked while looking at Josiah, who felt awkward being talked about in such a manner.

"Livy will take your place. He is a good shot and he can climb the church roof quite easily. Your research will be most helpful."

"Then I guess this is good-bye."

"What? You are leaving?"

"Maybe I have already left."

"Not without your supply." Josiah looked confused and stared at Carla. She had not told him about that aspect of her criminal career.

"Maybe I already have it."

"I highly doubt it," said Cato with confidence. "Because I am looking at the three and a half weeks' worth of emerald commitment." Carla's heart sank. "I must say, your grandfather is an interesting conversationalist." Carla's sadness turned to rage.

"If you touched even a hair on his head—"

"Oh, spare me the theatrics, Carla. I have said it once and I will say it again. We do not need to target your family; we can target you. For all your grandfather knew, he got a complimentary pest control inspection. He is none the wiser."

"What do you want?"

"Existential terror, my dear Carla," Cato spoke with sinister intentions. "Existential terror happens when a human being gets the epiphany that they will die at some point within the near future. That is what you are feeling now. Right now, you have two options. One is easy and the other very, very hard."

"What are you talking about?"

"Option one is that you return to the Eagle Factory, unarmed, and surrender. After you do so, Livy will put a bullet into your brain. As a result, you die a quick, and as I understand, painless death." Cato took a breath and then sounded ominous. "Option two is that you refuse to come in. As a result, the withdrawal symptoms happen and you slowly, painfully, suffer for the next 96 hours ... and then you die. Now if you took your last emerald commitment just before the robbery, then you probably have about three or four more hours before the pain begins. I hope to see you soon." Then Cato hung up.

X

It was a high quality restaurant. Many upper class people dined there. Businessmen, entrepreneurs, politicians, and wealthy tourists had their lunches or dinners at that locale. The menu included meals and drinks in the Romance languages and with prices double or triple the typical fast food joint. Waiters and waitresses dressed without pins or flairs, keeping a well-polished impression for the patrons. It was the kind of place at which gentry of old would eat, or nobility were it Europe.

The third floor of the restaurant was one that could be reserved for banquets, parties, wedding receptions, or Bar Mitzvahs. It had a Greco-Roman theme, with murals depicting gods and philosophers, forums and pillars, blue skies and a blue Mediterranean. There were a few statues of the old pagan deities, replicas of more expensive works. Square tables with cushioned chairs were the most common terrain feature. They were uniformly placed about a wood paneled floor, which could double as a space for dancing and ceremony should the reservation schedule demand it.

Mayor Mary Bhatia was seated at one of the many squared tables. Before her, and to her right and left, empty chairs kept her company. Along the walls, however, there were a few security personnel. They were dressed in generic black suits, black ties, white shirts, and sunglasses. Each had an earpiece and looked as stern-faced as the carved statues. Bhatia was not eating a meal; neither was she drinking any good bottled vintage available upon order. She was waiting, waiting for the guest. It was not her husband, who as often the case was overseas on business. Rather, it was a less desired presence.

He was a contrast when he appeared. While Bhatia wore a silver pantsuit and white jewelry on her neck and earlobes, he was in jeans and sneakers. His belly clearly hung over his waist, a tucked in t-shirt keeping it at bay. It was another political message, undoubtedly chosen to inflame his peer. Rafael Sanchez-Vargas did not care. He did this by choice, as he owned a fair number of formal and business casual clothing items. After getting the necessary check from security, he was allowed to walk through the maze of chairs and tables to the one where Bhatia patiently waited. Seeing the second half of the reserved guests present, a lone waitress approached the table.

"Could I get either of you anything to drink?"

"Your best red wine, please," said Bhatia without looking at the menu propped up on the table. The waitress nodded as she took a brief note on some paper on a pad.

"And you, sir?"

"A nice cold beer," he said with arms folded. "And none of that light garbage, I want the regular stuff. Surprise me with the brand name."

"Okay then," replied the waitress, "I will be back shortly."

There was silence at first. Sanchez-Vargas maintained his defiant expression, looking with a degree of disgust at the woman before him. Bhatia expressed a mutual feel, giving neither smile nor show of overt respect. She looked down at the white table cloth for a moment before she began to speak. "Do you know why I asked to see you?"

"Yes, but I would like to hear it from you, rather than some underpaid and underappreciated executive assistant."

"In everything truth surpasses the imitation," consented Bhatia. "I wanted to see you in order to forge an alliance of sorts."

"Just say alliance," replied Rafael, folded arms now placed upon the table top. "It sounds much better."

"Verbal nitpicking notwithstanding, I have realized that we need each other for the upcoming election cycle. Despite your contempt for both parties, even you know that your ideas have a better chance in my party than the other."

Rafael was about to speak, but then the waitress came balancing a dark brown server plate that had a wine glass, a bottle of red wine, and a beer bottle. She carefully placed each item before the person who ordered it, getting a fleeting expression of gratitude. "Are both of you ready to order or do you need more time?"

"We will need more time," spoke Bhatia. "I will have security let you know when we are ready. Thank you." Rafael offered no resistance to that point and so the waitress nodded and then walked away. "As I was saying, we could use your help in defeating them on the campaign trail. If you focus your activists against them, combined with my party's support you could do some great damage. And in return,

I and Governor Voxner will use our sway in the state party to adopt some of your ideas for the platform."

"Not all of them?" asked Rafael as he took the already opened beer and had a swig.

"You know what the word 'compromise' means, right? You are not that stupid, are you?"

Rafael took another swig and smiled. "Okay, so your plan sounds interesting. So, we are closer politically. I see that point."

"So, what is the problem?" asked Bhatia as tipped the bottle and filled the wine glass with the red fermented liquid.

"Simple," he said, leaning back in his chair, "I want to be mayor again."

"Good for you," replied Bhatia before sipping the contents of the glass. Rafael was a little confused by her contentment.

"That means, I will be running against you," he said as though he were trying to explain something to a three-year-old.

"No, you won't," flatly replied Bhatia as she sipped some more of the wine.

"What do you mean? Are you going to try and stop me from running?"

"No, by all means run," she replied. "Get elected and become mayor. You have never been a boring public official. I will endorse you if you like."

"You will endorse your own opponent?" smiled Rafael. Bhatia held up a finger that requested patience while she drank more of the wine.

"I am not running for mayor next year. I am running for governor."

"Uh-huh," said Rafael. "What does Voxner think about that?"

"Voxner is retiring."

"What?"

"Voxner is retiring. Comprendes inglés, sí?"

"Who says?"

"She does," replied Bhatia, opting to pour more wine from the bottle to the glass. "She told me that she has become sick of how politics has gotten. She wants to get out of the game. I told her she should stand firm, but I guess I am not convincing."

"But you're okay with not being convincing."

"True," acknowledged Bhatia as she took another swig from the newly filled glass. "But I did try. I do not mind playing in the muck, muck that your kind created."

"My kind," laughed Rafael. "That sounds kind of racist."

"And that is exactly my point," said Bhatia as she put down the wine glass. "People like you assume the most horrible interpretation of every comment, disrupt and shout down every person you disagree with, and love to pick fights with people who may, at the worst, respectfully disagree on things here and there. You're the reason why someone as qualified and accomplished as Voxner is calling it quits."

"Oh, it's my fault, huh?" spoke Rafael defensively. "Little local activist like me somehow ruined the country. Don't forget that like you I started my political career after the 2016 election. I was raised learning that if you use enough vitriol, identity politics, protests, and crass generalization you can win. So what if I take what I know to be a winning formula and use it to its fullest? If you truly hated it, we would not be here."

"A collective punishment?"

"Sounds good to me," continued Rafael as he finished his beer. "Neither party is clean and you know it. So if I am guilty of anything, it's taking advantage of the system your political class created."

"Your claim is not without merit," grudgingly conceded Bhatia.

"Besides, whatever my faults, at least no one turns up dead from my demonstrations. But the Cicero Organization, now those are people who want a zero-sum game. And I know people from both parties have used their services. You know, target activists, maybe kill a prospective candidate when necessary."

"Surely you have evidence for such wild accusations," stated Bhatia with clenched fists resting upon the table.

"Okay, so I don't have too many smoking guns. But I don't think I'm saying anything false here. We know they hit people from both parties. They don't have any principles, any stated ideological opinions. They are a means to an end, like me. They scare people into supporting the milder candidates, like me. The only difference is that they break bigger laws than disorderly conduct."

Bhatia took her time to speak, deciding instead to slowly drink the contents of her glass. The empty item was placed beside the bottle. "My late father was alive during the 1960s Civil Rights Movement. He remembers the days when most Americans considered Martin Luther King to be an extremist and a pariah to society. He used to always tell me that he believed the only real reason Dr. King became so beloved was because while most whites didn't care for his message, they still preferred him over the frightening ravings of Malcolm X and the Nation of Islam. Next year, I want you to be my Malcolm X."

"Now there's a comparison I like," smiled Rafael.

"Then it is agreed? Your help in return for getting a few of your ideas into our party platform and, of course, some financial backing?"

"My support will begin the moment the things I want in the platform are approved and not a moment sooner."

"Agreed."

"Then you have a deal," said Rafael as he stretched his burly hand across the square table. With a smile, Bhatia extended her hand and the shake was performed. After that, Sanchez-Vargas leaned back in his chair. "Now can we eat?"

***

She found the name in her phone and pushed it, causing the device to call the person. It rang a couple of times, giving added tension to an already tenuous feeling. She was nervous as she sat at the dining room table, Josiah being on the opposite end of the table. He was stoic, piecing together the situation in his mind. Even though this time Josiah had not asked for it to be so, the phone was on speaker. It had become a reflex. The ringing stopped and a familiar voice was heard.

"Hello?"

"Hi, Dr. Stephanie, it's me, Carla."

"Oh hi, Carla, how are you?"

"I'm doing okay," she said, not so much to lie but because good manners instinctively instructed her to make that generic statement. "How are you?"

"Doing alright, I guess," replied Stephanie. "I had a long shift today. Right now, I am counting down the minutes before I can leave."

"Stephanie?"

"Yes?" asked the doctor, detecting distress in her friend's voice. "Are you okay, Carla?"

"Thing is, um," she hesitated. "Remember when we had that talk? You know? The one about my drug issue?"

"Yes."

"Well, um, I, I am trying to quit now. I took my last dosage yesterday and I know that the withdrawal is going to begin soon."

"Okay."

"Is there any way I can get some sedatives or knock-out pills?"

"Yes, sure," replied Stephanie. "I can get you a spot in the ICU here at the hospital and then—"

"Stephanie, I am sorry, but can this be done somewhere else?"

"Somewhere else? What is going on, Carla?"

"Please," said Carla, trying to keep herself together. "Can you please meet me at a friend's place in the suburbs?"

"This is highly irregular, but sure I can do that. Give me the address and I will get there as soon as my shift is over." Carla provided Stephanie with the address, with the doctor repeating the information to confirm accurate record.

"Thanks so much, Stephanie."

"No problem. See you soon!"

"Bye," said Carla as she ended the call. From there, she turned her attention to the man who was giving her shelter.

"So, this is why none of you ever turn yourselves in."

"Correct."

"That man from the earlier call, Cato. He said that the withdrawal symptoms are extremely painful. Is that a certainty?"

"Yes, very," replied Carla. "One of the first things they do is have recruits swallow the substance. Near the end of training, they purposely lock us in a space and deprive us of it for more than 24 hours, just so we know what it's like."

"So it is painful, then."

"Quite possibly the worst pain I have ever felt in my life."

Josiah took a breath. He could see Carla was feeling downtrodden. Her immediate future was bleak. Her eye contact was nonexistent as she stared blankly into the carpeted flooring. The gaze was downward like peering into the freshly dug grave preserved for her usage. She moved only to brush aside some strands of her hair that fell in front of her face. With a line of fingers, she dragged the locks behind her ear. Getting up from his chair, he walked up to Carla, prompting her to look up at him.

"You are very brave for staying," said Josiah. "If I were in your situation, I probably would have given up by now." She smiled weakly. "Anything I can do for you now?"

"Other than what you are already doing?"

"How about I make dinner?"

"Do you know how to make anything?" she asked, her smile a little bigger than before.

"Now what is that supposed to mean?" he asked in faux outrage.

"Your frozen food supply outnumbers your cooking products," she said, this time making eye contact. "I noticed that when I made breakfast."

"How do you know I haven't just finished making a bunch of things?"

"That's your argument?" smiled Carla. "I thought lawyers were better at making arguments."

"Well, as the Good Book puts it, by their fruits shall ye know them."

"How does that apply here?"

"Follow me, and you can see how well I cook," offered Josiah.

"Okay then," she said as she arose from her chair. "But I get to help out when it becomes obvious you don't know what you are doing."

"Obvious?" grinned Josiah as the two walked to the kitchen. "Now what kind of attitude is that? Keep that up and I won't let you eat any of my marvelous cuisine."

"Reject my help and no one will want to eat your marvelous cuisine."

About a half hour later Josiah, with extensive help from Carla, was able to make a decent dinner for the two. Carla said grace and the two had a nice meal where they talked about anything except the very matter that brought them together. Josiah spoke about growing up in a town that was miles from the city while Carla talked about her many trips to the mother country. Josiah seemed especially fascinated with the conversation, as it referenced many places in the Old and New Testaments. At one point, he concluded aloud that her upbringing was more interesting than his own.

From dinner, they went to the living room to watch some television. They entered about midway through a movie on cable television that both had seen when they were younger. There was nostalgia talk, amusement over the little issues with continuity and logic within the action film. All in good fun, of course. Carla appreciated every moment of it all. The past twenty-four hours had been a time of great upheaval and dread. For the first time she was able to relax. She was starting to deeply appreciate Josiah for more than just his allowing her to hide at his place. Surely this was merely the aftereffect of the moment, but then again maybe it was something more.

As the credits rolled, there was a hush between them. That temporal flight into careless amusement was landing. The room gradually filled once more with solemnity and contemplation. They were sharing the couch at this point. Not touching, as the furniture piece was long enough to keep space between them and the armrests they used. Carla soon realized that Josiah was studying her with his eyes. She smiled at first, and then looking again noticed that his studying had not stopped.

"What is it?" she kindly inquired. He seemed deeply in thought as he looked about her appearance, which endured even the tumult of the past day.

"How did you do it?"

"Do what?"

"How were you able to kill people?" asked Josiah. "I get the ones who may have attacked first. But you admit few of them did." Carla stayed silent, while Josiah calmly continued. "So how did you do it? How were you able to kill someone who never wished you harm, who probably never knew you existed? And how did you do it, over and over again? That is what I find most bizarre about you."

Carla sat there silently for a moment. "I wonder about it myself. Then I hear about those people, mothers who save their kids by lifting cars. Or some peaceful father who kills the man who attempted to rape his daughter. Those stories. People can do horrible things when family are threatened. And if blowing up your boss, someone who means nothing to me, allows my grandfather to get the medical treatments he needs, then I will do it without question or hesitation."

Josiah wanted to interrupt, wanted to tell her how skewed her reasoning was on so many levels. He wanted to explain the better ways of acting and the more peaceable venues for resolution. None of this escaped his mouth. He remained there in silence, realizing that the person confiding in him was nearing a time of great suffering. Indeed, soon after her comment Carla squinted as her forehead began to throb. She was shaking her head as the pain increasingly began to manifest itself.

"No, no," she said continuously as the pain grew within her head. "It is too early, it cannot already be 24 hours. No, no …" The throbbing pain spread throughout her brain and head like liquid clay filling every crevice of the mold. It started to twitch and rent within her sides and chest, introducing itself independent of the spreading misery within her cerebrum. "No, not now. Please, it is too soon." She was desperate, her words becoming couched between growing breaths of desperation. Josiah jumped from his seat on the couch and rushed to her, grabbing her by both shoulders as her eyes became watery.

"Let's get you to my bed," he explained as she got up and the two rapidly walked to the bedroom. "I'll call your doctor and tell her to get here as soon as possible."

"Okay, Okay," said Carla, a third repeat of the word being countered by the piercing pain that was striking inside her head. The anguish flooded into her limbs next, making them feel extra sore. After a matter of minutes all four limbs felt sorer than the left leg felt yesterday when she arrived at Josiah's place. Shoes and belt off, she let herself fall upon the surface of the unmade bed. Her eyes were shutting for long periods and her fists were repeatedly clinching. A few tears finally escaped the ducts; more were to follow.

"Hello?"

"Dr. Greenwald? This is Carla's friend. We need you to come as soon as possible. The withdrawal is happening now and it's happening with a fury."

"I am on my way now. I should be there soon."

"Okay," said Josiah as he hung up. The height of dolorous sentiment reached the level of convulsion, with Carla erratically flailing upon the mattress. She pushed inwards entering the fetal position before increased pain from her back and neck made her shoot outwards to a nearly straight posture lying down. Lacking any better solution for the moment, Josiah took hold of Carla in an embrace as though he were trying to protect her from an external threat. She gripped hard, holding one of his hands with her right hand while the fingers of her left hand dug into his shoulder. For Josiah, it was not a pleasant feeling to have the digits digging into his shoulder or the crushing grip enveloping his other hand. Still, if it meant any alleviation of any kind for her misery, he was willing to endure it knowing that whatever discomfort he had was miniscule by comparison.

It felt far longer than it was, but in fact only nine minutes passed from when Josiah called to when a loud knocking was heard from the front door. By this point, Carla was crying aloud from the mounting pain. Josiah tried to pry himself away, with some struggle as Carla had to force herself to grip something, anything else. "That's the doctor. I'll be right back, I promise!" he said loudly as he had to talk over growing outward expression of uncontrolled excruciating sensory impact. She nodded between cries of agony and Josiah ran to the front to unlock and open it.

"Dr. Greenwald?"

"Yes," answered the guest who was immediately waved into the house. Josiah pointed in the general direction of the bedroom, which was easy to find because of the size of the house and the projection of the screams. After closing and locking the door, Josiah raced back to the bedroom as Stephanie was standing over a Carla whose was lashing about the unmade mattress. Stephanie quickly but carefully readied a needle filled with a temporary solution to what Carla was experiencing.

"Will that help?"

"It should," shouted back Stephanie. "But I need you to help hold her down. She's thrashing around too much."

"Okay," said Josiah who got to the bedside and did his best to hold her down. As the screams worsened and he struggled to keep her left arm still enough to get an injection, he felt like he was handling someone demonically possessed.

"Okay, Carla," calmly stated Stephanie, "I need you to try and help me, here. Try and hold your left arm still. It's almost over." Carla did not use words, but simply did what she could to not resist the grip of Josiah and the new piercing pain of the needle. The screams got even louder for those moments as the sedative entered her system. From there, the cries of agony started to lessen in their severity and the pain began to recede. Carla's eyes rolled about as her eyelids closed. About three minutes after the shot, the suffering woman was completely unconscious and appeared to sleep soundly. Stephanie and Josiah stood over her. "That should keep her out for about eight to ten hours. That is more than enough time to get her to an ICU where I can better monitor her progress."

"I am sorry, but that cannot happen."

"Excuse me, mister ..."

"Sharp."

"Mr. Sharp, it is very dangerous to give such heavy sedatives outside of a medical setting. She needs to be monitored. Given the severity of her reaction to the withdrawal, she must be kept heavily sedated at least for the next two to three days."

"Doctor," calmly explained Josiah, "I don't know how much she told you, but I am a lawyer and Carla is a very important witness for a case I am working on. The people who did this to her do not know she is here. If she gets moved to a hospital they may kill her."

"Are you serious?"

"Very," stressed Josiah. "And I need her awake, at least during the daytime. She doesn't have long to live."

"Long to live?" asked a surprised Stephanie.

"According to her, if she goes four days without the drug she dies. She still has more information I need for my case. Surely, there is something you can give her that will keep her awake and deal with the pain."

Stephanie thought a moment. "Well, there is a sedative we generally use for brain surgeries that keeps the patient awake during the procedure. I can give you some of that to help."

"Okay good."

"I will also need to get her hooked up to a device that will keep track of her vitals, especially blood oxygen levels which can be at risk for people heavily sedated for long periods of time. And I reserve the right to personally check in every so often."

"That works, yes, that works," said Josiah.

"Well, then. I guess I will be going back to the hospital to get the necessary supplies. I should be back within an hour."

"Okay good. Thank you, doctor," said Josiah as Stephanie went to the door, but then turned around briefly.

"A colleague of mine is analyzing the substance now. He might be able to find an antidote within the next four days."

"She might not have four days," solemnly spoke Josiah. Stephanie nodded and then exited the house. Josiah locked the door behind her and walked back into his bedroom. Carla was still. Josiah slowly sat down beside her, and stroked her hair once. "How can something so beautiful be so deadly?" He got up and paced around the room, his sore hand occasionally gripping his forehead as he gathered his paradoxical thoughts and more paradoxical feelings about the woman sleeping nearby.

***

All was void, all was absent. A nothingness for which the passage of time was undocumented and the ending of hours unmarked. There were no dreams, no lights or fancy. Only the heavy induced rest for which an entire evening quickly dissipated. From without the break of consciousness, Josiah Sharp kept vigil. He awoke early, having the couch for his evening slumber. Already fed and showered, he peered into the bedroom. After the second visit from Stephanie Greenwald, things looked more sophisticated, with Carla al-Hassan hooked up to a $300 machine that tracked her vital signs. The sheets were also made better, with her body from the arms down submerged below the covers. She was changed while unconscious into a pair of Josiah's sister's pajamas. While Josiah helped move the unconscious body, Stephanie did the disrobing and robing per mutually agreed upon moral sensibilities.

Carla was beginning to stir. Within her being, a gradual awareness of time and space began. Still bleakly dark, she was beginning to become cognizant of her positioning on the bed. Feeling was returning to her as well, and with it a slow rising of discomfort. A sense of gnawing pain was filling her head once more, like a plume rising into her cerebrum. Various proliferations were spreading through her legs and chest. It was starting up again, the escalating anguish of withdrawal. She felt too weak to tackle it again and started to shift more under the covers, her face beginning to prune in discomfort.

"Take this," she heard a masculine voice. Still blurry in her cognizance, she was not sure who it was. "Take this, Carla." Her eyes opened as the pain began to sharpen. She saw a blurry figure holding something in his hand. It was yellow and white, and looked like a tablet. With her right hand, she took hold of the pill and instinctively placed it in her mouth. She finally recognized Josiah as sitting at the bedside. He handed her a cup of water and she quickly tipped the cup into her mouth, swallowing the pill. The pill was a little bigger than she initially assumed, and so she had to drink all the water in the cup, requiring a second chugging of the cup's contents. Within minutes the pain began to plateau and then sink. "Is it working?" asked the voice. "Is it working, Carla?" he asked again.

"I don't know," she said. "There is still much pain." He put a hand on her shoulder and another on her hand. His own head bowed, he mumbled a prayer over her. She stayed quiet, her eyes still adjusting to the awakened morning. Several minutes later, the pain declined yet remained present, as though muted or kept under some defensive barrier. There was still head and chest pain, soreness in the limbs. Yet it was not brutal, neither was its sensation so grand as to incur screams of agony from Carla.

"How about now?"

"Better," she weakly smiled. "I feel like I have a head cold."

"Dr. Greenwald gave me some medicine that should sedate you, but keep you awake enough to, well, mostly function."

"Good," replied Carla as she mustered some more strength. "The more I can help your case the more I can get back at them. For this."

Josiah nodded in agreement. "Are you hungry for breakfast?"

"I think so."

"How about oatmeal?"

"Sounds like something to feed a sick person," faintly smiled Carla. "Yes."

"Be back shortly," said Josiah as he got up from the bed and left the bedroom. Carla looked at the simple ceiling, leaning her head back on the pillow. She felt very groggy, with the newly taken sedative relaxing her muscles. It took extra effort to get her upper body to a slouching position. Upon doing so, she grabbed the pillow next to the one she had used overnight and placed it behind her back. Leaning back, she slouched back more than she wanted, but it was an improvement over being completely flat on her back. As she began to gather strength to fix the pillows some more, the door opened and Josiah entered carrying a warm bowl of oatmeal with a spoon dipped in it. "Can I help?"

"No, I think I have it," said Carla as she took a few seconds to shift the pillows around just right. "Now I am ready."

"Okay," said Josiah, seated once more, gripping the spoon, which had a small dose of oatmeal within its small silver bowl. She raised her hand in protest, with a mild smile.

"That's not necessary. I think I can feed myself."

"You sure?"

"I want to try."

"Okay, then let me get you something to put it on," said Josiah, who quickly found a small table meant for breakfast in bed. He placed it above Carla's waist and then put the warm bowl on the top of it. Carla said a quick grace to herself and then slowly ate the meal. She was not as fast or steady with the spoon as someone of her age should be, but given the circumstances she did complete the meal without problem. With the dregs of the oatmeal still present, she discarded the spoon into the bowl.

"I am not that weak," she declared with pride as Josiah merely smiled and took away the small table with bowl. He was back soon after. "When can we get to it? You know, to my interview. My interview."

"Just as soon as I can set up the camera in here," replied Josiah with an amazed sentiment. After a few minutes he had everything ready, angling the shot just right to show not only Carla but the vital signs machine she was connected to. Carla had to adjust herself to keep a leaned-back, seated position. Every little action required more strength than usual. More effort but still accomplished. "Ready?"

"Yes," she said with a weakened, yet firm voice. Josiah nodded and then pushed the record button. The camera light was on.

"This is Thursday, May 18 at about 9:30 AM Eastern Time. This is day two of the interview recorded for the Cicero Organization investigation. The witness will answer questions regarding the nature of the Organization, her involvement, and other details of a similar nature. Please state your name once more for the record."

"Carla al-Hassan."

"Ms. al-Hassan, are you currently sedated?"

"Yes."

"What is the reason for your sedation?"

"I am experiencing. I am experiencing withdrawal symptoms."

"Withdrawal symptoms from what?"

"I quit taking a drug that the Cicero Organization ... that the Cicero Organization forces its members to take. To take."

"When did you start taking this drug?"

"The first night they recruited me."

"What happened if someone refused to take the drug?"

"They were shot. I remember ... I remember one person being shot that night. He refused to take it. So Livy shot him."

"Can you describe the drug and its effects?"

"Yes," said Carla with a pause. "It is green. Some call it the 'loyalty oath.' Cato and a few others call it the 'emerald commitment.' We have to take one around every, every 24 hours. When we stop, we get intense pain. This is why I am sedated. Sedated."

"Carla," said Josiah with some emotional pause. "What did they tell you would happen if you go four days without taking the drug?"

"I will die," said Carla. "Four days without it and I die …" Her eyes began to water. "Please, please turn it off. Please turn off the camera." Josiah did so.

"What is it?"

"Sorry," she replied, a few tears escaping her eyes. Her right hand covered her face as she cried for a few moments. Josiah did not know what to do, so he sat patiently, taking it on faith that the sedative was still working. "I am sorry, when I answered I, I started to realize that my grandfather will outlive me."

"I am sorry, Carla." Josiah approached her and gave her a hug, which she accepted. A few moments later, she patted his back.

"Okay, okay," she replied. "I am better now. I can continue now. Turn the recorder back on, please. I have more to tell you. I need to tell you as much as I can." Josiah patted her on the shoulder and then went back to the camera, Behind the lens, he pushed the recording button as Carla dried her eyes and after a deep breath, continued.

***

The next couple of days were tough, but stable. Carla's vital signs remained consistent, albeit weak. Her blood oxygen levels remained acceptable and there were no other signs of health risk. While not eating as much as before, she was still eating all three traditional meals. Josiah noted at one point that the small table got more usage from Carla in the past couple of days than from him in the past five years. Carla provided more details about the criminal actions she was involved in, especially matters like the robberies she used to perform with Tiffany. She explained why Josiah was being targeted, and the steps leading up to the assassination of Myles Talbert. After the third day of interviewing Carla, Josiah concluded that he had plenty of material. What he kept from Carla was that there were still certain pieces missing before a solid case could be created.

Dr. Stephanie made a few visits. She administered the heavy sedative for the evenings and checked with Carla on her overall health. Stephanie also updated Carla about her grandfather. Carla was relieved to hear that he was doing well and that presently his biggest source of worry was his plan to propose to Elnora. Stephanie was also there to help Carla with getting bathed and dressed. During the day, Josiah helped Carla to and from the bathroom, carrying her with an arm draped over his neck. She was strong enough to put some weight on her legs, but not much. He also gave her the occasional pill. This generally happened once every three to four hours. Stephanie had been forward-thinking enough to give them sufficient pills for the time period.

Carla was only in moderate pain during those days. The pills did not fully eliminate the anguish, but they at least made it manageable. On the fourth day, things were more emotionally draining than physically traumatic. Josiah informed Carla that he would get her whatever she wanted to eat. Carla kindly declined the offer, as she was not in the mood to have any particular favorite food. She did want to watch a couple of movies she was planning to see once they left theatres. It took a few minutes to get her comfortably situated on the couch, but it was done and the movies were watched.

It was when the credits rolled for the third film that the mood, which for the past several hours had been surprisingly upbeat, descended into realistic melancholy. That sense of finality, of ultimate end. Cato had been right about that strange feeling of existential terror. Josiah looked across the couch to Carla. She was distraught. Josiah exited out of the film and the television returned to the local station and its live newscast. It just so happened that the segment was about the violent robbery a few days earlier. No drawn description of the suspect, but the basic measurements of age and size matched Carla fairly well. Her sense of despair grew when she wondered if that was all she was going to be remembered as, that her great contribution to history was all vile.

In silence, Josiah helped her back to the bed. Midway through the trip the sedative was wearing off and the pain increased. Carla clinched her fists and bit down on her lip, almost to the point of drawing blood. Fortunately, Josiah hastily got another pill and some water to her just as things were becoming even more unbearable. Several minutes later, the pain returned to its mild lenient presence. Given the hour of the late afternoon, both concluded that it was the last pill Carla was ever going to take.

"It's going to happen soon," said Carla. "I can feel it." She was on the bed, a couple of pillows keeping her propped up, while Josiah sat in a chair placed a couple of feet away. He looked with pity upon her, beautiful even in this time of hardship. "Josiah? Josiah?" her queries sounded desperate.

"What is it, Carla?"

"Will God forgive me for what I did?" she asked with some tears beginning to form about her eyes. "Will He let me in, after all I did?"

"Of course, He will," replied Josiah, struggling as never before to maintain his own emotional stability. "He's let in worse people quite readily."

"There should be a priest here. I need a priest."

"I am sure you can confess just fine in your heart."

"You are such a Protestant," remarked Carla, making an attempt at humor. "Alright then, the Protestant way. I am sure God will forgive me of that, also."

"There are worse sins," smiled Josiah as he stroked the hair of Carla, who briefly smiled at the comment before returning to the morbid focus.

With mouthed words, Carla looked upwards, pleading with the Judge of All Creation to forgive her for everything. Crossing herself, she kept looking upwards while Josiah stayed close but silent. Her vision became blurry. It was probably the tears that continued to exit from both eyes, forming two small rivers along her cheeks. The tears could not explain what she saw next, a vision for her alone.

The nightmare was coming back. Before the ceiling were the growing waves of blood, the deluge enveloping her as it had in some form numerous times in sleep over the past eight years. Behind it was a grand icon of Christ. Branches stretched out, but then broke just as suddenly. The crests of the waves began to lower and then lower still. Soon the ground opened and the floods began to drain away. She began to smile greatly with teeth clearly visible, a sudden inward stroke of inexplicable joy. Clouds brightened and the once flooded route was dry and pure. She raised her right hand as though trying to grasp it. "The way is clear," she said sincerely. "The way is clear." Then her hand lowered to the mattress, her eyes closed, and her face slowly dropped to the side.

She was very still. Josiah presumed her ghost to have been given up. He sniffled in his own anguish and struggled to speak. "Carla?" he called out. "Carla?" No response. He was too drained to ask a third time. She was so peaceful. For a moment, he thought she was dead. Then he looked up and was instantly driven from his profound sorrow into a sense of enamored confusion. For when he looked at the tragic setting, he noticed that the equipment tracking her vital signs was still reporting life. No emergency alarm, no total flattening of the lines. The transmission was weaker, but the same.

Confused by this, Josiah placed his hand on her wrist and then lightly on her neck. While not a medical expert, Josiah knew enough to know that neither part of the body should have movement that could be felt. Something was not right, or maybe something was very right. Maybe she passed out in advance of the final moments, a merciful transition from this life unto the next. As he tried to make sense of the false alarm, his smart phone rang. Jolted by the disruption, it took a few rings to answer.

"Hello?"

"Mr. Sharp?"

"Dr. Greenwald?"

"Yes."

"What is it? Do you have an antidote?"

"Before I answer, how is Carla right now?"

"Well," breathed Josiah, trying to gather himself given the emotional chaos. "I thought she had died, but the machine says her vital signs are still a go and she seems to have a pulse."

"That's what I thought."

"Pardon me?"

"I just got the report from the toxicologist. According to him, the substance is a mixture of various opioids and NSAIDS. There also appears to be some chemotherapy drug components. When developed a certain way, these various drugs can be used to cause pain rather than relieve it," she explained.

"So do you have an antidote?" asked Josiah with a raised voice.

"Mr. Sharp. What I am trying to say is that there is no need for an antidote. All the substance is, is a kind of a chemical cocktail that induces intense pain when not constantly being replenished. There are no other side-effects. She probably passed out because the drug's effects finally wore off."

"Praise God, praise God!" said Josiah with great enthusiasm. "Should I wake her and let her know the good news?"

"It is best you let her sleep."

"Very well. Very, very well."

XI

Josiah Sharp's sister must have been into fitness. Amongst the things she left behind at his place while living abroad were items germane to an active life. There were two outfits of sweats, with matching colors. There were a couple of undershirts made for the gym and, to Carla's amazement, a punching bag. This was not located in the closet but rather among the things stashed away in the room where she first went on the record about her involvement in the Cicero Organization.

Carla converted the space into a fitness room, keeping the door open for ventilation as she worked out for most of the day. While she had spent a few days under varying levels of sedation, the drugs used for this purpose did not leave any lasting effects. She felt almost perfectly normal upon waking up to the morning she thought she would never see. Generally, the ability to maintain a certain exercise regimen is lost after more than two weeks of inactivity. Having been only a few days, Carla quickly and effectively returned to the issue of maintaining her prowess.

This included many pushups. She could do fifty at a time. After number fifty, she gave herself an extra heave and jumped to her feet in a crouched position. The punching bag was not as effective at staying in place as the one at the Eagle Factory. This was because it was not attached to the ceiling and floor. Still, it was heavy enough that it took several blows until it fell over. Carla made many imprints into the sides and front in her combinations of kicks and punches. She worked up another sweat by early afternoon, when she heard the front door unlock and then open. She kept at the punching, impressing the man she knew was watching her in action from the room's open door.

"I see you are back on the horse," commented Josiah. Carla stopped her exercise, breathing the panting of accomplishment and giving Josiah a pleasant if not slightly sadistic smile from her bout with the bag.

"How was work?" she asked as she took a towel left on one of the boxes and wiped her face and chest.

"It was interesting," replied Josiah, making way as Carla, still drying herself with the towel, went into the kitchen for water. "Not only did I have to keep my secret progress from my usual coworkers, but now even from my superiors."

"I must be a scandal for you," she smiled as he followed her into the kitchen. On the first try, she located a glass and turned the faucet on to fill it.

"All shall be revealed in due time," noted Josiah while she drank the cold liquid. "For now, I am hesitant to tell anyone, anything, until I know who the leak is."

"Fair enough," said Carla, breathing normally and water consumed. "And no one thinks it's strange that you spent so many days at home?"

"From time to time, I spend several days away from the office on assignment. You know, looking at case files, depositions, interviewing potential clients. Things of that nature. My coworkers rightly assume that that is why I was gone for most of last week and had to leave early today."

"So ..." began Carla, turning to a more controversial topic, "about a possible plea bargain deal. You know, now that I've helped you so much."

"Well," hesitated Josiah, knowing that she was not going to like the answer. "You have helped a lot, and I want you to know I am grateful. Very grateful."

"But?"

"It would shine poorly on the Justice Department to have someone who has murdered dozens of people and actively participated in one of our nation's worst domestic terrorist organizations to get only a small prison sentence."

"Seriously?" critically asked Carla, her pleasantry quickly evaporated. "So what would I look at if I officially turned myself in?"

"Ten to twenty years," stated Josiah.

"Hell, no," declared Carla. "I can't go to prison. It would destroy my grandfather. It might destroy me."

"This is not easy for me to say, Carla," reasoned Josiah, attempting to diffuse the moment. "I like you, a lot, but the law is the law and justice is justice."

"Justice is justice," she said in disdain. "What gives you the right to act all self-righteous at my situation? What gives you the right to judge me?"

"I think the fact that I haven't murdered forty people gives me the right to judge you," responded Josiah with a fittingly sharp tongue.

"I had no choice," angrily spoke Carla, imposing upon Josiah the same arguments she made with herself whenever she needed to convince herself of what she was doing. "It was either this or let my giddo die."

"There had to be other, better, more moral options. There are always better options."

"Oh really? Name them," she challenged. "Go on. I am listening."

"Well, um, as I understand, the Syrian Orthodox community is a strong one. Surely the Church could have helped you."

"The recession hit the Church hard. By the time I got to them, they were unable to help the ones already there. Next?"

"You could have, you could have gone to a bank and taken out a loan."

"Tried that. They rejected me. Called me a credit risk. Next?"

"Well, wait a minute," countered Josiah. "You're an American citizen, you have healthcare. You could have easily added your grandfather as a dependent. Given his emergency health needs, you could have gotten a special enrollment period to streamline it. You could have easily done that."

"Easily?" she said in great exception. "Josiah, it is not easy to add someone to an account. I went to the nearest HHS office and asked. They said it can take months, and even then the answer might still be no. By then, I would have had to pay for his treatments with money I didn't have. So, not easily."

Josiah gave Carla a look of perplexing uncertainty. The look was distracting and then unnerving for her, as she wanted to continue her tirade against Sharp's viewpoint on there being better ways to handle her situation. His expression became her expression as he eventually broke what seemed to be a lengthy silence. "Are you sure?"

"Yes," she insisted in a softer tone. "I talked with a man at the office and he said it would take several months."

Josiah shook his head. "I have a cousin whose grandmother was not a citizen. When she needed to be added to his insurance, he contacted HHS and scheduled an appointment. He brought in some paperwork, filled out a form, and everything was done after a few hours. His rates went up, but otherwise incident free."

Carla was dumbfounded. Things started to feel unstable. Her left hand gripped the kitchen counter as she started to feel a fundamental moment of her life story unravel. She looked at the floor rather than Josiah, still trying to process the contradictory evidence. Josiah slowly neared, feeling that he was dealing with a calmer person. Someone who was beginning to realize that something even more ominous had taken place years ago. It clicked for Josiah around the same time it began to be revealed to Carla.

"Could you identify the man you talked to if given the opportunity?"

"Maybe," replied Carla, right hand pressed against her head. "It's been over eight years. But I can try."

Josiah smiled and patted her on the shoulder. "That's good enough for me."

Soon after that the two made their way to the living room, where Carla sat on the couch, her legs bent inwards atop the cushion. She was still trying to process the epiphany. Thanks to the Internet as seen on Josiah's open laptop, they found the contact number for the specific office that Carla went to over eight years before. When she was desperate, when her world was painfully shattering, when all stability had abandoned her. She returned to that scene, that setting, in this new era of tortuous transition. Josiah paced as his smart phone rung a few times before a secretary picked up.

"Hello there," said Josiah within earshot of Carla, his end of the conversations being the only side she heard with clarity. "This is Assistant District Attorney Josiah Sharp with the Justice Department. I am conducting a white collar investigation and need to get some information from your office ... I need you to provide me with employment information, specifically the identities of every male person who was employed at your office between five and ten years ago ... Not too much, just name, head shot, contact info, and their address at the time of their hiring. When can you get me that? ... A couple hours? ... Sure, that should work. Let me give you my email address ..."

While the wait was about two and a half hours, the afternoon was still alive. During that time the enmity Carla had for the Cicero Organization compounded like it was on interest. Every awful thing she did, every life she took, was it all built upon a false foundation? Was she blatantly deceived? Did she, an intelligent creature with decent grades in school, fall for something that now seemed so obvious? Josiah got the email with the attached file. His laptop took a little longer than usual to download the document, but its effort was still successful and the file was quickly opened. It was formatted like a slide show, with each page having a photo of the employee, with name, contact information, and address placed at the bottom. Now came the time for sifting.

Josiah was seated on one side of the couch, his right arm leaning on the arm rest while the laptop was placed upon his legs. Having showered and changed into a new set of clothes, Carla now sat on the middle of the couch. One arm rested to her side while the other rested on the top of the couch, laying near but not directly behind the back of Josiah. With right clicks Josiah moved the faces along while Carla stared at each one intently. At first, she said "no" to each profile. Then she simply stayed quiet and after a few seconds Josiah would right click and a new face appeared.

Dozens had come and gone, none of them resembling her faint memory of that distressful errand. Most were obvious negatives, being clearly older than the relatively young man that gave her the deceptive news about her chances of adding George to her account. Others she struggled with, as they almost seemed to fit her mind's remembrance. Another click and a new visage. This one from the onset seemed familiar, but she was could not immediately confirm. After a few seconds, Josiah right-clicked again to a new face. Yet she kept thinking about that last one and made her thoughts known.

"Can you go back one?"

"Sure," nodded Josiah as moved the mouse icon to the arrow facing left and right-clicked it. Again Carla saw the face. After a few moments, Josiah spoke up. "Well?"

"I think that's him."

"Are you sure?"

"He looks more familiar than the others, I know that."

"Okay," replied Josiah with some optimism brewing. "The name is John Runfeld. Interesting, he has no contact information."

"Dead end?"

"Not yet," commented Josiah, opening a new window in the browser. "It still lists his apartment complex. They will have a number." He found the web page for the complex within a matter of moments and from there the main business number for the facility. Taking hold of his smart phone, he punched in the number. Once completed, he got up to pace again and heard a single ring before someone picked up. "Good afternoon, my name is Josiah Sharp and I am an attorney with the Justice Department. Can I speak to a tenant of yours named John Runfeld? ... Yes, I can hold." He directed his comment to Carla. "They're looking for him now."

"Or they are warning him that an attorney is trying to reach him."

"Now you're starting to get as paranoid as I am," smiled Josiah, eliciting a smile back from Carla. Josiah then returned his attention to the call. "Yes, I am still here ... he did? ... When was that? ... Five years ago. Okay, well, um did he leave a forwarding address? ... Good ... Hold on, let me get a pen and paper." Carla knew her cue and handed Josiah the two implements while he held the phone steady by leaning his head upon his shoulder. It was another apartment complex and the person he was on the line with was kind enough to provide their contact information. "Okay, thank you, bye."

"Now what?"

"Now we see if he has moved again," replied Josiah as he dialed the new number and soon reached the front desk of the other apartment complex. "Hello, I am Assistant District Attorney Josiah Sharp. I am conducting an important investigation and need to talk to a potential witness who lives at your building ... John Runfeld ... Yeah, I can hold." This time the complex was faster in their response, with a different voice responding. "Yes, I am an assistant district attorney. Can I speak to Runfeld?" Josiah's expression and voice changed. "Really? ... Three years ago? ... Sorry to hear that ... was it widely reported? ... Okay, I will look for more information ... Take care." Josiah ended the call and then looked at the seated Carla, curious as to what he learned. "John Runfeld died three years ago."

"Well, don't look at me, I didn't do it," defensively replied Carla.

"I know," laughed Josiah. "The super said it was a car accident. Apparently, the funeral got a fair amount of local media coverage." Carla naturally shifted more towards the center of the couch as Josiah sat back down and took to his laptop to search for the story. Within a few moments, he located an article about the accident and then another about the funeral. With Carla looking on with him, they scoured the local news piece.

"A literal dead end?"

"Maybe," said Josiah as he scrolled down the story, which had a photo at the center of the text from the funeral. As he did so, Carla felt a jolt of shock surge through her. She gripped the shoulder of Josiah as her eyes widened.

"Go back up to the photo!" she commanded. Josiah obliged, the screen showing a group of people exiting the church where the service was held. One of the figures to the left of the shot was too familiar, even with sunglasses on. Ironically, it was his well-dressed body that first made her think it was him. Only after seeing the suit did the face confirm it. As her right hand remained on Josiah's shoulder, her left hand pointed closely to the man in the photo. "That is Cato."

"Are you sure?"

"Far more than I was about Runfeld."

"Well," began Josiah as he looked at the photo caption. "According to this, he is listed as being family. Assuming it is not an erroneous attribution, he might be mentioned in the article itself." Carla found the list of those who survived the young man and directed Josiah to it. He then started to search each name. The fourth name put into the engine was Simon Runfeld, one of the uncles. As Josiah refined the search to focus on images, Carla again squeezed the shoulder of Josiah.

"That is definitely him."

"Then let us see what we can find out," commented Josiah, eyes centered on the screen as he clicked on a résumé posted online of Simon Runfeld. It was Josiah's turn to be surprised when he saw one of the company names listed. "Saddler & Frances. That one sounds a little too familiar."

"Like Saddler & Saddler?" inquired Carla.

"Exactly," replied Josiah as he immediately found the website for the business. He dragged the mouse icon to the "About Us" tab, clicked it and found a table that provided the option to see the "Board of Directors." A click on that, and the two found a page that had many names and photos, with brief biographies. The very first photo and name seen was that of the man Carla knew on a mysterious professional basis.

"Simon Runfeld," said Carla as she skimmed the biography information. "Second generation American, married with three kids and two grandkids. Chairman of the Board of Directors since 2012."

"I wonder who else is on this little board," said Josiah, who scrolled down. Again, Carla flinched in surprise.

"That's Livy!" she said, again pointing her finger close to the screen.

"Or as he is called here, Benedicto Velasquez. According to his bio, he served in the army and did tours in both Iraq and Afghanistan. Also claims to have special forces training and has won a few marksmanship trophies."

"I can believe all that," commented Carla.

"Also says he had a brief stint as a police detective."

"Which means the badge was real."

"Anyone else look familiar?" asked Josiah as he slowly scrolled through the photos of the other members. Carla found them all to be vaguely to strikingly familiar. While some of them she had only seen with cowls draped over most of their faces, they were seen enough by her to be recognizable as the other leaders within the Cicero Organization. There they were, all masquerading as honest entrepreneurs.

***

She was still in contemplation. A once tall glass of orange juice was reduced considerably while she sat at the dining room table. One leg touched the ground while the other was bent to rest upon the seat of the chair. Her arms folded atop the knee of the bent limb, her expression staring more into the polished wooden surface of the table. Blinking slowly, all the past crimes against the laws of God and man emerged to her conscious level. Below the mentality, rage was simmering. Like the bright lava bubbling underneath the readying volcano, so came those thoughts.

Another drink of the orange juice, the level of yellow liquid shrinking while the thin layer of pulp retained presence along the trail where the juice flowed. Back to the sedentary position, her body's movement slow compared to the rapid-fire action of her mind. Meanwhile Josiah Sharp was actively researching matters, typing away at search engines throughout the Internet. He finally reached a stopping point and put his laptop on standby. His excitability entered the dining room with him, drawing Carla al-Hassan's attention away from the internal considerations of a wasted cause.

"What's new?" she asked upon looking up.

"Saddler & Frances owns several properties throughout the metro area, especially many of the abandoned warehouses and factories on the outskirts," said Josiah. "Can you guess the name of one of the industrial properties they own?"

"The Eagle Factory," replied Carla sans emotion.

"Exactly," responded Josiah. "And I bet you know which downtown bar Saddler & Frances also owns."

"The Hopewell Bar," said Carla. "They're definitely guilty now."

"Very."

"Is it enough to arrest them?"

Josiah was silent. He struggled with the question also. "Maybe. Honestly, I would have called all this in if I didn't feel like someone was going to tell Cicero immediately."

"You mean you still do not know who Cicero or the leak are?"

"I pulled tax records on Saddler & Frances to see if there were any financial links. Turns out they've given money to both parties and the campaigns of both our current mayor and our current attorney general."

"Then you still need my testimony."

"And the punishment that must come as a result."

"Is there nothing I can do to get you to let me go? Is my only option to testify and then be thrown into prison until I am in my forties?"

"I am not sure what else there is. Someone needs to testify to the inner workings of the Cicero Organization. Unless I get my hands on something or someone that can tie up this case better, you are my best option."

Carla thought about it. Her grandfather had a weak heart. All these revelations about his granddaughter would destroy him. Going to prison, she might survive. Indeed, her fighting skills might make her the alpha predator among the inmates.

But the idea of losing all that time, all those years. It would be well-deserved. Her rationalizations for doing what she did no longer held merit, even for her. And then she remembered that she was still capable of doing violent things on behalf of others.

"Josiah," she said, her spirits lifting as she fixed her eyes upon him. "I know how I can get you all you need for your case. And in doing so, I will not have to testify or serve prison or anything like that."

"How?"

"Let me step into the darkness one more time," she said, giving Josiah a sense of unease that was apparent in his shifting physical stance.

"You mean go back to them?"

"You remember I told you about the rolodex that Cicero had? The paper one that includes all his contacts?"

"I do."

"I know where to find it. It is at the Eagle Factory. I get that and you will have plenty of witnesses and plenty of information on who the leak is and maybe even who Cicero is."

"Carla," critically spoke Josiah. "Are you telling me that you are going to take on the entire Cicero Organization?"

"It's not as challenging as you think," said Carla as she stood up. "The outside of the factory is always lightly guarded, because Cicero is more interested in being undetected. And during a time like this, what with your investigation and the campaign season not yet begun, there won't be more than a dozen or so personnel there altogether. If I get the surprise on them, then this can be done."

"And if you fail?"

"Well, I gave you several hours of recorded information. That's plenty to hurt them," said Carla, who then approached Josiah and put a hand on each shoulder. "Please, Josiah. I've wasted nearly ten years of my life on a lie. Let me make amends."

"The Good Book frowns upon doing evil so that good may ensue."

"You are assuming that killing terrorists is evil."

Josiah turned away, Carla's hand gently moving away from his shoulders in the process. She stayed silent but hopeful, cynically assuming that even if he rejected her proposal that she could find a way to still carry out her plan. He might have been praying, as his head bowed a little and he seemed to be talking under his breath. She stood there, wondering if he was going to reach a decision before dinner. Finally, he raised his head, straightened his posture, and turned around with a serious disposition.

"What do you need?"

Carla smiled. "Some weapons."

"Anything specific?"

"I'll write you up a list," she said as she went for some paper and a pen. "I am assuming you can get your hands on some of the arsenal that the police impounded from the raids."

"That I can."

List written, Josiah made his way to the police impound where he knew they were keeping the weaponry seized in the raids. Meanwhile, Carla was left alone at the house. She changed into the outfit she wore the night all things went awry. The shirt and pants were ideal for a night attack. They bore the small tears and rips from that violent evening, but were still fit to wear. No ski mask, but then again it was not going to take much for those at the Eagle Factory to realize who was assaulting them. In less than an hour, the front door opened and Josiah entered with a black duffle bag.

"I think I got what you need," he said, walking over to the living room couch and unzipping the bag to reveal various weapons. Carla searched through the contents and smiled. "I have a friend at the impound. He agreed to wait until tomorrow morning to file the paperwork on my removing evidence. I hope that is enough time for you."

"Plenty," said Carla, who got a couple of other things from the house before zipping up the duffle bag. She was about to leave when she saw Josiah standing there still. He looked intently at her and she at him.

"Carla," he said nervously. "I am very bad at this ... but ... I want you to know that, just in case, that I think I have very, very strong feelings for you. I know it doesn't mean much, given everything, but I just felt it was best you knew that." She was touched rather than embarrassed; a stroke of emotional sentiment went through her.

"For what it's worth," she said as she got closer. "I think I feel the same way."

"It can never work, can it?"

"No," solemnly replied Carla. "I guess it can't."

"I would kiss you if I didn't know it would make all this even harder," said Josiah with a weak smile. Carla smiled back and instead gave him an embrace that he reciprocated. Both gripped the other hard, but then after some moments realized that romanticism held no place in that real horrible world. With mutual regret, they let go. "You are the most fascinating woman I ever met. And the most violent."

Both laughed at the statement. "Don't wait up for me," said Carla. "This might take all evening. Just know that the morning will bring something."

"Indeed."

Carla took hold of the zipped duffle bag and slung it over her left shoulder. "Thank you, Josiah. For everything."

"No problem," he said, suppressing his emotion. She then went to the front door and had her hand on the knob. "Carla?" he said, prompting her to turn briefly. She looked with innocent dark eyes, her lips faintly parted. Her left arm was angled so that her hand gripped the top of the duffle bag strap. Black hair in a ponytail, the one bruise she received days earlier was already mostly gone. "As the old hymn says, 'God be with you 'til we meet again.'" She simply smiled in reply, opened the door, and departed.

***

The taxi driver was a little concerned about his passenger. An honorable man raised to respect women and be chivalrous when possible, the idea that she should be left alone on the outskirts of the city was a bit much. A middle-aged fellow with a couple of daughters, he feared the worst for the late twenty-something in the back seat. In his thoughts, he questioned her sanity when she requested that he stop the cab by the desolate darkened sidewalk. Even as she gave him a couple of twenties for his work.

"Are you sure you want to be here?"

"Not really," smiled Carla. "But I have to be."

"I could go an extra few blocks, drop you off closer to your place."

"Thanks, but it will not be necessary."

"Okay," he said with worry.

"You can keep the tip."

"Thank you, ma'am."

"Good night," she waved as she exited the vehicle with a black duffle bag slung about her shoulder. Without looking back, she walked down the broken sidewalk. She heard the cab motor rev up and saw the swinging lights as the taxicab made a U-turn and headed back towards the highway. As she neared the Eagle Factory, her steps became slower. Still covered by the shades of night, she crouched down and cautiously entered the crumbling asphalt foundation of the vacant lot before the factory.

Weak lights on the Eagle Factory made for her camouflage. After looking around to confirm her solitude, she unzipped the duffle bag and took out the weapons Josiah provided. There was not much ammunition provided. Josiah had limits as to just how much he was able to remove from the impound. Piecing together the sniper rifle, Carla placed the empty duffle bag to her side. To steady the weapon, she put down the two legs near the muzzle end of the weapon. Eye peering through the scope, she saw the guards outside of the clandestine compound. Several minutes went by of her lying prone on the asphalt, several small gravel pieces lightly grazing her pants and shirt.

As time progressed, she noticed the pattern of the three guards. All male, they each walked slowly in a clockwise direction. Two of them were closer together than the third, who was at the polar opposite end of the compound from the other two at all times. The two were rarely side by side, but rather one of them walked about ten feet ahead of the other. Their distance and pace was nonchalant, even arrogant. Though in their defense, Carla knew of no time in her over eight years with the Organization in which anyone, good or bad, rich or poor, religious or secular, had attacked the Eagle Factory.

She waited for the duo to appear next. The third man walked passed the main entrance, the side door that she had entered without incident many times in the past. For a few moments, all was still. Carla had time to wonder about what she was doing. "God," she quietly asked in the dark, "please let this work." She crossed herself after making the brief supplication. Then the duo appeared. She zeroed in on the one behind the other. Focusing the crosshairs on the head, slowly moving it as he moved, she slowed her breaths and then pulled the trigger. The sniper rifle made little noise, thanks to the affixed silencer. She saw her handiwork live, as the bullet instantly ripped through the man's skull, killing him.

The noise of the bullet impact and the thud of the body to the ground prompted the other guard to stop and turn. Carla saw his shocked face through the scope. His halt in movement made for an easier shot. The trigger was depressed and another bullet whizzed through the otherwise still eventide. This hit him in the forehead, landing just above the right eye and tearing through the brain before exiting out the back. Carla fired the shot with her aim at the side of his head, but a sudden movement on the victim's part made for an even better shot. For several seconds, the stage had only the two dead guards. Carla moved her rifle a little to focus more on the far end of the side of the Eagle Factory. She knew that the third man was coming from that direction.

A reliable person, he appeared moments after she fixed her scope upon the end of that side. Carla aimed for the head once more. Seeing the two bodies made him panic, causing more sudden movement than the second victim. When Carla pulled the trigger, the bullet hit his neck instead of the planned head shot. Slammed against the wall of the Eagle Factory, both hands gripping his wounded neck, he was choking on his blood. As he got to both knees, he was likely going to expire soon. Carla did not want to risk him somehow alerting those inside and so she fired a second bullet at the man, this time hitting the head and immediately ending his misery. Everything was tranquil.

Carla rose from her position on the asphalt. She took the empty duffle bag with her, slinging it over her left shoulder. Then she rushed towards the facility with her sniper rifle aimed forward. She verified that all three men were no longer living and then traded her sniper rifle for an assault rifle that one of the guards had. She also took a couple of clips of ammunition from the vanquished. Tucking them between her belt and her pants, she knocked on the door with adamancy.

"SPQR! SPQR! Let me in!" she shouted. As soon as someone answered the door and opened it, she sprayed him with several bullets from the newly acquired assault rifle. They variously went into his upper legs and chest, fatally wounding him. Pushing the closing door open with her left shoulder, she quickly saw a woman behind the front desk. Panic on her face, the woman was grabbing for the handgun Carla knew was under the desktop. Carla fired another flurry of bullets, punching holes into both the front desk and the woman behind it. She fell backwards, ricocheting off the wall and then forward onto the top of the desk, arms sprawled outwards. Nudging her with the silencer-affixed muzzle of the rifle, Carla confirmed her demise and then went towards the service elevator.

While all the gunfire below had been muted through a combination of walls and silencers, detection still occurred. On the second floor, Livy had exited a meeting with assorted leadership. At the encouragement of his peers, he was going to let the outside guards go home early and have another three take their place. When none outside replied to his communication, he realized something was amiss. As soon as Carla exited the floor via the service elevator shaft, the main elevator doors pulled open and out came Livy armed with a Glock and five other men armed with assault rifles. Everyone had their weapons drawn and ready, but the enemy was absent.

Carla climbed a few feet from the top of the elevator to the bottom part of the entryway for the second floor. She carefully undid the latch for the gate, pulling it open with one hand while holding on to the side of the shaft with the other. With the door opened, she swung herself from the side of the shaft so that both hands were grasping the second floor entryway. Using her legs to push upwards, she climbed onto the floor, duffle bag still around her left shoulder. She took hold of the rifle she had already placed on the second floor ledge in advance and walked cautiously to the double doors that led to the main hallway. They were blessed with windows. Looking through them, the only non-statue standing around was Cato in his usual well-tailored suit. Immersed in a state of caution and discipline, she pushed open the left door with her body while maintaining a good grip on the rifle. Cato turned to face her, offering only a faint show of surprise in his wrinkled face.

"Ah, my dear Carla. Good evening," he said, ignoring the fact that an assault rifle was clearly aimed at his body from less than ten feet away. "Even through it all, you remain as fetching as always. Care for a drink?" Cato directed her to the wine bottle and three glasses on the table. Carla shot all four items, causing the glasses to shatter and the bottle to break in two, the red wine spilling all over the table. Cato had a restrained look of disappointment at the sight of broken revelry. "I guess not," he said while returning his gaze to Carla. "You know, Livy and I had a wager going about what happened to you. He theorized that the withdrawal pain would be so intense that you would kill yourself after two days. I posited that you would survive, but then disappear. I guess we were both wrong."

"You were almost right," said Carla, gun still aimed at Cato. "I will disappear. But not until Cicero is no more."

"Are you going to kill me?" asked Cato, almost daring her to do so.

"I hope not," she replied. "I want you to live. To live and to testify against Cicero in a court of law."

Cato laughed for several moments. "You are quite the amusing little creature. Why should I even think of betraying Cicero in such a manner?"

"That assistant district attorney, Josiah Sharp," she said in a deadpanned tone, "he is getting closer. He knows a lot about the Organization and you."

"Prove it."

"Simon Runfeld," replied Carla, visibly shaking up Cato. "Oh yes, he knows your real name, Livy's real name, and the exact location of the Eagle Factory. And that is just the beginning."

Downstairs, the personnel kept searching the first floor. The intruder was nowhere to be found. One of them discovered the bodies outside, affirming Livy's initial suspicion. Two of them looked at the service elevator, but quickly dismissed it as an area of concern. Livy meandered around the first floor and the lobby. He wondered where the intruder was located. Walking about the space, he looked inside the service elevator. Unlike the first two who were inside, he saw small pieces of asphalt on the surface. Looking deeper he saw strewn along the side of the elevator some spent shell casings and small pieces of wood. Looking up, he realized that someone shot open the service elevator's top hatch. Turning from the elevator he saw a curious subordinate standing before him.

"You and the others stay down here," he commanded him. "I am going back up to the main hall. No matter what you may hear, everyone must stay on this floor. Understood?"

"Yes, sir," said the personnel. From there, Livy, went to the stairway on the other end of the lobby and cautiously made his way up the steps.

"What would you offer?" asked Cato to Carla, who continued to point the assault rifle at her company.

"Probably ten to twenty years, minimum."

"Ha," replied Cato, who instinctively reached for a glass of wine only to be reminded that all was dashed thanks to Carla's marksmanship.

"You will not get a better deal and you know it."

"Why me, Carla? Why not Livy or Cicero even?"

"Because, there has always been something different about you. You were always more averse to violence. You're the only member I know who does not carry a weapon. Something about this must seem wrong to you." Livy made his way to the top step, carefully pushing the door open with his left hand while holding the Glock with his right. He was in the vestibule area, but was about a hundred feet from Carla and Cato. "So you cooperate, you bring Cicero down, serve ten years, and still get out in time to live the rest of your days with your children and grandchildren."

"Do you know happened to the historical Cicero?" asked Cato, Carla giving no verbal reaction. "In Ancient Rome, Cicero tried to be principled. He tried to stand up to the tyrants of his day. He spoke out against the likes of Mark Antony in a very uncivil, vicious manner. In response, Antony had Cicero assassinated. While the death was pretty fast, afterwards Cicero's head and arms were chopped off and then nailed inside the Senate's main meeting place, to serve as a warning for any who dared to go against a virtuous terror." Cato raised his hands as though to emulate the theorized position of the historic Cicero's body. "Why should I be posed in a such a manner as this?"

Carla heard a faint sound down the hall. It was the slight shutting of the double doors that led to the stairway. She registered it but initially dismissed it. Then she saw Cato's eyes, which for a quick moment looked past her. Livy was nearing, using the one row of classical statues as a cover. Both hands were on the Glock as he darted from one statue to the next, his large frame barely able to use them as cover. Carla let a single bead of sweat roll down her face when she realized what was happening. Soon her ears were able to make out the faint shuffling of Livy's feet as he went from statue to statue. Silence. Waiting.

As soon as she heard the shuffling once again, Carla immediately turned 180 degrees and opened fire. The sporadic bursts fired in Livy's general direction hit the floor, the wall, and a couple of the statues. It also prompted Livy to fire a few shots back in desperation as he doubled his speed to get behind a statue. His shots wildly missed Carla, but one struck Cato on the right arm, ripping his suit, shirt, and flesh. Carla provided her own covering fire as she ducked behind the nearest statue on the opposite row. Cato grimaced in pain as he tumbled backwards into the wall and then collapsed to the ground, his back still to the wall. He breathed heavily and sweated as well as bled.

By the time Carla got behind one of the statues, her weapon was empty. Discarding the clip, she quickly grabbed another and kept spraying the statue Livy was crouched behind. To make her actions easier, she removed the duffle bag from her left shoulder and tossed it near the table dripping with spilled wine. Dozens of little pieces of the art, ranging from about a half inch to a few inches, were chipped away and flung into the air before landing on the red carpet dividing the two rows. A few pieces were thrown at Livy in high velocity, tearing into his clothes but leaving him basically unharmed. While Carla sprayed the statue in a failed attempt to wound him, Livy changed clips in his Glock and readied to return fire when time became convenient. Another clip emptied, Carla began to reload. She shifted to face the other side of the statue. Carla realized that Livy's size meant that he was positioning much of his body on one side of the statue. His unprotected hide was waiting to be shot.

Unbeknownst to Carla, Livy spotted her change of position. With precision, he wrapped his Glock-wielding arm around the statue and fired a single shot. Had there been no statue in the way, the projectile would likely have been fatal. Nevertheless, it did great damage as it struck a part of the artwork that had already been weakened by previous shots. The statue sent several sharpened pieces of varying sizes in the direction of Carla's left arm, shoulder, neck, and face. While her neck, face, and shoulder received only minor cuts, her upper left arm bore the brunt of the shrapnel as it tore deep gashes. The shot threw her down behind the statue with her hands briefly letting loose of the rifle. Wincing in pain, she quickly recovered and grabbed hold of the assault rifle.

She looked up expecting Livy to remain nestled behind the statue, but to her horror she saw that Livy was right in front of her. He raised the Glock so that it was before her face. Just as he pulled the trigger Carla lifted her rifle, holding it so the broad side faced the Glock. When Livy fired, the assault rifle deflected the bullet, but made the rifle unusable for firing back. The deflection threw back both combatants. Carla recovered first. With a swing of the assault rifle she hit the Glock out of Livy's hand. She then went to bat on her former superior, striking him multiple times with the rifle with such force as to bend the weapon. The blows knocked Livy down to both knees.

When Carla attempted to land the eighth blow, aimed at his head, he grabbed the mangled rifle as it was coming down. Gripping the weapon as tightly as Carla, he used the weapon as an aid in swinging her into the wall. Carla pruned in pain at the impact, the shock prompting her to lose control of the rifle. Throwing the rifle away, Livy grabbed Carla with both hands and flung her into the statue adjacent the one she used for cover earlier. She landed back first into the unfeeling figure, with impact intense enough to knock the statue down. Before she could fully open her eyes from the grimacing, Livy again grabbed hold of her and threw her at another statue, also knocking it down while causing great agony for his opponent. Finally, he grabbed hold of her again and threw her several feet onto the floor, landing her a couple yards from the Glock.

In desperation Carla attempted to crawl towards the equalizer. Amused and angered simultaneously, Livy easily caught up with the adversary. He then fell upon her, driving his right knee and shin into the lower back of Carla, who screamed in pain upon feeling the full weight of her enemy being driven into her. Knee keeping her in place, the Glock still several inches away from her fingertips, Livy used both fists to pound Carla's back. The blows bruised and battered her upper body, watering her eyes and obscuring her view of the gun as her eyelids closed as though on command from each strike. After more than a dozen hits, Carla stopped her attempt to reach for the Glock.

Feeling the resistance ending, Livy halted his barrage. With his left hand, he gathered most of the strands of hair scattered along her beaten upper back. Once in his hand he gripped them and pulled upwards, forcing Carla to arch her back with an agonized moan. After she was raised high enough, Livy let go and stretched out his right arm to catch her before she could fall to the floor. Knee still embedded into her lower back, Livy's right arm wrapped around Carla's neck like a sleeper hold. Both breathed heavily as the moments began to still, the quiet prompting a shouted query from Cato.

"What is going on?" asked Cato, his view of the fight blocked by the table and some of the statues both damaged and undamaged.

"The situation is under control," shouted back Livy.

"Is she dead?"

"When I am done with her, she'll wish she's dead," replied Livy with a sadistic smile. As he looked down towards the woman under his control, he felt a sudden cold touch to the bottom of his chin and a shot was fired. It loudly echoed for want of a silencer, sending a bullet through the chin into the mouth where it singed the tongue, and then through the roof of the mouth into the cranium.

While Livy was distracted in dialogue, Carla went for her right pants pocket. She quickly grabbed hold of Josiah Sharp's revolver that she had taken with her and then turned her bent arm backwards until it was stopped by a barrier of flesh. It was a last resort, for she knew that a possible forensic examination might directly tie her raid to Sharp. However, Sharp had failed to acquire a side arm from the impound, leaving her little option. With the shot fired, the weight upon her lower back subsided as the corpse went upward with the impact of the shot, and then tumbled to her right side. Looking to her side, she saw that Livy's eyes remained open in the blank shock of one surprisingly vanquished.

It felt like hours went by. The entirety of her back was in pain, as was her still bleeding left arm and irritated cuts along her neck and left side of her face. Her right ear was also screeching in agony, as the shot was fired very close to that side of her face. The echo of the shot produced a ringing in that ear which made it impossible to hear faint sounds from that side of the room. She wondered if it was only a matter of minutes before the personnel on the ground floor stormed the hall. With that fear in mind, she willed herself to get to her feet, ignoring the pain as best she could. What helped was the experience of withdrawal, which by comparison was still greater anguish than what she feeling at that point. Letting go of the revolver briefly, she turned her attention to the large corpse beside her. Tearing away some of his shirt, she tied it around her upper left arm, wincing in pain as she tightened the impromptu bandage. Taking hold of the revolver, she put it back into her pants pocket, and then took the Glock in her right hand. With redoubled effort, she arose to her feet, touching the statues as she limped towards the entrance to the office.

There she saw the anguished Cato, his sports jacket wrapped around his wounded arm and his tie loosened. Still seated, leaning upon the wall, he looked at Carla while he spoke into his smart phone. "Yes, I know you heard a loud shot … everything is okay now … we killed the intruder," he said between breaths. Carla stood there, the pain starting to ebb while she leaned with her left hand on the table. "You can go home now … we won't need guards now … are you second guessing my order?! … good … enjoy your evening." Cato pressed a button on the screen and with the phone conversation ended, directed his statements at Carla. "Cicero is in the office. It is best you do not keep him waiting." Carla nodded, grabbing the duffle bag and slinging it about her wounded left arm. She made her way to the large double doors. Amazingly, for all the confusion not a single bullet nor piece of shrapnel had grazed the exterior. With a deep breath, she opened the right door with her blood covered left hand and entered the presence of Cicero.

***

"You may close the door, Carla," said the mysterious voice of Cicero, a mask hiding any movement of the mouth. Seated as always behind the desk, wearing an elegant toga, sleeves and gloves. It was strange how untouched the room was by the travails of the evening hour. The statues continued to look towards the center of the room. The books were in good order and the rolodex was on the desk. Carla dripped blood on the carpet from her left arm. Despite the shirt wrapping, the occasional drops were escaping. "Do not worry about the mess, I can have some underlings clean it later."

"Remove your mask," she stated.

"I am impressed with your work. Combined with the guards outside, I believe you have passed the fifty-kill mark. I should remember to throw a party in your honor next week. After the Summer Ball of course."

"Remove your mask," repeated Carla with greater firmness. To press her demand, she raised the Glock to be level with Cicero's head.

"Very well. All shall be revealed in due time," said Cicero, who unhooked a couple things before pulling off the covering. Carla's eyes widened as she lowered her aim.

"I expected more surprise," casually spoke Mayor Mary Bhatia. Carla paused a moment before responding.

"Well, Josiah did say that he believed it was one of the people who he answered to," said Carla. "So you were on the list."

"A microphone device to distort my voice," stoically explained Mary. "I took that from our Justice Department. They sometimes use them for anonymous calls, witness protection. I also took bullet proof vests from our SWAT chapter to offer padding for my chest. This of course aids in hiding the most obvious evidence of my gender." Carla stayed silent. At least the pain in her back was transitioning to soreness. Her left arm throbbed with misery. Mary gave a sick smile while the mask, placed on the top of the table, stared at the guest. "Do you not have questions for me?"

"Why?"

"Politics," she stated in response. "Politics is a man's world. That was what my late father used to always tell me. He used to say, 'Mary, politics, the military, these are the worlds of men. They are too horrible, too brutish, too vile for the fairer sex.' If only he had lived to see me, or for that matter, you. If only he saw us, what we can do, the extents that we can accomplish, and how much fear we can put into the minds of any man alive."

"Why me?" asked Carla. "Why did you go to all the trouble to recruit me years ago?"

"I didn't," replied Mary. "For years, I had loyal people placed throughout our fair city to snatch anyone, man or woman, young and desperate. I have people at various health care offices, law firms, and even a bank or two. They always give the worst possible news, get the contact information, and then the Organization swoops in. It could be learning that you cannot add a loved one to your health insurance, or it could be learning that you can't get a loan because you're a credit risk." That comment provided more visible shock to Carla, which Mary quickly noted. "I see, you heard that one also. You must not have provided a phone number to keep in touch."

"As a matter of fact, I stormed out in anger."

Mary laughed. "But you came to us eventually. And that is what matters." Mary studied Carla some more. "You must have some more questions. Feel free to ask them. This time you really can do so with impunity."

"Who else knows you are Cicero?"

"Cato. He helped found the Organization."

"But he refers to you in the masculine tense."

"Part of the ruse."

"Why did you have us attack people in your own party?"

"Bipartisanship. Through occasionally arranging hits against my own party to the benefit of my friends on the opposite wing, I am accruing influence."

"You mean blackmail."

"Same idea," countered Mary. "Next year I will run for governor. And I will win because several politicians from the other side will endorse me."

"You sound very optimistic for someone who is about to be arrested."

"By who? You?" Mary asked with disbelief. "I go down, you go down. You know that."

"If that is what it takes."

"It doesn't, you know," replied Mary. "I think something better can be done."

Carla lowered the Glock, letting her right arm hang to the side while still holding the weapon in case it was necessary. "I am listening."

"Good," said Mary. "My offer is simple: become the new Livy."

"Excuse me?"

"You really think Benedicto Velasquez is—was—the first Livy? Oh no. His rise to prominence was remarkably like yours. Some differences. His weakness was alimony payments. The Livy at the time became paranoid of his success rate and tried to kill him. Velasquez was cut off from the substance and left alone for a whole week, using an old war buddy's loft and post-surgery pain-killers to survive. When he killed his former superior, I made him the same offer I am making you. He was smart enough to say yes."

"And look what happened to him."

Mary laughed. "Good point. But you are better than him. You always were. You lack the same weaknesses as the first three Livys. So you will endure. I need someone like you for next year. It will be a statewide race. The Organization will need to recruit like never before, we will have to strike out in more cities than ever. You will, of course, be compensated far better."

"How much?"

"A salary. I cannot promise six figures, but I can say that it's all tax free."

"What would I have to do?"

"Kill Josiah Sharp at the Summer Ball later this week. Basically do what you were going to do anyway until Velasquez acted like a fool. What do you say?"

"Can you pay me something upfront?"

Mary smiled. She got up from the desk and walked towards the safe in the corner. Carla watched her as she did so. It turned out that the toga only went as far as just below the waist, with pants covering the rest of her legs. Mary kept smiling at Carla as she did the combination and opened the safe. "How much do you want? Maybe seven thousand for killing Velasquez. That is usually the price for assassinating a prominent figure and he was technically prominent. Sound good?"

Carla responded by raising the Glock and shooting Mary Bhatia between the eyes. Putting the Glock between her belt and her pants, Carla then took the duffle bag she had brought with her and approached the opened safe. With Mary staring blankly at the ceiling, Carla opened the duffle bag and proceeded to fill it with all the money she could, using her right arm to push the bundled bills off the shelves and into the bag. Then she went over to the desk and dropped the rolodex into the bag. She zipped the bag, slung it upon her right shoulder and walked away. As she entered the ruined main hallway, Carla looked at Runfeld. His breathing was at a resting pace. He nodded at her and she smiled, taking the stairs to the first floor and from there into the outside world.

XII

Josiah Sharp slept surprisingly well that evening. He did not take any sedatives or medication; neither did someone slip something into his food or drink. He struggled to eat dinner, so maybe the lack of sustenance aided in making him faint and thus better able to rest. Sleep came deeply for most of the evening. Dreams flooded his consciousness, most included him and Carla al-Hassan marrying. They were only dreams. At one point during the evening, his slumber was faintly disrupted by what sounded like a door slamming. However, the sound wave was not strong enough to cause him worry.

With the morning came the sunlight. A rested Josiah automatically went towards the bathroom to get ready for the day. Showering and getting dressed, he was in casual gear and did not expect to get to the office as early as everyone else. They assumed he was still working on a case that required attention outside of the cubicle. As he prepared in the morning he wondered about what happened. There was no noise on the other side of his locked bedroom door. No one was making breakfast or exercising. It was a lonely time; the first time he had been alone in his place for over a week.

Pessimism crept into Josiah as he finished shaving. Putting down the disposable razor beside the faucet, he presumed the worst. Guilt swept over him as he thought about how he allowed her to go to her death. Then again, she wanted to go. She was the agitator, not him. Aside from personal distraught, Josiah turned to thinking about the overall case. He had plenty of information and was ready to, at the least, arrest the board and staff at Saddler & Frances. Surely rattling their cages some more might turn up something even more concrete. Then again, there was always the mole issue.

Unlocking his bedroom door and opening it, Josiah saw something peculiar on the living room couch. Getting closer he realized that it was a box. He was hesitant to get near it, wondering if this was another explosive device planted by the Cicero Organization. Mouthing a brief prayer of mercy, Sharp got closer and saw that a note was taped at the top of the box. Removing the folded paper, he opened it to see in cursive writing Proverbs 28:1, "The wicked flee when no man pursueth: but the righteous are bold as a lion." Confidence building, he took hold of the box and opened it. Inside he found the old-fashioned paper rolodex, delivered straight from the Eagle Factory.

Josiah smiled. He took hold of the rolodex and peeled through its content. He found the paper card with Carla's name, contact information, and home address. For whatever reason, she had not removed it when bringing it to him. "Just this once," he said to himself aloud as he tore out the card, crumpled it up, and threw it into his trash can. He then went to the landline phone and dialed a familiar number.

"Detective Frank Cooper," replied the professional voice.

"Good morning, Frank, its Josiah."

"Morning."

Josiah looked down at the rolodex while he continued his conversation. "Frank, how would you like to make the bust of the century?"

***

"Continuing to follow up on our top story today," began the local news talking head on the television screen, "more than fifty individuals including members of both major political parties have been arrested in a series of raids conducted by police. Most allegedly belong to the Cicero Organization." She was watching from the comfort of her apartment, a finished lunch on a small table before her. Carla's upper left arm was bandaged earlier that week courtesy Dr. Stephanie Greenwald. Her other cuts were dealt with as well and were fast healing up. There was still ringing in her right ear and soreness in her back and limbs. However, the severity of these things was in entropy.

The anchor continued as the screen showed more footage of authorities arresting various folks, including a couple who did not hide their faces from the cameras and were thus recognized by Carla. She almost blurted out the name "Bill" when seeing the acquaintance of her late friend dragged off. George al-Hassan was seated in his wheelchair a few feet from her, eating the last remaining bites of his lunch. The anchor continued: "According to the Justice Department, a key leader of the Organization has agreed to fully cooperate with authorities. Most of those taken into custody were discovered by the investigative work of Detective Frank Cooper and Assistant District Attorney Josiah Sharp." Carla smiled as she saw the video feed showing Sharp speaking to the press.

"He looks like a nice man," commented George. "I do not see any wedding rings on his fingers. What do you think?"

"Oh, Giddo," said an amused and lying Carla, "there's no way someone like him would want a woman like me."

"Worth a shot," replied George while Carla got up to take the dishes and utensils to the kitchen sink.

"Don't tell me you are starting to miss me already," smiled Carla as she turned the faucet on to rinse the plates.

"No, not at all," responded George. "Just wanted to make sure you considered everything before leaving."

"Of course, I have," said Carla as she returned to the television area. "I told my boss that I was quitting, I told Dr. Stephanie, and yeah, that about covers it."

"You're not worried about me?"

"I trust Elnora," replied Carla, standing before her wheelchair bound kinfolk. "Besides, I plan to visit every so often. That's why I am keeping most of my stuff here."

"Okay, I can see that," agreed George. Carla had explained her injuries as being work related and that her sudden increase in finances was connected to a rapid settlement. "And Dr. Stephanie will occasionally visit. And not even just to see me."

"Yeah, she told me the other day that you two were going to have your weddings on the same week. I will definitely be here for that."

As the news continued, explaining how both state party chapters were actively helping the investigation and how shocking it was that Mayor Bhatia was the leader of the terrorist group and how tomorrow's Summer Ball was cancelled, Carla gathered the things she was taking. There was the blue and white duffle bag. It had the various toiletries and some sets of clothes. Then there was the black duffle bag, which contained all the bundled untraceable bills. She placed them both by the door as she turned to her grandfather. They hugged and she kissed him on the cheek.

"Good bye, Giddo."

"See you in a couple months, my favorite granddaughter."

Carla smiled that perfect smile as she went to the door, opened it, and took hold of the bags. Her left arm had some pain when having to carry the weight, but it was nothing compared to other pain she had felt over the past month. She placed the two bags down as she waited for the elevator, and then carried them in when the doors opened. The apartment complex was mostly vacant at this hour, with the majority of tenants either at work or sleeping in. When the doors opened to the ground floor, she took hold of them again to carry them out of the complex, a kind neighbor holding the door open for her. She walked across the flat paved walking space to get to the bus stop. A few minutes later, the large vehicle came towards her from the left and halted in front of her, lights blinking.

"Good morning, Max," she said as she struggled a bit up the steep, narrow steps of the vehicle with the two bags.

"Morning, Carla," said a cheerful yet curious driver. "What's with the baggage?"

"Going on a long trip, nothing serious," she replied as she swiped her fare card. He was still curious.

"And what about your injuries?"

"Oh, it's nothing. Accident at work."

Carla made her way to her preferred seat, stacking the two duffle bags on top of each other to allow for more space for other riders should they come aboard. For the time being, she was the only passenger. "Well, if you are okay, then I am okay." Both smiled at the comment the bus driver made. "Off we go."

"Thanks, Max."

With a guttural revving up, the bus veered left into the lane without problem and charged onward towards the next stop on the route. Carla saw her world blur by, the various buildings and communities that held sentimental value. She had lived in that city for nearly all of her life. Now it was rushing away, passing along as though into oblivion. Yet it was still there, it and all the people in it. The streets and the structures, the people and the machines, the criminals and the law enforcers. She felt it all lift away as she leaned back into the seat, turning her gaze to the passing city, seeing her future come ever closer, and a new world in which for her to begin, even at age 29, a whole new life.

About the Author

Michael Gryboski was born and raised in the Washington, DC metropolitan area. He graduated from George Mason University with a Bachelor of Arts and then a Master's, both in history. He previously had seven novels released by the small California-based publisher, Inknbeans Press. In addition to writing fiction, Michael also writes news articles for an online publication based in DC, as well as other works including church hymns and the occasional opinion piece. Michael would rather be correct than widely accepted.

Carla al-Hassan will return next year in *Carla: The Antithesis Killer*.

Feel free to follow Michael on social media at the following accounts:
www.facebook.com/MichaelCGryboski/
www.twitter.com/Puritan1986
www.instagram.com/michaelgryboski/

CPSIA information can be obtained
at www.ICGtesting.com
Printed in the USA
JSHW051551200423
40480JS00006B/225